BOOK THREE OF THE STARBLOOD TRILOGY

THE DEATH AND RESURRECTION SHOW

Carmilla Voiez

The Death & Resurrection Show

This is a work of fiction. All characters and events portrayed in this novel are fictitious and are products of the author's imagination and any resemblance to actual events, or locales or persons, living or dead are entirely coincidental.

Cover by: Paul Grover

Dedicated to Colleen Stevens who may be gone but shall never be forgotten.

With thanks to Beth, Scott, Paul, Vanessa, Faith, Ann, and all the other people who have offered their time and support to help me develop and rewrite this novel. Thanks to my daughters who inspire me every single day, and my partner who gives me strength when needed. And thanks to my father, who reads all my books and loves me anyway. My life and art are richer for all of you.

SUGGESTED READING ORDER
Starblood
Psychonaut
The Death & Resurrection Show

If you have ever wondered why I used these titles for the trilogy, they are all songs I love and that I believe resonate with the themes of the books. Thanks also to Cranes, Fields of the Nephilim, Killing Joke, and the many other bands and musicians who have brought me joy.

Trigger Warnings

The Starblood Trilogy deals with potentially distressing topics including mental illness, depression, self-harm, suicide, murder, sexual assault, castration, rape, incest, drug references. Please be aware that this list may not be exhaustive.

THE DEATH AND RESURRECTION SHOW

CHAPTER ONE

BLACK CURLS wrap around Star's throat like a scarf. Satori's breath tickles her neck as he hooks a stick-like arm around her waist and pulls her close. His skin is warm against hers, and she realises how much she has missed that.

'Star,' he murmurs. 'I found you.'

He found her, but she saved them both. She sighs and moulds herself into his angular frame.

'We're home,' he says.

The room is tiny. No more than two metres by three. An aluminium toilet squats in one corner and a metal door is set into the opposite wall. *Home?*

She laughs, but her laughter is gentle, not mocking, happy to be alive and with him, wherever they are.

'Well, almost home.' His laughter joins hers.

'Where are we?' she asks.

'A prison cell,' Satori says. 'They arrested me for your murder.'

'I wonder how that will work out now I'm not dead…' Her laughter morphs into sobs. 'Raven?'

He strokes her hair. 'Shush, it's okay.'

She faces him, her wide eyes begging him to understand her fear.

'We won't tell them you're alive.' He kisses her forehead and brushes her tears away with his thumb.

Star scowls. 'Umm, I think they'll notice I'm here.'

'Not if we escape.' Satori's eyes shine in the half-light: one grey, the other red.

Star shudders. He has worn this manic look before: the one that says anything is possible. Evidence supports his belief. A few hours ago, she was dead. Now she's lying in his arms, heart beating and lungs drawing oxygen from the stale air. *Anything is possible.* His law, not hers, but their reality confirms its validity. Part of her hates him for being right.

Star stares at the metal door. 'Escape? That's all I've ever done. Maybe it's time I stood my ground — took some responsibility?'

'We'll figure it out.'

She gazes into his eyes. One sparkles with steely brilliance. The other is ruined. His aborted rescue attempt in the mountains; the battle with Lilith. Both lifetimes ago. She kisses his lips and snuggles into his chest, allowing his steady heartbeat to calm her.

'Satori, I don't want to keep running.'

He cups her chin, holding her gaze. 'You don't belong in prison. It will be easier to make amends, earn the forgiveness of those we have wronged, when we get out of here.' His voice is soft and calming, his logic impossible to dispute.

Hairs rise across her naked flesh as the air chills. She tugs the blanket, trying to burrow inside the scratchy nest.

'You're cold,' he says and folds the thin wool in two, pressing it over her with the weight of his arm.

The fluorescent light flickers above them. Energy crackles around the room, making her scalp tingle and her teeth ache. Star clings to Satori as freezing air whirls around the cell like a dervish.

Satori sits up and pats her shoulder, instructing her to stay down. The light flickers again then fails and the cell falls into darkness. Congealed air punches Star's ears and throat and frost prickles her skin.

'Satori!' she screams.

'It's okay.' Satori grips her shoulders and pulls her toward him. They sit on the narrow bed together, shaking.

A cyclone tugs Star from his embrace and drags her to the centre of the room. She stands alone, whipped by vicious air, heart hammering and legs shaking. It spins her until she cannot tell which direction she's facing then floors her with a heavy blow. The room stinks of blood and decay.

'What's happening?' Star screams.

'I... don't... n... know,' Satori stammers. He sounds far away. 'Stay down. Breathe.'

Resting on her knees and one hand, she reaches into the space in front of her, searching for him, fingers flailing through the bitter wind.

'Where are you?' she wails.

'I'm here, Star. It's going to be okay.'

'How can you be sure?'

'Because we survived, I found you and we survived. We're not about to die here.'

She shakes her head.

'Talk to me,' he says. 'I'll move towards your voice.'

'Fuck! When will this punishment end? We don't deserve this. I never meant to hurt anyone. I don't know why things happened the way they did. It was like I was sleepwalking.'

Satori's fingers brush her knee. 'Here you are.' He crawls to her side and puts his arms around her. 'It's going to be okay; I promise.'

As their eyes adjust to the dark, shapes take form in the air around them. Three terrifying faces, with hollow eyes and gaping mouths, drip blackness onto the floor. They move like reflections in agitated water. Arms appear, reach toward Star and Satori then vanish again. The faces remain — soulless, angry and tormented.

'... know what... is,' Satori says. '... idiots! ... begged them not ... do it, ... opened the vessel.'

The whirlwind snatches syllables from his mouth before they reach Star's ears, and the words she manages to catch don't make any sense. 'What?'

'Paul... he ... prison ... demons. The police ... here... wanted to ... what ... inside... fools.'

The demons hiss at the huddled couple. 'Where is he?'

'Who?' Star asks.

'The one who enslaved us. Where is he?'

'Paul's dead,' Satori yells.

'Where issss he?'

'… morgue.' Satori's voice shakes. '… dead… can't hurt you.'

'Then we can't punish him, but we can eviscerate both of you.' The menacing voices echo around the room, moving closer and closer to the cowering couple until they are harsh whispers in their ears and sour breaths on their faces.

'Star!' Satori yells. 'Do something.'

Why is he asking her to take charge? Satori lives for moments like this, the battles against magical forces. The thought that he might be powerless terrifies her. 'Me? What can I do?'

Her mind rushes through images — the toad she expelled from her mind; the goddess she subdued with forgiveness. Closing her eyes, Star reaches for the light inside herself, searching the dark tunnels of her mind, running through empty corridors, turning every corner. 'I can't find my light.'

'Hold … hand … do … to … ther,' Satori says.

She squeezes his hand, and his warmth guides her. Drawing on his strength and magic — this tragic hero, the man who loved and destroyed her — she concentrates their combined energy inward. The world outside ceases to exist, and she floats through grey-pink chambers and crimson corridors until she finds a speck of light fluttering deep inside her mind. She races towards it, concentrating only on its brightness, willing it to grow, blowing on embers until her skin burns. She wraps herself in the light, stretching her mind, forcing it outwards until it fills the cell.

Demons growl and the floor trembles. Air roars in rage as it rushes from the room to escape the scorching brightness. In the still silence that remains, the oxygen feels too thin. Star clings to Satori's arm, afraid she might pass out. Her light fades, and the darkness is deeper than ever.

'There's not enough… air. We must get… out of… this room,' Satori wheezes.

They crawl blindly until her outstretched hand touches metal. 'The door.'

'Open it,' he gasps.

'Me?'

'What… the fuck? This again! You. You're a… fucking… goddess! I think… you can… open a… locked… door.'

'I… don't know.' Her head spins, and she collapses onto the floor.

'You… can… do… it.' Satori gasps for air. 'Please…'

Star rests her palm against the metal and closes her eyes. 'Open,' she says.

The door swings toward them, bending Star's wrist, stopping only when it smacks her forehead. Cold air rushes into the cell. Star and Satori lie on the floor, gulping oxygen.

Satori laughs. Flickering light from the hallway highlights his beautiful face.

'Your eye.'

'A scratch. Don't worry.' Satori moves to stand up.

Star touches Satori's face and closes her eyes. Her fingers tingle and grow hot. When she removes her hand, he is healed. The scar has vanished, and two grey eyes blink at her.

He stands up, wobbling unsteadily, gazing at Star's face. His lips curl upward in a warm and loving smile. 'Thank you.'

Star extends her hand, and he helps her to her feet. Satori kisses her fingers before guiding her through the doorway. She holds his gaze for one eternal moment, before he looks away.

'It's too quiet. Where is everyone?'

They stagger to the next cell. Satori opens the viewing flap. 'Empty.' He checks each one. 'They're all empty.' The pitch of his voice rises in panic.

Star shares his unease. 'We should leave, but my god, I'm so tired I could sleep for a year. Maybe I'm not meant to use that power in this world.'

Satori rests against a cell door and strokes her cheek. 'You just need to learn how to recharge.'

She shakes her head, grabbing his hand again, dragging him towards the barred gate at the end of the silent hallway. 'I don't trust it. Magic comes from Lilith.'

'Not from Lilith, from you. Just take it easy until it feels natural. Although, fuck knows what those demons would have done to us back there if you hadn't...'

Star coughs, embarrassed. 'We. You helped.' She tugs the gate. 'This one's locked too. Help!' Her voice echoes around the corridor, but no sound answers her call, not even the rush of heavy boots.

'We should go to Donna and check she's okay,' Satori says.

'Donna?'

'She helped me reach you. She's in hospital, long story, but she needs to know you're okay.'

The corridor is empty, but Star senses the demons' presence. They are close. Waiting. Waiting for what? And where are all the people?

'Can you feel them?' Star asks.

Satori nods. 'Help me with this gate.' Satori entwines his fingers with hers, and they wrap their hands around the steel bars.

Star closes her eyes and reaches for her light. 'Open.'

The lock clicks.

Star's skin glows gold. The demons' auras retreat into the shadows like cockroaches. *They fear my light.*

Satori turns the handle and pushes the door open into another dimly lit, empty corridor. He leads the way through a maze of narrow hallways. When they encounter dead ends and turn back, Star glimpses a deeper darkness at the edges of the ubiquitous gloom, then it vanishes, retreating around corners or seeping into walls. Eventually, they find the stairwell and ascend.

As they reach the ground floor of the police station, death greets them, and the full effect of the demons' rage becomes apparent. The first body they encounter has its back against a blood-stained wall. The man's mouth stretches wider than any scream; pink liquid oozes from hollow eye-sockets, staining his cheeks, and the flesh of his nose hangs in front of his mouth. Cartilage clings to his Kevlar vest.

Satori grasps Star's arm. 'Don't look.'

Star shudders and turns away. Strewn across the hallway

are five more corpses in police uniforms: four lie face-down. They step over fallen bodies toward the exit. The final corpse is female. Its spine is twisted, broken, and one arm reaches for her colleague, seeking solace, fingers stretching across the floor of carnage a few inches short of their target. Star cannot help but look at her face. The skull is concave, as though a giant fist punched her features into the back of her head. Thankfully, her eyes are closed, but her nose, cheeks and lips point inwards as if her face is an empty mould.

Dark despair smothers Star as the mindless cruelty and carnage extinguish her light. Air freezes around her. Her hair stands on end as evil races along the corridor towards them. Satori tugs her arm, pulling her away from the horrors. Demons chase them, their fingers piercing her with frost, scratching her spine and heels as they run. No one alive, police, prisoner or civilian, crosses their path, and Star wonders whether anyone else survived.

'Come on,' Satori urges.

Finally, they reach the exit and burst out of the doors, emerging into the dark street. Turning back, they see blackened windows of cracked glass. The building shakes as if in fear.

'It's going to collapse,' she says.

Hand in hand, they sprint past strangers who stare at them. Star assumes their shocked faces are in response to her nakedness and tries to cover herself.

Satori takes off his shirt and passes it to her. 'I'm sorry. I don't know why… I didn't think…'

She stops running to button it over her chest then kisses his cheek. 'Paul's demons might have done us a favour.'

'I'm not a fan of cops either, but isn't that…'

'I mean the evidence room,' Star says. 'If all the evidence against us is gone…'

That thought follows them as they move through busy streets towards Donna. Have they been offered a fresh start?

'Satori!' Donna says. 'You're back. I thought…'

Star steps out from behind Satori and smiles at Donna.

'Oh. My. God! How?' Donna stares at Star in disbelief. 'Am I fucking dreaming?'

'We did it,' Satori says.

'Sarah, you're alive. I can't believe this is real… How did you?'

'He found me.'

'I knew he would.' Donna pushes herself upright. 'Come here. Let me touch you. I can't believe my fucking eyes. Are you real?'

Star crosses the hospital room and sits on the edge of Donna's mattress. She reaches out and grasps her friend's trembling hand. 'It's real. I'm alive.'

Tears pour down Donna's face as she squeezes the hand. Love fills the room. The unbridled devotion makes every cell in Star's body buzz. It's energising, this worship, and sunlight fills her mind, restoring and recharging her.

'Donna, I brought something back from Binah. Some sort of power. Let me heal you.'

Donna shrugs. 'I'm okay, honestly. It's just good to see you.'

'I want to do this. I need to. Please.'

Donna nods. 'Okay, sure.'

'Your scar from the bar brawl, shall I get rid of that too?'

Donna touches her eye. 'I haven't thought about that in a very long time. What do you think?' she asks Satori.

He smiles and nods. 'You've earned a fresh start.'

Star fixes her lips against Donna's. Warmth spreads from Star's mouth, making Donna's face glow with healing light. When Star moves away, Donna's lips are pursed in the remembered kiss.

'Thank you.' Donna's face shines, pale and fresh, unblemished.

Star's mind soars, and her heart races. 'You're welcome.'

Satori puts his hand on Star's shoulder. 'Are you okay?'

Star nods. 'I feel wonderful.'

Donna stares at the blanket. 'Sarah, when they discharge me, I'm going home with Mum.'

'Donna…'

'I love you, but you'll never feel that way about… Like Satori said… a fresh start…'

Star nods and kisses her friend's cheek. 'Promise me you'll write… and visit sometimes.'

'I promise.' Tears soak Donna's cheeks and nightdress.

Star blows her one last kiss. 'We have to go.'

'Take care… both of you.'

'You too.'

'Thank you, Donna,' Satori says.

'You're welcome.'

Satori and Star hold hands as they leave the hospital.

'What now?' Star asks.

'Got any of that juice left?'

'A little, I think. Why?'

'There's one more place I want to take you before we go home and start the rest of our lives. A wrong to put right. I'll explain when we get there.'

Streetlights hang above busy roads, and beyond those, countless stars. The occasional beeping of car horns reminds Star that she is only half-dressed. Satori leads her to large iron gates set between high stone walls. The handle squeaks as he pushes it down, and the gate judders as he shoves it open.

'What are we doing here?'

'One more friend to visit,' he answers.

He steps through the gateway, skin glowing in the moonlight. Star pauses for a moment before following. Loose stones dig into the soles of her feet as she walks behind him.

Graves tower on both sides of the driveway. Satori turns left onto a mud path. The earth is soft, and her soles sink into his footprints.

'What are we doing here?'

Satori doesn't answer. He keeps walking. Angels and dogs give way to simple crosses and the occasional teddy bear as they progress to newer graves.

Satori stops in front of a black cross. A tree stretches its bare branches across the grave. Star stands beside him and reads the marker. The name on the tombstone is Rhiannon Sanders.

Satori's head is bowed; his hands pressed together as if he is praying. She kneels at the edge of the turf. The earth embraces her knees, and she trembles.

'Raven,' Satori says.

Star stares at the glossy blackness and remembers her friend. A teardrop gathers in her eye, rolls down her cheek and splatters onto the wet and yielding ground. 'I'm sorry.'

'Can you?' Satori asks.

'Can I what?'

'Bring her back?'

Star shakes her head. 'I don't… Can you… give me a moment alone… please, Satori… Leave me alone!'

He pads softly along the path toward the older graves. When she can no longer hear him, Star breathes deeply and studies the convex mound of grass covering Raven's final resting place. Sepia-toned petals stick to the base of the cross. 'Oh, Raven. I'm so sorry.'

She touches her forehead to the earth that covers her beautiful friend's feet then reaches out with her consciousness, trying to find Raven or some remnant of her. The earth teems with life; industrious insects and worms push through crumbly soil. Star dives further, beyond a wooden barrier and into the satin embrace of Raven's coffin. Her body looks peaceful. Pins hold her jaw in place, and a chiffon veil softens her features, obscuring most of the damage to her once perfect bone structure.

Star shivers. 'Raven, are you there?'

'I fucked Satori.' The weight of Raven's declaration crashed through Star's skull. Images of Raven and Satori's bodies moving together filled her brain.

Something shifted in Star's belly — *the baby?* — as she grabbed Raven's shoulders and dragged her into a narrow stall. Raven's boots slipped on the wet floor and her ankles buckled. Star grabbed a fistful of hair and smashed Raven's cheek against the porcelain toilet, forcing the face down again and again, pummelling Raven against the grubby white seat, streaked with ribbons of red.

Raven's face cracks open like an eggshell in Star's hands, and rivers of blood pour from Star's fingertips, staining the chiffon shroud. Raven's dead eyes open, milky white; her shattered cheek and jaw hang lower on one side. A triangle of pain.

'Why?' Raven gurgles as broken lips form the word.

'I don't know. I'm sorry.'

'What do you want?' Bubbles of blood explode like fungal spores against the veil.

'Satori wants me to bring you back.'

A sound between a laugh and a cough adds more redness to the darkening material.

'Should I try?' Star asks.

'What you did, the way you smashed my skull into shards, cannot be undone. Let me rest in peace. Tell Satori he is not to blame.'

'Who is?' Star's voice trembles, and she immediately regrets asking the question.

'You. Binah may have taught you how to thrive, but to me you'll always be a murdering bitch.'

The venom of Raven's words jolts Star back. She hits the top of the coffin and smashes through it. Blades of wood tear and bruise her skin, and the earth is cold and damp around her. It presses into her nostrils, making her cough as her throat convulses. She claws her way to the surface and spits mud onto the grave, rejecting both the choking earth and Raven's vicious, unforgiving words.

She hears Satori's footsteps as he approaches. The pain as splinters tore her flesh and the cloying, suffocating earth she escaped were real to her; their echoes have the quality of memories not dreams, yet the grave appears undisturbed. No gaping hole marks her desperate journey.

'I'm sorry. I can't.' Star turns away, bristling with fury. His grief makes her tremble with jealousy.

Magic grants them access through Paul's gates and unlocks his front door — a fitting tribute to the dead sorcerer. Star has no desire to stay here, but it is preferable to sneaking into Satori's bedroom and risk facing his mother's interrogation.

As they sit together in Paul's library, a fire banishing the damp chill from the air, Satori shares his plans for the future, 'We'll rent a cottage of our own and live peaceful lives. You'll have time to paint. There are plenty of ways for me to earn a living. Let me support you financially and emotionally. All you need to do is heal yourself and learn to be happy.'

Star shudders, unsure whether her unease comes from the thought of relying on Satori or the distant sobbing of children that seeps through the floorboards.

When they can no longer keep their eyes open, they stumble up the staircase to Paul's bedroom and fall asleep on the four-poster bed. Satori wraps his arm around her, and she falls asleep with her head on his chest, listening to the beat of his heart. That night, she dreams she is an unmanned vessel, drifting passively along the gentle current of a river.

When Star wakes, the symbolism is clear. Satori's idealised version of the future will require a similar passivity. She cannot blame him. The Star he knew followed the crowd, did what she was told, accepted the names and roles she was given. The first time she swam against the current was when she left him. A decision that caused Satori to take drastic measures. He brought Lilith to Earth and thus started a chain of events which led to her pregnancy, death and rebirth. Without a plan of her own, a dream she yearns to fulfil, to tug her in a different direction, it might be easier and safer to sit back and discover where Satori takes them.

CHAPTER TWO

'M-M-M,' THE infant says.

It has been months since Lilith said goodbye to Star, but each day the determined baby crawls to the spot where his mother vanished and holds out his arms, begging her to return. Before he can speak or walk, the child understands loss.

Lilith misses Star too. Her handmaidens do their best to distract her, but the three sisters are hedonists, and Lilith misses Star's exquisite agony.

Siloth is the baby's guardian and his teacher. The serpent's devotion is a source of wonder to Lilith. Never angry, never bored. The attention he craves, the omnipresence he demands are too great a strain on Lilith's nerves, but Siloth remains by his side, infinitely patient.

'What should we call him?' Lilith asks.

'You want me to name your son, Mistress-sss?'

'Of course not, Serpent. I want you to suggest names, so I might name him.'

Siloth bows his head. 'Well, may I sss-suggest a name that represents-sss both his-sss mothers-sss? Moonstar? Edensun?'

Lilith taps her clawed fingertips against her hip, staring at the baby. 'Edensun. I like it. It suits him. Come home, Edensun, your other mother won't return for you today.'

Edensun crawls behind Lilith, up a steep bank of earth and toward the villa. Lilith's stride is too quick for him to keep up, but he will not lose his way, not after travelling the same route every day since birth.

Edensun grows quickly. Before a year passes on Earth, the boy acquires two distinct forms, human and demon, and can shift between them at will. In his human form, flesh replaces scales, earlobes extend beyond sculpted cheeks, and his teeth resemble tiny tombstones rather than needles; his hair is jet black, his green eyes bright, and his olive-toned face is beautiful. He no longer pines for his mother. Instead of sitting, arms outstretched, willing Star to return, he sprints across the soft earth, yelping with delight. He somersaults through the air, landing perfectly on his feet or bouncing on his bottom in fits of giggles.

Lilith has fulfilled her promise to Star. She looked after their son and watched him grow into a happy and exuberant little monster.

Under Binah's twilight sky, Edensun admires his body, revelling in its beauty and strength. He stretches his legs and increases his speed while his will creates a door in the air ahead, a rift into darkness where Chaos reigns, where the air is active and directionless like his thoughts.

He prepares his muscles to leap, like a rabbit returning to its warren. Earth trembles beneath his feet. Guiltily, he seals the unauthorised entrance. A blunt nose pushes through the grey earth between Edensun and the now closed gateway.

'Edensun.' The voice in his head commands his full attention while the eyeless face and thick cylindrical body of the giant wyrm curl outwards from Edensun's feet.

'Siloth.' Edensun's voice trembles. He sits within the spiral and crosses his slender legs.

'You are sss-supposed to ask Lilith before jumping.' The wyrm's huge jaws do not move as he speaks.

'I know, but…'

'Lilith understands-sss you find comfort in Chaos-sss, but you must obey her rules-sss.'

Edensun nods. 'I'm sorry.' Not for opening the doorway but for getting caught before he could jump through. 'Has she sent you to fetch me?'

'No. She is working. Instead of tearing holes-sss in the air, perhaps you should distract yourself with the charms-sss of Magenta, sss-Sapphire and Violet.'

Edensun pushes himself from the ground. Siloth unfurls his body, giving the boy space to change into his demon form. His skin cracks into grey scales, and wings spread from his shoulders. His back bends and two legs merge into one, forcing him to balance on tripod limbs. From each of his three feet, a scimitar-shaped claw extends. He nods at the eyeless, all-seeing wyrm before rising. Powerful, leathery wings agitate the air, making clouds of sand. He hovers for a moment before shooting toward Lilith's villa, seeking the company of her three handmaidens.

The handmaidens rush to greet him as he lands in the garden. Exotic scents embrace him, and the women's clothing outshines the glorious blooms surrounding them. Edensun lets their soft hands caress his rough skin. Magenta's tongue flicks into his mouth and licks his fangs. Violet guides his left foreleg towards her. He sways on two claws, anchoring them into the dirt for stability, while Violet wraps her lips around the captive appendage. Sapphire strokes the scales on his shoulders and lower back, singing a song that fills him with lust and joy and encourages his demonic urge to dominate. He growls and bites Magenta's lip, swallowing her sweet, warm blood. Violet's yielding flesh rips as he scratches the back of her throat, and Edensun's body pulses with desire while Lilith's handmaidens croon and adore him, accepting each sensation of pain he offers and begging for more.

Despite their attempts to distract him from his yearning sorrow, his mind shifts from the handmaidens to the fading memory of Star's face. When will Lilith let him go? His body throbs with impatience.

Lilith stands before the black mountain in Yesod. Her red hair is covered with a grey silk veil. Her green eyes are directed downward in a demonstration of respect and humility. She has come here to seek guidance.

A door opens and she enters.

The air is thick with heat and moisture. She follows the winding corridor to a gigantic cave full of lava and fire.

'Good day, sister,' Hecate says. 'Would you care for some tea?'

Hecate's spirit is chained to a human form on Malkuth; the plane that humans call Earth. Four years earlier, Lilith killed the magician who worked the spell, but the man who ordered it still lives. Strangely, Lilith senses no resentment from the goddess. Instead, she has internalised certain human affectations, including a love of tea.

Hecate steps into the light. She shifts through her three aspects: maiden, mother and crone, before choosing the appearance most suited to her current role.

Lilith lifts her head and smiles. 'It's good to see you.'

The ancient, wizened crone lowers herself onto a padded chair at a circular table where a teapot and two cups send steam into the humid air. She waves her hand graciously to indicate that Lilith should join her.

'How can I help you, Lilith?' Hecate asks, although Lilith is certain the goddess already knows why she has come and what she will ask.

'Edensun is restless. He wants to find his mother.'

'And you are afraid he is not ready.' Hecate lifts a china cup and sips the hot beverage. Her pupils widen with pleasure and a contented sigh escapes her wrinkled lips.

'He's a child. If she rejects him again…'

'She will not reject him. She misses him as much as he misses her, though his father might stand in his way.'

'That damn magician.'

'And there are others who wish him harm. He will face tragedy. He will win Star only to lose her again. In the end, it is all about sacrifice.' Hecate empties her cup and leans forward to refill it from the pot.

'So, I should prevent him from leaving?'

'You cannot, and he will hate you for trying. Summon that follower of yours, Freya, the one with the ribbons. She will push him to complete his mission. All Star's friends, dead and alive, have a role to play. I will guide him. He will be tested, but he is strong enough to do what must be done.'

'I sense you have a vested interest in making this happen, Hecate. Do not make me your enemy.'

'Lilith, sister, great and terrible mother, it is Edensun who forces your hand, not I.'

Lilith snorts. She does not trust the triple-faced goddess, but Hecate is right. Edensun will head to Malkuth and search for Star with or without her blessing.

CHAPTER THREE

A BABY cries. The wail pricks at the edge of Freya's mind, nudging her into consciousness. 'Oh, for fuck's sake, shut up.'

Her eyes open in slits to protect her sensitive pupils from the dawn light that nudges between the curtains and paints the white wall peach. 'It's your turn.' She reaches behind to poke Rob in the ribs. *Lazy bastard!* Her finger sinks into his side, but he doesn't respond. His t-shirt is sticky. The night wasn't hot. It's still early spring. Why is he damp?

She struggles to turn around, but sleep doesn't want to free her from its grip yet; midnight feeds take their toll, and she has never felt so tired. *Why won't he wake up? It's his fucking turn.* Rotating slowly, degree by tortuous degree, she braves the light from the window and opens her eyes. Rob's face looks pale; his eyes are open.

'For Christ's sake, Rob, Ava's crying; sort her out. I need to sleep. I can't keep doing this by myself.'

He doesn't respond. His lips are slightly open but do not tremble with breath. She pulls back the duvet so the cold air will shock him awake. His t-shirt is torn; his torso stained red with blood, and his cheek is cold to the touch.

Freya's scream drowns the baby's cries. Long after she has drawn breath the echoes of it shake the room. 'Rob! Oh my god! Rob!'

She jumps out of bed and stares in horror. *How? Why?* She flees the room and checks on the baby. Avaline's arms reach towards her mother, the screams growing more demanding as Freya steps closer to the cot, but Ava is okay, unharmed.

Freya reaches into the cot and picks up the beetroot-faced infant. Bloody handprints smudge her yellow onesie. Freya shakes, torn between returning her daughter to the cot or taking her to her dead father. The room spins. Freya blinks. Her stomach does somersaults, and she puts the baby back into the pine cot mere seconds before her back folds and she vomits on the nursery floor.

Freya covers her ears as Avaline's screams grow louder. Slicks of blood from her hands tangle her hair and stain her cheeks. Avaline's legs and arms punch air. Freya turns and runs back to the bedroom. Back to Rob's inert body and the crimson liquid which stains his torso. Shaking, Freya approaches. Her fingers tremble as she pulls the hem of his t-shirt toward his throat. Six deep cunt-like wounds gape across his blue-grey chest.

Freya backs away and turns around, searching the room for clues. Shadows skulk in the corners, watching her as she opens wardrobe doors and checks behind the curtains. She creeps from room to room in the apartment peering behind every door, but no one pounces out at her, and the only sound she hears is the insistent scream of her six-month-old daughter.

The front door is still bolted on the inside. She rushes around, tearing open the curtains. Every window large enough to admit someone is closed and locked. Almost blinded by tears, she searches the apartment again. Avaline's cries are frantic. Panic makes Freya sluggish; she tastes iron on her tongue; her limbs are heavy; her legs shake.

The attic?

She grabs a hooked pole and thrusts upwards, snagging the handle. Steps unfold. The pole doubles as a weapon — a makeshift spear; gripping it tightly in one fist, she climbs. A naked bulb hangs at the centre; its feeble light does not reach the outer edges. Anyone could be hiding there or behind the dozens of cardboard boxes. Her eyes flick around the room, wishing the baby would be quiet. Screams drown out all competing noise, meaning Freya will be unable to hear footsteps until it is too late. Still, she must look.

She steps onto the plywood floor and tiptoes across the space. The attic is self-contained and there is no access to or from the other apartments. Only seven by ten metres in which someone could hide, but in that space dozens of boxes create bolt holes, sheltering anything or anyone from her gaze. She looks behind them all, ready to strike with her hooked stick, but finds no one. She is alone.

If Avaline doesn't quiet down soon, a neighbour will call the authorities. *Bloody neighbours.* Always complaining, never sympathetic to the mother of a demanding child. A child who grinds Freya's soul into dust while her skin ages with disinfectant and her clothes grow tatty from scrubbing off baby vomit. She descends, shutting the trap door behind her. After stashing her pole in a cupboard, she fetches Avaline. The baby is hot to the touch. Freya suspects it is because she has cried for so long, but she undresses her and leaves the blood-stained onesie on the nursery floor.

'What are we going to do, Ava?'

The only answer is a weak hiccup of protest. Freya opens her pyjama top and lets Avaline latch on for her feed. She paces around the nursery, frightened to return to her bedroom.

'Should I phone the police?'

The baby suckles contentedly.

'What if they take Mummy away? What then, sweetheart? They might think I killed him… Fuck! What should I do?'

Avaline finishes feeding and falls asleep in Freya's arms. Freya places her back in the cot and tucks the blanket over her. She does not look for a clean onesie or redress her daughter in the blood-stained garment on the floor, hoping Ava will be warm enough for a couple of hours.

The baby's body relaxes. Freya sits beside the cot, crosses her legs and places her palms face up on her knees. She breathes in and out and tries to purge the tension from her body, but when she visualises the cleansing light that should wash away the negativity and stress, it becomes her bloodstained lover. She squeezes her eyes tighter, trying to push the image away, but it refuses to be ignored. Her mind will not let her pretend the carnage does not exist, not even for one blissful second.

She tiptoes silently into the room, convincing herself Rob's playing a trick, that she'll catch him grinning, amused by her over-reaction. But he isn't smiling, and he hasn't moved. She approaches the bed by a circuitous route, so that the window is behind her, casting her shadow across him. Keeping the open door in sight, she grips Rob's wrist — no pulse. She lowers herself to the floor, kneeling beside him as if in prayer. 'Who did this to you?'

Rob's corpse does not reply.

His mobile phone is on his bedside table. She picks it up and dials her brother's number.

Ivan's voice sounds like a yawn. 'Rob?'

Freya weeps into the receiver.

'Sis?' Ivan's voice trembles. 'Is Ava okay?'

'She's sleeping, but I'm in trouble.'

'What sort of trouble?'

'Rob's dead.'

'Did you kill him?' Ivan asks.

'No, of course not. How could you ask that?'

'Then call the police.'

'I can't.'

'Why?'

'They'll think I did it. They'll lock me up, and I'll lose Avaline.'

'They won't. You have to call them.'

'No.'

'It'll take me at least five hours to reach you. You and Ava can't stay in the flat with…'

'A corpse,' she finishes the sentence, so he doesn't have to. 'Tell me what to do.'

'Call the police.'

'No.'

'Then get out of the flat. Take Ava. I'll call you when I reach York. We'll go back to the flat together. Shall I call you on this number?'

Tears run through her fingers onto the screen of Rob's phone.

'Call my mobile. I'll take that.'

'Will you be okay?' His voice is soft and full of concern.

Her chest squeezes her heavy heart like a vice. 'I don't think so, Bro.'

'I'll be there as soon as I can. I'll bring Dad. He'll be more use than me.'

Freya sobs into the receiver. 'He'll hate me.' Freya's weeping grows louder. Her body shakes as hysteria grips her shoulders.

'We'll sort this out, you, me and Dad. It'll be okay. Look, I'm going to put the phone down. We'll call you when we're in York, okay?'

Freya nods.

'Okay?' Ivan asks again.

'Please hurry,' Freya says.

Freya pushes the pram around town. Its wheels bounce over cobblestones at the Shambles; the market stinks of fish and rotting food. Dozens of voices fight each other for her attention, offering her the best deals on fruit, vegetables and electrical goods. She glances at her phone; the signal is strong, but no message yet.

Avaline wakes with a piercing cry. Freya pushes her faster around the marketplace, ignoring the other people and staring at her daughter through a veil of tears. She's grateful for the size and weight of the old-fashioned pram. No one tries to push past her; they avoid her as if she is driving a tank rather than pushing a baby.

She checks her phone again, no call from her father or brother, but it has only been two hours. She must try to keep calm, avoid drawing attention to herself; stop Avaline's crying.

Freya nudges the pram into a coffee shop at the edge of the market and sits at a table with plastic flowers in a metal vase. She lifts her baby from the pram and opens her blouse. Ava settles — she's just hungry, always hungry.

A woman eases across the room, holding a notepad and

pencil. She smiles at the baby and then at Freya. 'What can I get you?'

'Tea, please,' Freya answers.

'And water to top up your fluids?'

'Sure, thanks.'

'How about something to eat?'

Freya shakes her head. 'Just tea for now, okay?'

'No problem. Shout if you change your mind. Nursing mummies have to stay strong, right?'

Freya shrugs. 'Yeah, I guess. Look, I don't want to be rude, but…'

'I'm sorry.' The woman blushes. 'I'll leave you in peace. Your tea and water will be with you in a minute.'

Freya nods. 'Thanks.'

She looks at her phone again and considers dialling Ivan's number, but what good would that do? She can hardly talk about Rob's murder in a café, better to wait until they get here. *Maybe they can help me understand what happened?*

Avaline falls asleep in Freya's arms. When the waitress returns with a pot of tea and a cup, she nods at Freya's open blouse and exposed breast. Freya lays Ava in the pram and buttons her blouse, but within seconds the baby wakes and screams again. The waitress pulls a sympathetic face and hurries away. Freya sighs and picks Ava up again. The baby reaches for her mother's breast. *Always hungry.*

They repeat this familiar dance for one hour then another. Feed the baby, place her in the pram, listen to her fuss until she starts screaming again, pick her up. *Motherhood feels too much like Limbo,* Freya thinks.

At last, Freya's phone buzzes. She picks it up. 'Where are you?'

'Outside your apartment. Where are you?'

'At a café off the Shambles. I'll leave now.'

'Dad's heading inside. I can meet you at the café.'

'Meet me at the city wall. I'll be there in fifteen minutes.'

Freya pays the bill and tucks Avaline into her pram. Her cup

of tea sits untouched on the table. Scum floats on the surface —
grey — the colour of dead flesh. She never even got to taste it,
although she sat there for hours, cuddling her daughter through
sleep and wakefulness, staring out of the window at the Medieval
city. Customers have come and gone; snippets of their conversations overheard — tourists, students, lovers, families, each
with their own lives.

'You're a good mum,' the waitress says.

Freya weaves the pram between tables and out of the café.
Avaline sniffs the air.

'Hush,' Freya urges.

Avaline pushes her blanket up with her tiny feet, looks into
her mother's eyes and makes a hiccupping sound.

'Don't cry.' Freya blinks back her tears.

Avaline smacks her lips noisily and reaches for the blue and
green giraffe beside her pillow. Freya picks it up and passes it to
the baby, steering the pram one-handed, glancing up every now
and again to avoid other pedestrians. 'Grampy and Uncle Ivan
are coming.'

Ava suckles the misshapen nose of the giraffe and sleeps.
Freya pushes the pram faster towards her destination — the wall
and Ivan. She spots him in the distance under the arch of the city
wall and smiles, forgetting for a moment her fear and grief until
it all comes flooding back. Ivan puts his arm around her shoulder
and pulls her towards him.

He bends his neck to glance into the pram. 'She's beautiful.'

Freya nods.

'Let's get you to Dad.' Ivan touches the handlebar of Avaline's
pram. 'May I?'

'Sure.' Freya hooks her arm through his. Elbow to elbow,
they walk under the arch, out of the old city and into the new.
'I'm sorry.' Freya's voice breaks into sobs. 'What will we do?'

'I haven't even seen the flat yet,' Ivan answers. 'We'll see
what Dad and Bill say when we get there.'

'Bill?'

'Dad's friend. Don't you remember? Maybe not. You were

young.'

They turn the corner onto Freya's street. 'Where's Dad's car?' she asks.

'It was here.' Ivan pulls out his mobile phone and calls their father, but there's no answer.

Freya unlocks the front door and pulls the pram inside. 'Dad?'

The house is silent. Leaving Avaline and the pram in the hallway, Freya and Ivan squeeze past, climb the stairs and head for the bedroom. The bed has been stripped. A dark stain on the mattress is the only trace of Rob which remains.

'Help me,' Freya says, lifting the side of the mattress.

Together they flip it over, but the stain is larger on the other side, so they turn it back.

'I guess Dad couldn't fit this in the car,' she says. 'Do you think we can wash it?'

Ivan sits on the floor in silence, shaking his head.

'He's protecting me,' Freya says. 'It looks like I did it, so he's protecting me. He always protects me.'

Ivan looks away.

'What about this mattress?' Freya is rambling but cannot stop. Despair stalks her, and she dare not give it room to grow. 'Maybe I should burn it? Help me drag it into the garden, Bro.'

Ivan shakes his head. Worry lines cast the shadows of his doubts across his forehead. 'We should have called the police.'

'Well, we can't now. Dad's made sure of that,' Freya answers.

'Rob has work and family. It's only a matter of time before people come looking for him.'

'Ava and I won't be here. We'll come home with you. Help me get rid of this mattress.' She tugs the heavy corner, cursing its weight and bulk.

'You can't burn the mattress in the garden. Think of the smoke. Someone will call the fire brigade.'

'What do you suggest?' Freya snaps angrily.

'Wait for Dad and Bill to get back.'

Freya shudders. Her eyes fix on the bloodstain. She sniffs

and takes a deep breath. 'Okay. Do you want a cup of tea?'

Ivan stares at her. Thoughts seem to dart behind his eyes. 'No, thanks.'

Freya heads to the kitchen and switches the kettle on anyway. She moves from foot to foot, unable to be still. *Dad's doing what needs to be done. He's saving Avaline and me.* The kettle bubbles as the water warms. She holds her hand in the column of steam, letting it scald her skin.

From the top of the stairs, Freya watches her daughter sleep while she sips her tea. It feels like the calm spot at the centre of a hurricane, and she imagines Rob kissing her goodbye before heading to work.

The front door opens, and her father steps inside.

'Hi, Daddy.'

Mike glances in the pram then climbs the stairs. 'Hey, Freya. Is that tea? I'm parched. Could you make us a cuppa?'

Bill trudges after him, grunting. 'What happened here anyway? I haven't seen a mess like this since…'

Mike pushes him into the bedroom before Bill can complete his sentence. When Mike returns, he is alone. 'I need to make a quick phone call then Bill and I will take the mattress while you pack.'

'I'm sorry, Daddy. I woke up and…' A tear rolls down Freya's cheek. 'He was already dead.'

Mike looks at Ivan then Freya. 'Okay. We can talk about it later if you want. First, we'll clear the apartment of everything, make it look like the three of you skipped town.'

Bill and Mike man-handle the mattress downstairs. Ivan follows them. Freya hears whispers then the front door closes.

Do they think I did this?

Well, did we?

No, of course not.

Are you sure?

We didn't, Deya. You'd remember if we did. Now think. Dad wants us to get rid of everything. Passports, credit cards, clothes.

Yes. Grab a suitcase, and we'll pack.

She recognises Ivan's tired footsteps as he trudges upstairs. 'Dad told me to clean everything. Here, put these on.' Ivan hands her a pair of latex gloves.

Freya opens every drawer, leaving cutlery and kitchenware behind, but packing everything else — toiletries, books, clothing, money and identification are squashed into suitcases while her tears dampen the fabrics. Her skin itches, and she wants out, wants to leave this place and never return.

Freya, do you think it's odd that your father knows what to do? No one found those boys, did they? Do you think?

Do I think he killed the kids who murdered our sister? Yes. I think it's possible.

Should we ask him?

Absolutely not.

Mike returns without Bill. By the time he arrives, Freya and Rob's belongings are packed.

'Is this all of it?' Mike asks. A nerve beneath his eye pulses.

Freya nods. 'What did you do with…'

'Bill's taking care of it.'

In the reflection of the rear-view mirror, Freya catches glimpses of Mike's face while his eyes study the road with cold concentration. Ivan keeps turning around in his seat to frown at her or smile at the baby.

'I'm sorry,' she says.

'It's what dads are supposed to do, sweetheart, get their daughters out of trouble. Did he hurt you?' A rush of hot anger floods the car. To her father, she is the perpetual victim; throughout these difficult years, he has never blamed her, always himself. Now he must make up for letting her sister die by ensuring nothing can ever hurt his little girl. Even if he believed she was a cold-blooded murderer, he would still want to save her, whatever it took.

'He didn't hurt me… and I swear I didn't hurt him either.'

Ivan faces her again, his stare penetrating her skin. His jaw is clenched, and his mouth trembles.

'I didn't, Ivan. I loved him.'

'No one is saying you killed Rob, are they, Ivan?' Mike's voice is hard.

Ivan turns to face the windscreen and the road ahead but doesn't answer.

'Who's Bill?' Freya asks.

'Just a friend. Someone I can rely on.'

When Freya tries to probe further, her father ignores her questions.

The three of them and the baby travel silently for half an hour while Freya rubs the handle of Avaline's car seat, trying to ignore the void in her stomach which grows and stretches through her body, pressing against her lungs and making it hard to breathe.

'Do you think I'm mad?'

'Insane?' Mike says. 'No, you're not ill. You're strange, but who wouldn't be after all you've been through. You're a survivor, Freya.'

She stares at her brother's ash blond hair while he watches the road steadfastly.

'I searched the flat after I found him… like that. There was no one else.' She is unsure whether she is speaking to herself, her father or brother, but the words spill out of her. 'I looked everywhere. The house was locked. What could have done that to him if not me?'

'I don't know, Freya, but if you say you didn't kill him, I believe you. We just need to get you away from there and things will work out.'

'Dad.' Ivan's voice trembles from the weight of his thoughts or maybe fear of his father's reaction. 'What about the police?'

'We didn't leave anything there. There was no murder. Rob, Freya and Avaline left town.'

'What did you do with the body, Dad?' Ivan asks.

'There is no body. Leave it, son.'

'How can you be so calm about this? You… you… I don't get it. What are you not telling us?'

'Drop the subject.'

'Dad?'

'Ivan,' Mike roars. 'Shut the fuck up!'

Ava wakes and whimpers. Freya places her hand across the baby's stomach and sings softly to her. Her mother's voice and the movement of the car soothe Avaline to sleep.

'I'm sorry, Freya, I didn't mean to wake her. Your mum's looking forward to seeing you both.'

Freya studies the back of her brother's head. He stays perfectly still, eyes forward as if meditating, and she wonders what he is thinking. *Is he working through all the questions our father refuses to answer, or has he escaped to his sacred space?* She remembers her own sacred space, the snakeskin, shell, skeleton and athame. She remembers going in search of Lilith and returning to the body she created with magic. She remembers everything, all of it, so why doesn't she remember killing Rob?

Deya, do you think Lilith killed Rob?

Why would she?

I'm not sure. Maybe she wants us to return home or maybe she simply enjoys fucking with my life.

CHAPTER FOUR

STAR OPENS the kitchen door and steps into fresh air. Satori found this cottage almost four years ago. It is almost identical to the home Star dreamed of before she fell in love with a demon, died, and was resurrected. It surprises her that she isn't as happy as she imagined she would be, living in a place like this.

The verdant lawn blurs into shadow below the ivy-laden stone wall of the garden's borders. At the centre of the far wall is a wooden door with weather-worn green paint that has peeled away in places like stripes. The door is bolted and locked, and beyond it, a Victorian park with trees and a duck pond waits. With no swings or seesaws, it is a space used solely by adults, who come to read or think or walk their dogs when they come at all.

She crosses the lawn, bare feet sinking into the damp grass, juggling her load as she takes an iron key from her pocket and draws back the rusty bolt at the top then unlocks the door. She rolls the anachronistic key across her palm, studying it before returning it to her pocket. It reminds her of churches and mausoleums. She turns the domed knob and lets the door sweep outwards, taking care to scan the ground for sharp stones and broken glass before skirting around thick trunks of oak and chestnut trees.

The air smells sharp and sweet like freshly cut grass, but she cannot hear a lawnmower and it hasn't trimmed the area behind her garden wall. The soft blades tickle her soles while moss caresses her toes. She finds the same spot as yesterday. The light is too harsh. She will have to adjust her palette to compensate. The bluebells looked rich yesterday, but today their hue seems dull.

She lays out her rug and opens her easel and watercolours. The half-finished picture rests before her as she opens her mind to the magic of nature. The plants and trees have voices; they speak to her. Her brush dances across the paper. Greens, blues and purples stain the landscape. Bluebells spring up before her and between them glimpses of other lives and other worlds.

Each morning, Satori leaves their cottage. He returns after the sun sets, having entertained believers and non-believers alike, reading tarot cards and performing illusions. Star wonders how much of the magic he uses is real, whether he still plays with forces beyond his control. Satori's life is as speckled with light and darkness as the parkland behind their cottage. He visits the cemetery. However often she asks, Satori will not tell her why he goes or what he gains from his time knelt at Raven's feet. The thought of it humiliates her — a bitter betrayal.

Putting down her brush, she studies her painting. The violence of her memories is echoed in her brush strokes and the half-concealed faces with hungry eyes that watch her from the shadows. To the right, one bloom drips blood which congeals on its stem while a similar sticky dampness spreads between Star's thighs.

Star screws the lid back onto the jar of water and the pigments weave around each other, merging into russets and browns. She shakes the jar and stares at the dull brown liquid, folds her easel and rolls up her rug. Arms laden, she trudges back to the cottage.

After cleaning herself, she studies her reflection in the bathroom mirror. Her blue eyes are listless from too many troubled nights. Her wild curls need taming, yet she cannot motivate herself to pick up the brush.

She wanders along the hallway and into her bedroom. A plum velvet bedspread wrinkles into valleys and peaks as she sits at the foot of the divan and tries to remember why she came into the room.

The house is quiet, like a breath held. *What is it waiting for? What am I waiting for? I have everything.* She can paint all day if she wishes, but like everything she does, her art is an echo of what she has lost.

Star lies on her bed, lifts her legs and turns her ankles, watching the play of shadow and light on her skin. A face fills her head: a male face, similar to Satori's but with darker skin and vivid green eyes. She reaches out to stroke the warm cheek of the familiar stranger, smiling as his lips move to kiss her fingertips, soft as butterfly wings against her flesh.

'I'm sorry. I'm sorry. I'm sorry,' she repeats until she falls asleep.

When she wakes, the room is dark. She wonders whether Satori has returned. 'Satori, are you here?'

There's no answer.

She imagines her son, the tiny sharp-toothed infant she discarded. He will be four now, walking and talking. 'I shouldn't have left you.'

Satori sits at a circular table covered in black velvet. At its centre rests a crystal ball, between that and him, a pack of cards. The chairs opposite are empty. People move around the room, women mostly. He lifts his gaze and smiles at a passing woman, and she smiles back.

He has read the cards for ten people already today, each with unique problems, all searching for solutions and guidance. He is their confessor. Their minds open to him, and he strolls through their memories, but some memories linger in his mind long after the customers have paid him and moved on, unwelcome stories to add to his own. He shares their pain, some of it minor, others almost overwhelming: loss and degradation, confusion and humiliation. He understands. He too has lost. He thought he found it again but realises he has been fooling himself. Star is not the woman she was. She is more and yet she is less than he hoped. She doesn't need him. Perhaps she never did.

He thinks of her beauty: her fragile, ivory face, blue eyes full of sadness and regret and her soft lips. He wishes he could make those lips smile and light her eyes with joy. *When she looks at me now, what does she see?* He has not lost his looks. Other women's reactions to his attention assure him of this. When he reaches for Star, why does she pull away?

His ears strain to hear her profess her love for him, wanting to be admired and adored. His desire, his need to lose himself in her arms is eternal and continues to burn while Star grows cold. Their lovemaking, if it can be called that, is always on her terms and simply for her gratification, an itch she must scratch that obsesses her for a few nights then leaves as quickly as it arrives. She feeds on his love like a black hole absorbs light, never satisfied and unable or unwilling to return his adoration. His eyes follow a woman around the room, watching her red hair bounce on her shoulders as she moves, and the way her white shift dress caresses her curves without clinging.

At four, Satori leaves the community hall, his crystal ball heavy in the black sports bag which he slings over his shoulder. He marches toward home, pockets bulging with notes. The air is warm and smells of freshly cut grass. He hopes it means winter has ended. He hates the cold, has for years.

His feet lead him to Ivan and Freya's house. He hurries past, turns a few more corners and stops. This isn't the way home. He's heading towards his mum's house. Here is the street where Star once lived with Raven and Donna. He approaches their old front door. A pilgrimage to his past. Memories resurface, parties hosted by Raven at the top of these stairs, including that fateful evening when he met Star. It seemed like a dream at the time. Her beauty, youth and fragility enchanted him, and he sensed something about her, something she tried to hide, that excited him. He retraces his steps out of the cul-de-sac and decides to visit his mum before heading to the cottage. It isn't far. How closely they all lived. It was inevitable that their lives would become entangled.

He passes the park gates. More memories. Some good, like drunken picnics on summer weekends and others bad, like the death of Ivan's older sister.

As he turns onto his mother's street, a thousand memories assault his mind: he hid behind this hedge to phone Star the day he returned from Paul's; he sat on this wall while Donna screamed at him; he sat on that front step for hours, waiting for his waste-of-space father to return.

Satori pushes the gate open, strides along the short path and rings the doorbell. He has a key, but he is a visitor now. He hears movement and voices from within then the blinds twitch. He waves and smiles. Marian opens the door and embraces him.

'I'm sorry, love,' she says. 'You should have phoned; told me you were coming.'

'Do you have company?'

'Yes, but they'll be gone in a moment. Come in. Grab yourself a coffee and wait in the kitchen.'

As he passes the open living room door, four faces stare at him: two men, one not much older than Satori, the other around his mother's age, and two women — dominant, strong looking women with stern faces and cold stares. One has white hair and milky cataracts, the other looks younger than Satori and pretty, despite her scorn. The young woman holds a mobile phone against her ear but does not speak. He waves at the eclectic group and heads to the kitchen.

'Pour yourself a coffee, sweetheart. I'll only be five minutes.' Marian closes the living room door behind her, and Satori cannot make sense of the hushed voices beyond.

He pours a coffee and waits obediently at the kitchen table. Soon, the guests filter along the hallway, nodding, shaking hands and saying goodbye.

'Who were they?' he asks, after Marian closes the front door.

She shrugs and pours her own coffee. 'Friends,' she answers. 'So, what brings you here? Not that I mind of course. You're always welcome, but I wasn't expecting you until Sunday.'

'I just wanted to…'

'Is everything okay?' Her mouth trembles, and he waits a moment in case she has more to say.

'Of course. It's just… things aren't how I expected.'

'Sarah?' She frowns.

Marian has never approved of Star, but he feels protective of his girlfriend. 'In part, I guess, although it's not her fault.'

'It isn't yours either.'

'Mum, did you ever fall in love again after Dad left?'

'I have plenty of love in my life. I'm not lonely. Baby, you can come home whenever you want. You've proven yourself time and time again. If it isn't working between the two of you, you don't owe her anything. You repaid that debt in full, remember?'

'I still love her.'

'Does she love you?'

Satori stares into his mother's eyes; their colour changes with her mood. Today, her grey irises are cradled within golden haloes. If eyes are the windows to the soul, her soul must be in constant flux. He shakes his head.

'You deserve love,' she tells him. 'You deserve someone who will make you happy.'

'Maybe I'm like you, Mum. Destined to be alone.'

'I'm not alone, Steve, and neither are you. Stay here a while. Let me spoil you.'

'You have your own life, and she needs me.'

'Are you sure?'

Satori shudders. Marian's words remind him of those spoken in another land years ago. *Are you sure she needs you to save her?* 'Yes, I'm sure.'

'Steve?'

'Yes, Mum.'

Marian's eyes dart towards her son. 'It's nothing. I'm just… I worry about you.'

Satori stares at the empty hallway. Shadows of Marian's friends pass the open door, tugging at a distant memory. 'Who were those people?'

'You met most of them years ago, although I doubt if you'd remember.'

Satori exhales sharply. 'Who are they?'

Marian frowns. 'You can keep secrets, but I'm supposed to

tell you everything. Is that what you think?'

'I just… I feel like I'm missing something.'

Marian fetches the pot and pours dark liquid into both cups. She speaks without facing her son. 'We're helping a friend who's in trouble. Do you remember Freya?'

Satori's chest tightens. 'I haven't seen her in four years.'

'She moved away. I… Mike… well, anyway…' She takes a sip of coffee then purses her lips.

Satori reaches across the table, but his mother leans back, out of his reach.

'Is Freya okay?' he asks.

'She had a baby. They're coming home… I… where did I go wrong?' Her eyes moisten with the word baby, and she gazes wistfully across the table.

Satori stretches his arm further and reaches for his mother's hand. 'You did nothing wrong, Mum. You're perfect.'

She stares at their joined hands before pulling away to wrap both palms around her mug of coffee. 'I wish… I could protect you. A storm's coming.'

Satori shakes his head. 'What are you talking about? I don't need protection?'

'You'll always be my son. If you had children, you'd under-stand. Is it too late?' Marian shivers.

Satori moves around the table and squeezes her tightly. 'What are you afraid of? Let me help you.' His voice carries no authority and the sense of calm and wellbeing that he wants to wrap around his mother is tainted by his eagerness to understand. 'Mum, remember those times I said strange things and you despaired because I didn't make any sense?'

She nods.

'Well, now I know how you felt.'

'I'm sorry.'

'Don't be sorry. Why are you afraid?'

Marian stands up, places her cup on a work surface and stares out of the window. Her shoulders rise and fall as she breathes deeply, but her voice sounds unsteady when she speaks.

'Your magic isn't unique, but you never learned discipline, always determined to do it alone, and now it's too late. If you'd made different choices… We'll do everything we can.' Marian covers her eyes, and her body shakes to the sound of her sobbing. 'I have a splitting headache. Can you fetch me some pills?'

Satori heads for the medicine cupboard, brings her some paracetamol and fills a glass with water. She downs the pills, and he returns the glass to the sink then holds her shoulders, hoping to reassure her.

'I think I should lie down until the headache goes away. Are you okay to let yourself out?'

'Don't avoid me, Mum. If I need protecting, at least tell me from what.'

'My head… it… hurts.' She closes her eyes and rubs her forehead. 'Look, I don't know, okay? Something's coming, but we think we might be able to stop it. I'll feel safer if you're here, with me.'

'Who can stop it? Those friends?'

'I can't do this right now, Steve, please.'

Satori is dizzy chasing after her words and trying to make sense of them. It isn't the first time his mother has gotten stuck like this, acting as though she is privy to some greater power, sounding muddled and confused. 'Will you be okay?'

'I'll be fine. I just need to sleep.'

Satori watches as Marian leaves the room, hunching her shoulders as she walks, looking ancient and weak. He is bereft without her strength. 'Sleep well, Mum. I love you.'

When Satori reaches his front door, he hears sobbing. His skin prickles, and he shivers. *What now?*

'Are you okay, Star?' he asks as he steps into the cottage.

Star doesn't reply, but the crying grows louder.

He closes and locks the door then strides across the living room. The hallway is dark, and the door to their bedroom stands ajar. He pushes it open a crack further and peers inside.

An empty bottle of tequila lies on its side on the bedside table. The hair on her bowed head is wild and tangled, and the tip of her bright red nose pokes through the curtain of locks. She rocks herself, holding a vibrator with traces of blood on its shaft.

He rushes over and envelopes her with his arms. 'Shush, it's okay.'

He takes the vibrator from her clenched fist and places it beside the empty bottle then strokes her hair, pushing tangled and damp strands away from her face. Ginger roots provide a vivid contrast against the black dye.

'What happened?'

Her sobs grow louder while their bodies rock together.

'It's okay now, Star. I'm here. You're safe. I love you. We'll get past this, okay?'

She presses her cheek harder against his chest.

'I love you,' he whispers.

Her body remains stiff as if she tolerates his touch without enjoying it.

'Star, what happened to us?'

Her shoulders move as she shrugs.

He asks nothing more, holding her while anger gnaws his stomach. He wishes he was beyond caring, but he isn't. Star will always be his responsibility. He takes care of her, hoping that one day she will come back to him, like she did four years ago. The memory of that temporary success chills him. If he knew then what he knows now, would he have bothered to travel worlds to save her?

In Binah, her body had been torn apart, but he didn't realise how deep her wounds were. Lilith's taint remains. Star internalised it, and her obsessive behaviour is becoming more pronounced and dangerous. No doctor can prescribe her pills. Officially, she is still dead. It seemed simpler at first, and now it is too late. Satori cannot help her and day by day she pushes him further and further away.

'I should go back,' Star whispers.

Satori straightens. 'Did you say something?'

'I should go back. We have a son.'

'And we left him four years ago. Give it time. Give us time, please.'

'How much time?'

'You survived a nightmare. That place was torture, but it made you stronger not weaker.'

'I miss him.'

Satori sighs. 'Our son isn't human. Who knows what he is or what he will become?'

Star puts her arms around him and squeezes as if she wants to crush them both. He doesn't struggle. Instead, he strokes her hair until the tension flows out of her and her grip loosens.

'Why do I feel like this?' she asks.

'I don't know.'

'It's a hunger. Like I'm always searching for my next hit. It took all my strength to resist today. I'm scared, Satori.'

'Let's meditate together; cleanse your spirit; start again; be who you are meant to be. Fulfil your potential.'

'My potential.' Star snorts.

'When we escaped, you healed me, got us out of prison, and helped Donna. You can heal yourself in the same way.'

'It isn't that easy. When I saw Donna and felt how much she loved me, my light shone so brightly, it flooded my mind. That's how I healed her. I reflected her own energy back. With you, in the prison cell, then all those locked doors, all that death… it exhausted me.'

'I love you,' Satori says.

'No, you love who you want me to be.'

'That's not true, and there are other ways to recharge. Use my energy, or the earth's, or the sun's. Meditation helps. It's stupid to turn your back on who you are.'

'I'm stupid because I don't want to mess around with this stuff like you do, because I think it's dangerous? You say I am strong because I survived where you couldn't. Yet you question every fucking thing I do then wonder why I can't stand to be around you.'

He pulls away and stares at her hate-filled face through narrowed eyes. 'Look, I know about Ivan. Honestly, I get it. You think he's clean. I wish you'd told me though. Not tried to keep it secret.'

'He didn't want me to tell you.' Her voice is softer this time.

'Why?'

'Maybe he's scared of you.'

'I doubt it. What does he want from you, Star?'

'To help me heal and give me time out. Pretty much what you want, except he understands the answer isn't always magic. Magic, that's all you understand, Satori. When you look at me, you see yourself with tits, but I'm not you. I don't want to be.'

'Do you want me to move out so you can be with him?'

'I don't want to be bullied and challenged. I don't want to always hear that you know best when you clearly don't.'

Satori's hands become fists and his arms tremble. 'You think I bully you?'

'I think you live your life assuming you are the most important person in the world and deserve to have everything you want. I think you want me to be someone I am not. In fact, I think that the moment I finish this sentence, you'll try to convince me that you only want me to "fulfil my potential", my potential as you perceive it, of course.'

Satori frowns. 'Maybe I should go?'

'Maybe you should.'

He stares at her in silence, and she wipes her nose with the back of her hand, returning his stare. 'I'm sorry,' she whispers.

'What for?'

'For not being what you want me to be.'

Satori shakes his head. 'I only want you to be happy.'

'Exactly.'

CHAPTER FIVE

EDENSUN'S LUNGS drag oxygen from the air as his swift feet propel him forward. Movement is his medium, and he will not be still, not until he loses them, those figures in black cloaks who shadow his every step. This weakness, powerlessness frustrates him. Lilith warned him it would be like this at first. She said it takes her twenty-four hours to gain her full strength after entering a new realm. He wonders how long it will take him.

Clothes cling to his body while rain plasters his black hair to his olive-skinned face. His green eyes dart around him, aware of shadows in doorways and scowling faces. The human form he has adopted for this mission is a thirteen-year-old youth.

His eyes search every direction for potential threats, spotting three men gathered near a doorway with a shivering dog, talking to each other. One gesticulates wildly while the others nod sagely and open their mouths to speak, filling the gaps between the roars of their companion's excited voice. The boy cannot grasp the subject of their conversation but reassures himself that they are oblivious to his presence. Ten metres or so further along the street, two children kick a football against a stone wall; they glance at him before looking away.

He pushes wet hair from his eyes and spots an open door that leads into darkness: an abandoned factory or warehouse. As he creeps towards the building, one of the three men glances at him, smiles a toothless grin and holds his gaze. He pulls his eyes from the man, checks the doorway then glances in both directions along the dilapidated terrace. Now, all three men face him, and their grey, weather-worn skins crease as they peer through the drizzle. The dog barks, and the boy is sure it smells his difference and knows he doesn't belong. He chooses not to trap himself inside and moves on.

He reaches a dank subway. A fire crackles in a metal bin near the centre of the tunnel. Its promise of warmth calls to the youth like a siren, but the people standing in a circle around the flames warn him to stay back. Greedy faces stare at him expectantly. Everyone wants something from him. Their motives are unclear, but he is certain they want something he isn't willing to give them.

A can rattles at the far end of the tunnel. A group of young men stride through the darkness toward the fire. He hears cruel laughter, and his body stiffens.

The people around the fire notice the strangers; mud-stained heads turn, and grimy bodies jerk inelegantly around the flaming bin while the light shifts and dances, making the men vanish and reappear like ghosts as they progress. Edensun hides in the shadows as the strangers converge on the hobos around the fire.

'Fuck off!' A drunken man lurches towards the group of skinheads.

'What did you say, Grandpa?' The leader strides towards the swaying man, twisting his wrist to uncoil the metal chain at his side. A sombre note resounds through the tunnel when heavy links hit the cracked concrete.

The drunk shakes his head, thinking better of his plan, but the man with the chain lifts his hand and cracks his metal whip against the skull of the staggering drunk. The vagrant's knees buckle, and he falls to the floor, disturbing stagnant water. The skinheads gather around the fallen body like hyenas. A thread of blood flows from the man's head, making the water around him pink.

With a growl, one man pulls back his leg and kicks the hobo in the lower back. Bones crunch, but the man does not cry out.

Stifled gasps of shock and confusion rise from the vagrants as they watch their fallen comrade, but none seem willing to help. The homeless people in the tunnel far outnumber the three angry men. Yet the audience scatter, fleeing the brutality like mice scuttling from cats.

The unconscious body becomes a rag doll, lifted by kicks and crushed by chains and stamping boots. Fingers of red liquid point at Edensun as he tries to comprehend what joy these men might gain from ruining the lifeless body of a stranger.

The kicks become slower and less intense. The men put arms around each other's shoulders like teammates after a winning goal. Then one of the men catches sight of the lingering witness.

'Over there,' he says.

'Enjoy the show?' the leader asks. 'Want an encore?'

Bending his back, the man holds his forearms towards the youth. Eight fingers waggle, beckoning. The man grins. His knees are bent slightly, and his face is cocked to one side. His shaven head, his heavy, black boots and the turned-up cuffs of his jeans are all spattered with blood.

Edensun stares at the waggling fingers and bloody clothing, while the other men move to flank him, cutting off every escape route.

He checks the positions of his enemies then addresses their leader, keeping his voice calm. 'We're good here,' he tells the jeering skinhead. 'Move along.'

Howls of laughter echo through the tunnel, bouncing off curved brick walls and making the youth's eardrums vibrate.

'Yeah, we're good,' one of the tribe echoes.

The others nod.

The boy picks something off the floor and rises.

'Uh, uh, uh.' The leader shakes his head. 'You're not leaving. Not when the fun is just getting started.'

Edensun grins. His teeth grow sharp.

The men's faces betray their confusion.

The leader drops his chain, and the clatter echoes around the tunnel, making bones and teeth shudder. When the echoes stop, the men ball their hands into fists and step closer until they are an arm's reach away from the boy.

Edensun ducks and lunges forwards, punching upwards and knocking the leader off his feet.

'Fuck!' The leader sits in a dark puddle, rubbing his jaw. 'Wait,' he tells the others as they move to grab Edensun. 'How old are you, kid?'

'Thirteen.'

'Thirteen.' The man rises to his feet and nods at his cronies, motioning for them to join him. 'That kid has a killer right hook. I reckon he could be the one Garlow's looking for.' The others mumble their agreement. 'Hey, kid. Come have a drink with us. I reckon you could make a pretty penny or two.'

'Doing what?'

The leader laughs. 'Nothing kinky. I ain't no ponce. Fighting. You're a lot stronger than you look. Of course, if you prefer not to let me manage your fighting career and get you out of this dump, we can always go back to plan A,' he says, bending to retrieve the discarded chain. 'What's your name, kid?'

'Mark,' he says, nodding towards the motionless body of the vagrant. 'What will you do about him?'

'Nothing. He'll wake up with a sore head and drink the pain away. Stinking wreckage, just like my ol' man. Yours too I bet, Mark. So, what do you say? Fancy getting pissed?'

Edensun pockets the rock clenched between the fingers of his right hand. 'Sure,' he says. 'Why the fuck not?'

Kevin's flat is dingy. Empty cans and bottles cover the floor around the sofa and chairs like pebbled shores around volcanic islands. Edensun steps across reefs of glass and aluminium to curl his legs up on an empty armchair the arms of which are pitted with black circles as if someone has used them as ashtrays. When he rubs his fingers over the scars, the melted fibres scratch his skin.

The three men sit shoulder to shoulder on the sofa. When Kevin offers him a cigarette, he shakes his head.

Simon lifts a bottle of Grolsh to his lips and pours the lager into his throat. 'This stuff will kill you, but who wants to live forever, huh?'

'Why did you hurt that man?' Edensun asks.

'Filthy, stinking drunk,' Kevin replies. 'He got what was coming to him.'

Edensun leans back in the chair, mulling over the skinhead's answer. His eyelids are heavy, and the oppressive warmth of the room pulls him towards sleep.

'Sure kid, get some rest. You're safe here,' Kevin assures him.

When Edensun wakes, the settee before him is empty. He picks his way across the carpet, between mounds of debris to the kitchenette. An antique fridge hums and the surfaces are covered in dirty plates, dishes, take-away cartons and mugs of cold, half-drunk tea. The bin overflows, and the oven, covered with unwashed crockery, looks grimy and black.

He leaves the kitchen and heads to the front door. It has three keyholes and two sets of heavy bolts. Edensun pulls back the bolts and pushes the handle down. The door opens. The staircase is empty.

Remaining inside the apartment, he closes the door again and looks at an alcove to his left. Two other doors hang between magnolia walls; both stand ajar. He peers into a dark room. A bed rests in the centre and a pale body in boxer shorts is sprawled across the sheet. The upper sheet and blanket have been kicked away and lie tangled like a caterpillar beside the shaven-headed sleeper.

The second door leads to a tiny bathroom. This room, although grubby, does not have rubbish strewn across the floor. A small blue bathtub, sink and toilet huddle together around a grey towel which has been spread across a vinyl floor.

He heads for the kitchen and searches for bin liners. The empty cans, bottles and cartons he stuffs into four large sacks and carries down the stairs and out of the building, placing them in a nearby bin. He looks for washing up liquid but finds only hand soap which he uses to drag grime from plates and dishes before tidying them away into empty cupboards.

By the time the sleeper rises from the bedroom, the kitchen

and living room have been cleared of rubbish. The carpet still looks dirty, but it's less hazardous to move around the room and easier to find a clean vessel from which to drink water.

'Did you do this?' Kevin asks.

'Yes,' Edensun answers.

'Why?'

Edensun shrugs. 'I had time to kill.'

The man returns Edensun's shrug and sits on the sofa. 'Thanks. Get us a cuppa will you, kid?'

'Sure.' Edensun heads to the kitchen to fill the kettle.

A cloud of cigarette smoke and the chatter of a television waft into the kitchenette. *Better than a subway tunnel*, he tells himself.

Edensun passes a mug of strong, sweet tea to the man, who grunts. 'Thanks, kid.'

'I'm going out,' Edensun tells him.

'Wait ten minutes and I'll come with.' Kevin lights a cigarette and takes in drags of smoke between sips of tea.

Edensun shakes his head.

'Okay, two minutes. I'll get my kit on, and we'll head out. Where are you heading?'

Edensun waits in the living room, easier than trying to avoid the man while he scouts the unfamiliar city. 'I'm looking for my mum, but I only know her name.'

Kevin's grunts of effort and the rustling of denim and cotton escape from the bedroom. 'How long since you've seen her?'

'Most of my life.'

Kevin strides into the room, fully dressed. 'That sucks. How old is she?'

'About your age.'

'No fucking way, kid. I'm only twenty-six. I couldn't have a kid your age.' Kevin looks at Edensun askance. 'We should hang tight and ask Garlow. He's got connections. If anyone can tell you where to look, it's him.'

'Sure, you can ask him, but I'm heading out now. I want to get a feel for the place.'

'Okay.'

Cobblestones, flattened and worn by millions of feet, many of whom were in chains, suggest a time when the harbour thrived. Now it's all shops and apartment blocks.

'Wait here a minute,' Kevin says. 'Need anything?'

Edensun leans against the shop window, gazing at men in suits and women in high heels as they hurry past. A movement, caught in the corner of his eye, attracts his attention, something in black weaving between shoppers, heading straight for him, cloak billowing like a spectre. Its steps are slow but purposeful. In the opposite direction, another figure in black stands motionless, watching him.

Edensun's heart hammers, and he looks left and right between the two robed men. Kevin is waiting in a queue and doesn't look up when Edensun taps on the glass with his knuckles. Edensun balls his fist and considers fleeing into the store, but what can Kevin do, and does Edensun really need the thug's protection?

'Come with me.' The grim smile seems fixed in place. The stranger's mouth barely moves when he speaks.

'What do you want?' Edensun's voice is loud.

A woman glances at them and an auburn curl falls across her eyes. She frowns, tucks her hair behind her ear, shrugs, then hurries away, checking over her shoulder to assuage her guilt.

'To talk,' the cloaked man says. 'Somewhere quiet.'

'I'm waiting for someone,' Edensun answers.

'We know who you're looking for,' the man says. 'We can take you to her.'

Edensun's eyes widen. 'You do?'

The man nods. The top of his head has a bald patch the size of Edensun's fist, and the skin glows pink within a halo of grey.

'What's her name?' Edensun asks.

'Not here,' the man answers.

A movement to Edensun's left as the second man strides

toward them. Edensun knocks on the shop window again.

The bald man looks past Edensun through the window. 'He won't help you.'

'What's going on?' Kevin strides toward the trio. 'Are these men bothering you, kid?'

'Do you know this boy?' the bald man asks.

'Sure,' Kevin answers.

'Do you know what he's capable of?'

Kevin sighs. 'We're not interested, Grandpa. Get lost.'

The man nods towards his companion who is less than two metres away, and his hand slips inside the black wool.

'Run!' Kevin shouts.

Kevin's punch catches the bald man off balance, and he stumbles. They sprint out of the mall, across a road and onto a grass bank that overlooks the river. Chests inflate and deflate rapidly, hyperventilating from the rush of adrenaline. Kevin laughs then wheezes, bending to rest his hands on his knees, unable to catch his breath.

'Who were they? What did they want?'

'They wanted me to go somewhere with them.'

'Fucking perverts.' Kevin spits. 'There's too much of that shit around here, kid. This city ain't what it used to be.'

'Did we lose them?'

'They'll be long gone. I'd like to know what that bastard was gonna pull from his pocket though, wouldn't you? Couldn't get into a decent scrap there. Too much fucking security.'

'Can we go back? I think they know my mum.'

'Didn't seem that way to me, kid. If you wanna go back, I'll be right beside you, but we can't be late for Garlow. It just doesn't happen. We'll look for them tomorrow if you want.'

'Thanks.'

'No problem. Gotta keep my prize fighter in good nick, huh?' Kevin punches Edensun's shoulder playfully.

Kevin nudges Edensun's shoulder.

'Hello, Mr Garlow, sir,' Edensun says.

Garlow sits in the corner of the public bar, back straight and face proud. A golden throne would suit him better than a cracked and grimy leather couch. His beard is black and grey and his suit a deep blue. He doesn't smile, but his pale blue eyes shine.

'Hello, Mark,' Garlow replies. 'Kevin has told me a lot about you. Please, take a seat.'

Edensun sits on a wooden stool, towering over the man. He slouches to reduce the height differential.

'Kevin tells me you're searching for your mother. How did you lose her?'

'She left me. One day a man came, and she left with him. I haven't seen her since.'

'How old were you?'

'A baby.'

'Kevin tells me she was very young.'

'I guess so.'

'Do you know why you're here?'

'To find my mum.'

Garlow smiles. 'No, here with me.'

'Kevin says you want me to fight.'

Garlow leans forward and taps Edensun's knee. 'I wonder…' Garlow rises and pulls his coat over his shoulders. He nods at Kevin who follows him out of the room.

Edensun straightens up in his chair. Dotted around the bar are five other bald-headed men. Some wear suits, others wear jeans and short-sleeved shirts. They drink and chat together. Occasionally one or two of them glance across at Edensun before resuming their conversations.

Edensun presses the palms of his hands together, folding his fingers over his knuckles and bouncing his chin against their peaks. He scratches the top of his head then his neck, shuffles his shoulders and moves about in his chair, leans forwards, rests his elbows on his knees and breathes into his palms then repeats the movements until he can remain seated no longer. He stands up and strides to the door.

A large man moves in front of him to block his way. 'Where are you going, kid?'

Edensun glances at the door then faces the man. 'Toilet.'

The man nods and steps aside. Eyes follow him as he walks through the door marked "Gents".

The door opens while he is washing his hands, and Kevin's reflection fills the mirror.

'He's gone,' Kevin says.

'What did he say about me?' Edensun asks.

'He's got a job for you. Not a fight, nothing happening there for the moment. A delivery.'

Edensun reaches for the towel but recoils when he notices the black and cream patina of mould, rubbing his wet hands on his jeans instead.

Kevin takes a package from his pocket and passes it to Edensun. He goes to open it.

'No.' Kevin shakes his head emphatically and passes Edensun a piece of paper. 'The address is on that.'

'Are you coming with me?'

'Not this time, kid. Meet me at the flat. Do you like curry? It's curry night.'

Edensun stares at the address on the piece of paper. The streets all look the same. 'Excuse me,' he calls to a woman striding past but, if she hears him, she fails to show any indication.

Edensun sighs and sits on a bench, turning the paper over and over in his hand as life passes him: businesspeople, mothers, children, elderly couples and lonely looking people wandering aimlessly. Clutching the paper in his hand, he walks towards a white-haired man sitting quietly on another bench.

'Excuse me.' Edensun sits beside the old man. 'Can you help me?'

'What's the trouble, kid? Shouldn't you be in school?'

'Day off.' Edensun passes the man the piece of paper. 'Do you know where this is?'

The man pulls a pair of glasses from his coat and studies the note. 'Yeah, I grew up around there. You need to catch the… number nine. Head out of town and under the motorway. Get off at a rank of shops… what's there now? Hmm, a ladies' hairdressers… a hardware store, and a flower shop, yeah.' The old man nods thoughtfully. 'I'm pretty sure they're all still there. Get off there and walk up the hill toward a telecommunications tower. Impossible to miss. Pierces the sky, it does. There's a road called… Church Lane, no Church Terrace… well, Church something. After the church, you'll come to a bend…' The man's body sways as if he is turning a corner in his mind. 'There used to be an old play park on the right. Dunno if it's still there… probably houses now. There's a steep, narrow street. That's the road you're looking for.'

Edensun scratches his neck. 'Thank you, sir. Number nine bus?'

'Yup. They're pretty regular. There's a stop close to the cinema, just over the way. I can't remember the name, but it's one of the old ones — pretty. I took dates there when I was young. Always took my lady friends to the pictures. Do you like films, son?'

Edensun stares at the road sign and checks the paper in his hand. It's a match. Blocks of flats on either side narrow the street, creating a claustrophobic tunnel. He reads numbers on the sides of buildings. 'Forty to Fifty two… Fifty four to sixty six… Sixty eight to Eighty.' He checks the note again, one hundred and six, walks up to a narrow door and studies an arrangement of buttons on the right, locates 106 and presses. No answer. He waits a few moments and presses again.

'Hello,' a female voice crackles.

'It's Mark.'

'Mark who?'

'Garlow sent me.'

'I'll be right down.'

The door clicks open, revealing a woman with short, blonde hair. She wears a dressing gown and exudes a smell like nothing he has encountered before — repugnantly sweet and bitter. He considers thrusting the envelope into her clawed hand and leaving. He dips his hand into his pocket, but she shakes her head. Her touch is soft like a gnat flitting between the hairs on his forearm.

'Come inside,' she says.

He looks around the empty street again, longing to be gone from this place.

'Inside.' Her breath makes his stomach churn.

He stands at the doorway shaking.

'Come on. Hurry up.'

He removes his hand from his pocket, leaving the package inside. She nods and steps back from the doorway into the shadows.

They climb three flights. The sharp bones of her slender hips stab at the air as she moves. He has never felt more uncomfortable in the presence of a woman.

She draws a key from the deep pocket of her velour robe and opens the door to her flat. The windows are shuttered, and the room is dark, but she does not switch on the light. She moves effortlessly around the room, seeming not to notice the darkness. He watches her movements with fascination as she bends to remove papers from a drawer. One of the two envelopes has the letter G scribbled on the front, the other is hidden behind the first.

'This is for Garlow,' she says, passing the envelope to Edensun. 'Do you know where you have to take this one?'

Edensun shakes his head as she passes him a second envelope with the letter J written in what looks like a red felt-tip pen. She taps the envelope with her forefinger. Her nail is long, curved like a talon and stained brown along its edge.

She scribbles an address on some paper and passes it to him. She is obviously a witch, young and yet old as if the magic she accesses has aged her prematurely. Her appearance, like her apartment, is chaotic. She seems oblivious to the true nature of the presence she has welcomed into her home. He would have expected some sign of recognition, a positive or negative reaction to his existence, but she displays neither, so wrapped up is she in the chaos in her head that she appears detached from the world outside.

She snorts and holds out her hand. 'What have you got for me?'

He pulls the package from his pocket and passes it to her.

'Ta,' she says. 'Is my address written down anywhere?'

He nods and passes the scrap of paper to her. 'I'll dispose of this.'

'Can I go?' he asks.

'You don't want to stay for a cuppa?'

He shakes his head.

'Give my regards to G.' She leans past him and pulls the door open. 'You can find your own way out, right kid?'

As he starts to move, she grabs his wrist. Her face darkens, her eyes roll back, and her breaths become shallow. He tries to pull himself from her clutches.

'I see you,' she whispers.

Edensun prises her fingers from his arm and hurries down the stairs. He rushes out of the building, pinching his nose, trying to squeeze remnants of the smell from his nostrils. He coughs and gulps air into his lungs. He runs away from the building, hoping he never needs to return. By the time he reaches the bottom of the hill, calm is restored and his heart and breathing slow.

Edensun delivers the second envelope without incident but, as he turns away from the street, he feels a furious tug in his stomach. He closes his eyes and investigates, picturing a chessboard. The black bishop fades and becomes translucent.

Satori is practising magic. Somewhere in the city, the magician is leaving Malkuth and travelling to the planes of existence.

It is time to visit his father. When Marian opens the door, Edensun is acutely aware of his oversight. She belongs to the group of robed strangers who have dogged his steps. Her eyes darken as she recognises him and invites him inside. His mind works quickly to change this unexpected problem to his advantage. When she raises a brown bottle from an occasional table, he blusters around the room as noisily as possible, begging her at the top of his voice to have mercy on him. She screams at him and swings the makeshift weapon.

CHAPTER SIX

SATORI SITS on the edge of their bed. 'See you Monday.'

Star stirs under the duvet. 'Oh, yeah. Have a good weekend.'

He considers kissing her lips, soft, supple, frowning. Everything from her chin downwards is cocooned in black cotton as if her head was decapitated and left on his pillow as a warning.

He sighs and blows her a kiss before hoisting his bag onto his shoulder. Her cheeks twitch in what might be an uncertain smile. He turns away and leaves the cottage, locking the door behind him.

'Steve!' Marian kisses both his cheeks and ushers him into the house. 'I made up your bed for you. Dinner will be ready in half an hour. Do you want a drink?'

'Hi, Mum.' Satori embraces her. 'Can I help with anything?'

'No, no. Just relax. Wine, whisky, coffee?'

Satori nods. 'Whatever you're having will be great. I'll just pop my bag upstairs.'

'Coffee's already made. Shall I bring a cup up to you?' She studies his face, perhaps searching for cracks in his armour.

He protects her from his tears, holding them back with a smile. 'I'll grab it in a minute. Thanks, Mum.'

'There's no hurry, love.'

Satori takes his bag to his old room. His possessions drag on his arm as he trudges up the stairs. His door groans when he opens it, protesting his long absence. Marian has placed a

Turkish rug over the bare floorboards and a dark red armchair by the window. The bookshelves are filled with novels, and his old, black duvet is tucked into his single bed.

He opens his wardrobe. Empty hangers wait to be filled. He closes the door again and drops his bag on the bed then sits beside it, bouncing, remembering times spent in this room, studying, practising magic, making love. Memories flow through his mind, not swamping him with their weight, simply visiting, saying hello then making way for the next one. He sits with his hands on his lap and closes his eyes, letting each memory come and go in their polite and orderly fashion. This was where he lived. He may have been flawed, he may have been selfish, but here he truly lived.

He could leave Star and start again, put it all behind him; be free. *Why is it so hard to leave? She doesn't need me. She never has. I needed her once, but now? I should leave. This weekend I'll find out whether I miss her. Maybe I won't?*

He unzips his bag. His clothes are folded neatly inside, and he piles them on the bed before hanging them in his wardrobe. Next, he removes a toiletry bag, two books, three pens, a journal and his MP3 player, the earplug wires coiled snugly around it. He pushes the bags under his bed then places the books, pens and journal on the floor within easy reach. Finally, he unravels the wires of his MP3 player and places it on top of the bookcase.

He sits with a pen in his hand and his journal on his lap and writes the word Star, following it with a question mark. Turning the page, he doodles. The glyph resembles an elaborate figure 8 drawn diagonally. He stares at it while tapping his pen on his bottom lip. After sitting like this for five minutes, he closes the journal, puts it and the pen with the others, and returns downstairs to his waiting mother.

After dinner, Satori stretches across his bed, rubbing his back against the familiar cotton, creasing the duvet around him like a nest. *Home.*

He imagines a place where he can be himself without fear of judgement. The planes were the only places he felt free. He went there to find Star and found much more.

He closes his eyes and tells his mind to return to Yesod with its violet shifting sky and bone white earth. He yearns to see Gabriel again.

The brightness of the purple sky is blinding. He shelters his eyes with his hand and salutes the world. Air moves around him, touching him, stroking his body, embracing him.

The ivory soil beneath his feet is hard and cool, and he leaves no imprints. He scans the horizon for hints of life, something to head toward, but the agitated sky makes him dizzy. He closes his fingers around a metal object in his fist — his athame. Lifting it to the sky, he calls, 'Gabriel, come to me.'

Light bounces off the curved blade, whirling in a vortex, a tunnel of air and colour. Satori waits, but Gabriel does not appear. The vortex expands until he is part of the whirlwind. He holds his knife up again and whispers, 'Take me to him.'

His body is tugged to the right. His neck jolts violently and he grabs it with one hand trying to relieve the pressure. He is flung onto the ground, landing awkwardly on his knees. The beautiful naked man towers above him, a gentle smile on his perfect lips. The angel extends his enormous hand towards Satori who grasps it, allowing himself to be pulled to his feet. Even standing, Satori barely reaches Gabriel's chest.

'Welcome back. I suspect years have passed since the sun and moon embraced. Did you save the woman?'

'That sun was Star, the woman I came to save.'

Gabriel's eyes widen. 'You said she had power.'

'Not anymore. She's thrown it all away,' Satori says.

'You sound bitter.'

'She doesn't love me.'

'And?'

'I don't think I love her anymore.'

Gabriel shakes his head. 'You're merely feeling sorry for

yourself. Remember your love is not for one woman but for everyone and everything. All is one. It's a beautiful truth if you can accept it, Satori. I'm about to make crupta, will you eat with me?'

'I can't. The rules will not let me eat here.'

'Then what can I offer you?'

Satori smiles. 'May I?' he asks, widening his arms.

Gabriel smiles back. 'You wish to hold me?'

'Yes.'

Gabriel cocks his head and stares at Satori. 'Why?'

'It's hard to explain. I guess love for me needs physical expression to feel real.'

'Physical expression?' Gabriel shrugs. 'You need the physical to express the metaphysical?'

'Umm, yes. I guess I do.'

'You may hold me.'

Satori wraps his arms around Gabriel's waist. The angel's muscles are hard and lumpy against his skin and Gabriel's energy prickles him, making Satori's hairs stand on end. He shakes as he tries to keep hold. His teeth chatter and his eyes roll back in their sockets; he bites his tongue and blood drips down his chin. He lets go and looks up at Gabriel.

Gabriel smiles. 'Sit with me while I prepare my meal. I enjoy listening to your wisdom and folly.'

Satori sits on the hard earth beside the newly made fire. As before, a pot stands above the flames. The gentle aroma grows stronger as the broth warms.

In the distance, Satori hears the splintering of glass then a cry of rage. 'Did you hear that?'

'What?' Gabriel asks.

Satori strains his ears and hears shouting and the thud of something heavy hitting the floor. The violet sky fades until he is surrounded by the whitewashed walls of his bedroom. He sits up on his bed and hears his mother scream.

He pushes himself to his feet, shaking the remnants of Yesod from his mind. *Mum!*

He races down the stairs, leaping over the final four, and runs into the living room. His mother is there, the neck of a broken wine bottle in her hand, while at her feet, curled into a foetal position, is a boy.

Satori squeezes Marian's shoulder. She looks at him through glazed eyes as he removes the broken bottle from her hand.

'What happened?' he asks.

She nods towards the boy on the floor. His shoulder-length, black hair is matted with blood, and his skin looks frighteningly pale.

'Help me tie him up, before he wakes,' Marian says, her voice bordering on hysteria. 'Rope, get some rope, Steve. I need to tie him to a chair.'

'Who is he? What did he do?'

'I'll tell you, I promise, but first we need to make sure he can't hurt us.'

'Hurt us? He needs an ambulance, Mum. Is he still alive?' Satori bends down and touches the boy's wrist. The pulse flutters, weakly.

When he looks around the room, his mum has gone. He hears her voice in the kitchen. 'That's right. Yes, hurry.'

She puts the phone down as Satori joins her. 'How long until they get here?'

'Not long,' she answers, picking up a chair.

'What are you doing?'

'Just in case, Steve. It will make me feel safer.'

'Mum, you can't!' Satori tries to wrestle the chair from her.

Her grip is firm and, however hard he tugs, she does not let go. 'He came here to kill us, Steve.'

'I didn't see a weapon.'

He grabs the chair again, but she refuses to release her hold; he sidesteps to block the door, preventing her from reaching the living room and the unconscious boy. Marian swings the chair. The blow knocks Satori off his feet. His head hits the edge of the freezer, and he blacks out.

Satori hears the front door close then voices, whispers. He tries to sit up, but his head spins, and he vomits. The whispers grow louder. He lies down and watches through the narrow slits between his lashes. A red-robed woman hovers in the open doorway, glaring at him.

'He'll be out for a while,' Marian says.

The other woman's voice is deep and soft. She speaks as though she expects to be obeyed without question. 'What will you tell him when he wakes?'

'Don't worry, Jessica. I'll think of something.'

Jessica leaves the room, and Satori wriggles across the floor, ears alert for sounds of their return.

'How did you find him?' Jessica asks.

'He rang our doorbell. He said he was drawn here.'

'By what?'

'Morrigan only knows. I invited him in and...'

'Did he attack you?'

'No. He insisted on seeing my son. When I said he couldn't, he was about to leave. I stopped him.'

'Well done, Sister Marian. Brother Bill, help us get the demon into the van. We need to get him out of here before Marian's son wakes up.'

Satori hears a groan. 'He's heavier than he looks,' a male voice says. 'Grab his feet, Mike.'

The woman snorts. 'What's wrong with you? He's only a child.'

'He isn't only a child, is he?' Marian says. 'He's the one she predicted.'

Satori peers around the kitchen door. The hallway is empty. Satori takes a key from under the bread bin and unlocks the backdoor, opening it slightly. Breeze freshens his face, and his strength returns.

He creeps into the hallway and listens to grunts of exertion as the men struggle with the boy. A shoulder nudges into the hallway, and Satori runs straight for it, hitting it with the full impact of his elbow and knocking a man to the floor.

Satori grabs the boy. Freya's father stares at Satori in anger and amazement.

'Steve!' his mum shouts as he sprints toward the back door with the boy over his shoulder. 'Steve, come back!'

The boy isn't heavy at all, although his body slams against Satori's stomach and lower back as he runs.

'Help me,' a weak male voice begs.

'I am,' Satori answers.

Satori races along a shadowy lane between the gardens of his neighbours. 'I'll… get you… to the… hospital.'

'Don't. They'll find me there.'

'Your head's bleeding. You need to go to a hospital.'

'I heal fast. You can put me down. I can walk.'

'Are you sure?'

'Yes. I just need somewhere safe to hide, where they won't find me.'

Boy and man march side by side. Their steps are urgent, and they keep to side streets, away from traffic.

'Where do you live?' Satori says.

'I don't have a home.'

'I know a place. I can take you there. What were you doing at my house?'

'Looking for you.'

'Why?'

'I was drawn there by your magic.'

Satori grinds to a halt. He frowns and narrows his vision to a graphite stare. 'My magic… Why did Mum hurt you?'

'They've been watching me for weeks, trying to get close, trying to kidnap me. I don't know why.'

'Who?'

'The people in your house.'

Satori paces, flapping his arms, trying to think. 'Do I know you?'

'We met a long time ago.'

'Who are you?'

'I'm Mark. Look, we need to go somewhere safe. What if they find us?'

Satori stops pacing and marches along the lane without checking whether the boy is following in his wake. 'We'll find a taxi. There's this place. I think it's empty still.'

'Thanks.'

Headlights sweep around the street corner and an orange rectangle glows on the roof.

'Taxi!' Satori shouts, lifting his hand.

The taxi pulls up and Satori and Mark climb onto the back seat.

'Where to?' the driver asks.

'Snuff Mills,' Satori says.

Grunting, Satori pushes the iron gates, but they do not yield. Frustrated, he shakes them before finally admitting defeat. 'We'll have to climb the wall.'

Mark nods, peering between the bars of the gate at the long driveway and Gothic mansion beyond. 'Who owns this place?'

'An old friend. He's dead, but I don't think it's been sold yet. We should be okay to stay here for a while.'

'Should?'

'There are no guarantees in this life, kid.'

'Please, don't call me kid. Everyone calls me kid. Call me Mark.'

'Sorry, Mark. There are trees around the side. That'll be the easiest place to climb, and the drop shouldn't be too challenging.'

'Go through the neighbour's garden?'

'Their wall is lower at the front.'

'Lead the way.' Mark makes a sweeping movement with his right arm; the theatrical gesture charms Satori.

He grins at the youth. 'Feeling strong enough for this?'

'Never better.'

'How's your head?'

'It was just a scratch. Your mum hits like a girl.'

Satori snorts. 'When we get inside, you're going to tell me what all that was about.'

'I would if I could. I'll tell you as much as I know.'

'Deal.'

Satori and Mark scramble over the neighbour's wall. As they drop to the other side, they hear barking. Three Rottweilers race towards them, jaws hanging open, saliva soaking their chins and dripping onto the claws of their huge front paws. The dogs stop a metre away, eyeing the intruders suspiciously and growling.

Satori backs away.

'It's okay.' Mark's voice is low and calm. He squats, putting his arms out at either side of his body. 'You're not going to hurt us.' He faces each dog in turn. The dog at the centre growls louder, but the others quieten down. 'You have nothing to fear from us. We're just passing through. Do you understand?'

The Rottweiler takes a step towards the youth.

'Watch out,' Satori urges. *The boy is mad!*

The dog shakes its head and saliva sprays in every direction. Mark wipes some from his cheek and laughs. The dog takes another step forwards. Now, dog and boy are muzzle to muzzle, and the Rottweiler's nostrils expand and contract as it sniffs the intruder. Mark's right hand edges toward the dog, and it growls again.

'Mark!' Satori warns.

'It's okay. Isn't it, girl? You don't want to hurt me.'

The growling softens, and the crazy kid continues to move his hand toward the dog. The bitch glances at the boy's hand and cocks her head as if trying to make a decision. Mark strokes the short fur between her alert ears. She growls when he touches her, and Satori's skin crawls at the warning.

'That's good, isn't it?' Mark says.

She lies down and stops growling.

'Good girl,' Mark tells her. 'We're going to climb the wall

over there. Neither of us is going to hurt you, and we won't stay in your territory for long.'

Satori stares open mouthed. 'How?'

'I have a way with dogs,' the boy says. 'Shall we?'

'Are you sure it's safe?'

Mark grins. 'Nothing can be guaranteed, right?'

Satori grins back, appreciating the kid's sense of humour. 'Okay. Let's do this.'

They cross the well-kept lawn, the three Rottweilers following on their heels. They keep a measured pace, sticking to the edges of the garden and the shadows. A conifer stands about forty metres ahead.

'There?' Mark asks.

'Looks likely.' Satori moves to overtake the boy, but growls of warning make him change his mind.

When they reach the wall, Satori tests the branches of the tree. They are supple and bend when he pulls them. They should hold Mark's weight if not his own. He looks at the wall, testing for hand and foot holds. Memories of scaling the sheer wall of the obsidian mountain in Yesod chill him. This should be much easier and only a twelve-foot drop onto grass if he falls.

'Stand clear. I'll check what the drop on the other side looks like, okay?' Satori says.

'Sure, but just so you know, I could scale that tree in five seconds flat, old man.'

Satori scoffs. 'Go on then… kid.'

'Touché. See you on the other side.'

'Check the drop before doing anything stupid.'

Mark pulls himself through the branches and twists his body to sit on the apex, king of the proverbial castle, swinging his legs like a little boy and smiling down at Satori.

'What's it like on the other side?'

'Drop and roll.' Mark vanishes.

Satori scales the wall and lands with a bump on the other side. 'You okay?'

'Not a scratch.'

'We'll try to get in through the back. If not, there's always his summer house.' Satori points at a white building to their right then strides ahead through the overgrowth.

'How long has it been empty?' the boy asks.

'Four years.'

'What happened to the owner?'

'He was murdered by a demon,' Satori says.

'Which one?'

Satori halts and stares at the boy. 'You believe me?'

Mark shrugs. 'Which demon murdered this guy?'

'Lilith.'

Mark chuckles. 'Nobody important then.'

Satori cocks his head to one side, intrigued. 'How old are you? Thirteen… fourteen, do you practise?'

'Practise?'

'Magic.'

'No, but I've picked up a thing or two along the way.'

Satori's fingers tingle. He forces himself to look at the house rather than the strange boy. A memory lurks in the far reaches of his mind, something his mother said, and he tugs at the memory, but it makes him dizzy.

They reach the side of the house and follow the wall to the rear.

'There might be squatters here,' Satori says.

A panel of the French doors has been smashed and the door forced open. Glass covers the entrance to the kitchen and words and drawings have been scribbled in black and red across the white tiled walls. Mounds of debris are scattered across the floor and surfaces — cigarette butts, bottles, takeaway boxes, tissues and blankets. Satori steps sideways through the open door and the kid follows. There's no one in the kitchen, but the wreckage defies all logic. Why would someone do this?

'Do you think they're still here?' Mark asks.

'Probably,' Satori says.

The two of them cross the kitchen and open the door to the hallway. The hallway is untouched. There are no footprints on the dust-powdered floor.

'Why did they stop in the kitchen?' the boy asks.

'Maybe something scared them.'

'Lilith?'

'No,' Satori answers. 'Something else.'

Satori steps into the hallway, his footprints marking the dust like virgin snow. The dark wood panelling, the grand staircase and dramatic portraits make it seem like the house of an old maid rather than the lair of a vibrant magician. It is easy to imagine Miss Haversham descending the staircase in her flaming wedding gown.

Mark moves behind him. 'Wow!' the boy exclaims.

Satori shakes his head to clear the fog-like dust motes in his eyes and points to a door. 'That was always my favourite room. Paul's library.'

'Shall we see if it's been damagzed?' The youth opens the library door.

The library is exactly how Satori remembers it. He remembers Star stroking the spines of Paul's paperbacks. 'Sit down.'

Mark does as he is told and settles himself in one of the two leather armchairs. 'Do you think we could light the fire?'

Satori grabs pre-cut blocks of wood from the box beside the fireplace and sets them in the grate then looks for a bin. There's one beside Paul's desk, and Satori pulls a crumpled piece of paper from it. The paper is dry and lights easily.

'Who are you?' Satori asks.

'My name is Mark. I came here looking for my mother, but this city is crazy; people have been chasing me ever since I arrived — those men in black and some guy called Garlow with his gang of thugs. I don't understand any of it, or why they think I'm important.'

Satori's mind struggles to fit the pieces of the puzzle together. He remembers the robes from his distant past — an argument, and his father calling Mum a witch.

What else can I remember? Dad hit Mum, and she fell onto the sofa, laughing. Dad didn't see me, too busy trying to stop Mum laughing. I remember blood, so much blood. Dad fell onto the coffee table and glass exploded beneath him. His blood on Mum's dress.

A woman pulled me from Mum's arms. I fought and bust the woman's lip. More red. I hid in my room.

The next day the coffee table was gone. Mum made me eggs. She smiled and told me it was a bad dream, but her cheek was bruised.

Mark fidgets in his seat. 'It's so cold. Can we move closer to the fire?'

Satori rubs his hands together. 'It'll warm up. Tell me about your mum.'

The boy wraps his arms around his body and shivers. 'That's my business.'

'You promised to tell me everything, but nothing you've said so far makes sense. What about this man Garlow?'

'I met him through... well that doesn't matter. He gave me some delivery jobs.' The teen fumbles in his pocket and pulls out an envelope. 'I had to drop a packet to a woman, and she gave me two envelopes. I delivered one, and I was supposed to hand this to Garlow, but I came to you instead.'

'What's inside?'

'Money probably.'

Satori leans forward and holds out his hand. 'Can I see?'

'Are you going to open it? What if I piss Garlow off? He has the eyes of a shark.'

Satori's hand, palm up, hangs in the space between them. 'If you want my help, you'll show me that envelope.'

Mark hands the envelope to Satori who turns it over. Apart from the letter G scribbled on the front it has no further information on the outside. He squeezes the paper. The envelope is too thin for a wad of banknotes and too stiff for a single note.

The boy leans forwards as Satori tears it open. He pulls out a photograph, turns it over and studies the image. He shows it to Mark before looking at it again, more closely. It's a photo of a raven's head with a red ribbon tied around its beak; there's nothing else inside. He shows the empty envelope to Mark then passes both to the kid. *More questions and no new answers.* 'Any ideas?'

Mark stares at the photo. 'A warning?'

'Who gave it to you?'

'A woman. She smelt bad. I think she's a witch.'

'A curse?' *A face nudges into Satori's thoughts, pale and beautiful. Raven? Can it be a coincidence?*

'You think she's cursing Garlow?'

'Or he ordered a curse for someone else, and this is proof that she's carried out his instructions.'

'Garlow didn't seem… he's just a guy who has a load of skinheads doing stuff for him. A gangster or something, but he didn't seem spiritual in the slightest. He runs illegal boxing rings, probably money lending and that kind of thing, intimidation maybe. He's got the muscle for that, but the photo, the bird, it doesn't make any sense to me.'

'It reminds me of a friend. Someone I should have treated better when I had the chance.' *One regret among thousands.* His mind is full of the bird's image. He squeezes his eyelids tightly together then opens them again.

Satori lets his gaze wander over the bookshelves, recalling the time he was here with Paul and Star and how different things had seemed. *She didn't love me then, either.*

'It's getting late. Let's check the rest of the house. Maybe the bedrooms are usable. Are you hungry? I doubt there's anything here, and I'd prefer to head out and buy some stuff tomorrow when things have died down a bit,' Satori says.

'I'll be fine. I'm more tired than hungry.'

'Are you sure? It could be concussion. Do you feel sick?'

'I've had worse. Shall we check the house or curl up in these chairs in front of this lovely fire?'

'I won't be able to sleep until I check the house is empty. You can wait here if you want,' Satori says.

'I'll come with you.'

'You've seen the kitchen, or what's left of it. This is the living room.' Satori wanders into the room where he once burned Paul's clothes. Shivers run up and down his spine as he remembers the ticking sounds of the scurrying scarab beetles which devoured his friend's remains.

The furniture still holds much of its sumptuous splendour. Most of the ornaments are missing, probably removed as evidence by the police or stolen by whoever broke through the French doors. Paul's paintings remain, gracing the walls — huge oils, water-colours and original sketches including a uniquely disturbing framed picture by Crowley. Satori moves the heavy curtains and opens the large cabinet aware that the boy is studying him.

'No one here,' he says. 'Dining room next.'

The dining room and downstairs bathroom are checked thoroughly for signs of human occupation. The bathroom looks unused, and the dining room is still laid with plates and glassware as if awaiting dinner guests.

'We should check the cellar as well,' Satori says. 'I hope the lights still work down there.'

Multiple light bulbs must have failed over the years; there is barely enough light to descend the narrow staircase safely. They search the shadowy rooms for anyone who might be hiding there.

'Do you hear that?' Mark asks. 'What happened here?'

Satori stands still. Wind whistles through a gap in the tiny window frame at the top of the room. 'It's just the wind.'

'No, it isn't,' Mark says.

Satori listens again. On the edge of his perception, he hears the cries of children and shivers as he remembers the remains he discovered here before. The bones of children had lain in this cellar, casualties of Paul's magical experiments and carnal lusts. The police removed those too. The flagstones are uneven where they were carelessly replaced.

'I don't hear anything.' Satori strides towards the stairs. He spots an upturned flashlight on a worktable and grabs it. It is heavy in his hand, like a bludgeon. 'There's no one here. We'll check the bedrooms.'

Satori hovers in the doorway of Paul's bedroom. The rest of the house is empty. Despite the chill in the damp air, it is perfectly habitable. In the morning they would do well to grab clean bed linen and tidy the kitchen, but it will do for the night. *One last room to check.*

He pushes the door further open. The curtains are drawn, and he reaches for the light switch, but like many others around the house it doesn't work. He sweeps the beam of the borrowed flashlight around the furniture.

Mark shuffles about behind him. 'Satori?'

'I'm okay. Just… memories.'

'I'll check it out. Hand me the torch.'

Satori edges away from the doorway and passes the torch to the youth. 'Thanks.'

Mark steps into the room. The invisible barrier Satori felt in the doorway does not seem to bother him. The beam from the torch flashes around the room. 'Empty. If you don't want to sleep here, I'll take it.'

'Feel free. I'll take the room at the rear. See you in the morning.'

'Goodnight, Satori.'

Satori shrugs out of his clothes and collapses onto a meagre single bed. The blankets smell musty, but he pulls them around himself. In one corner of the shadow-filled room stands a large wooden wardrobe full of clothes and on the wall opposite his bed is a chimney breast with a guard in front of the fireplace. Moth-eaten drapes attempt to cover the window, and a full-length oval mirror tilts away from the bed.

Sleep comes quickly. In his dream, Satori greets his tower, the one he created before his journey across the planes of existence. He wants to climb the cairn and gain entry, but the staircase is missing, and the hill is too steep. Every time he pushes himself upwards, he slips back to the base.

A bleak and endless desert surrounds the hill. Dirty mustard-coloured sand. When he returns his gaze to the tower, the hill has vanished and its foundations rest on the sand. He steps toward the building, imagining the warmth inside — the library, chair and whisky.

A low rumble echoes around the desert. Sand crumbles and

parts as a shape emerges, rising between Satori and his tower. Black curls and a pale oval face — Star. She rises higher, holding her arms out on either side. In each hand, she holds a terracotta jug. Her body is broken, defiled and ruined. The gaping cavern of her stomach reveals bloodied entrails. Heart and lungs, still pulsing, frame the horrifying void. Her legs are held within the mouth of a giant wyrm.

She tips her head to look at Satori.

'Star,' he mumbles.

She nods and twists her wrists, tipping the jugs. From the left, a thick red liquid drips onto the sand and, from the right, flows a white liquid. Behind her, the tower shudders.

'What are you doing?' he asks.

'Nothing,' she answers. 'It's disintegrating because you don't need it now.' The corners of her lips turn up a little. Her smile is cold and humourless. The tower shakes and stones bounce off the walls before hitting the ground. More follow, shaken by the blows of other stones; the speed increases and more of the building crumbles and falls.

Everything is wrong, nothing is stable, and he doesn't understand any of it. He holds his ears and closes his eyes.

'Satori… Satori, wake up, darling.'

Satori stares at the shadowy ceiling, removes his hands from his ears and looks around the empty room. His eyes settle on the oval mirror and the soft glow that emanates from it. He approaches the looking glass, unsure whether he is awake or asleep, holding his breath while terror fills him. It reflects part of the room, but the lighting is different. The furniture is the same, and the bed he just left has creased covers where he pushed them from his body. Everything is present, but the light makes the objects less solid.

'Satori. Satori, darling, wake up.'

He recognises the voice. 'Raven?'

Something hits his chest and the sudden blow forces him backwards. His body drops, sinks and plunges, not hitting the floor; the floor has gone. He tumbles into a void. All he can see is an oval far above, glowing with golden light, getting smaller and smaller until it disappears completely, and still he falls.

CHAPTER SEVEN

STAR FIXES two drinks, pouring a generous measure of Satori's favourite whisky into a tumbler and adding ice before opening a bottle of beer for herself. She gulps the foamy head and carries both drinks to the table beside the sofa. Sinking into the second-hand settee, she closes her eyes, cradling the brown bottle in one hand.

Ivan will arrive soon. They will talk as friends before they embrace as lovers. He expects nothing from her, not even love.

A gentle knock at the door breaks through her thoughts, and she rises from the settee. *He's here.* As she fumbles with her key, she listens to his steady breathing on the other side of the wooden barrier. He looks flushed, fresh and warm; he smells intoxicating. He chuckles softly as he wraps his arms around her.

'I've missed you,' he says.

'I've missed you too.' She pulls herself away from his warmth to let him move inside the cottage and locks the door behind him. 'I made you a drink.'

'Thank you,' he says. 'Although I'm driving. I probably shouldn't.'

'You could stay here.'

He nods, smiles, lifts the glass, and sips the rich golden liquid, watching her intently. She squirms under his gaze and blushes.

'Ivan, why do you like me?'

He coughs and splutters, and his cheeks redden, but she cannot tell whether it's from nervousness, embarrassment or the whisky burning his throat. She wishes she could take back the question and has a sudden urge to run from the room.

'You're the most interesting, complex and melancholic woman I have ever met.'

She stops shaking and sits beside him. 'You mean I'm sad. He hated that part of me.'

'Satori?'

'Yes, my sadness threatened him, but it's been the one constant in my life, and I don't know how to stop.'

'You experience joy too.'

'And those moments are exquisite but fleeting.'

'We can experience a full spectrum of emotions and find value in them all.'

'Yes.' She brushes her lips against his. The whisky tastes peaty on his mouth.

He puts their drinks on the table. His whiskers scratch her chin, awakening her senses. There is no space between them. She straddles his lap and clings to his torso with all her strength while passionate kisses bruise her lips, and she explores his mouth with her tongue — tasting freedom; freedom to be herself without having to justify every thought and emotion.

'Fuck me,' Star breathes into Ivan's ear.

He pulls her top over her breasts and strokes the soft pale skin of her stomach before returning to their kiss. She pulls away, just a few inches, but enough to look into his cool blue eyes. There is no judgement in those clear eyes, no expectation. His desire fills her head with warmth and light; it makes her fingertips tingle.

He lifts her arms and slides her t-shirt over her head.

Her breasts swell beneath the black lace of her bra, and he traces her cleavage with his fingertip, making her shiver. Every cell in her body is alive with excitement and anticipation.

'I love you,' she tells him.

'I know,' he answers.

Her ears strain to hear him declare his love. He worships every inch of her body and will spend hours kissing and caressing her even after sex but has never uttered those words. If he told her he loved her, would it be to stake his claim on her? Would it mean he wanted more than she could give him? Yet, she wants to hear him say it. Why? A hangover from her lack of paternal approval and affection or more than that?

Ivan flicks her nipples with his thumb and index finger. Her bra tightens as her breasts swell beneath his touch.

He kisses her throat while she tugs his hair, strokes his ear, cheek, throat, and sculpted, hairless chest. He frees her of her bra, and she crushes her breasts against the muscles of his chest.

The words "I love you" rise in her again but she swallows them. *What does it matter, anyway?*

'Ivan.' His name is a prayer in her mouth.

She tears off her panties and returns to his lap. As he sucks her breasts, his fingers play between her thighs. She unzips his jeans, pushes her hand inside and pulls his cock between the teeth of his zip.

His fingers work her clit even as his penis fills her. She rises and falls, hair bouncing, curls obscuring her vision, but sight is the least important of her senses. She feels, tastes, hears and smells him. Ivan carries her to the bedroom. She falls onto the mattress and laughs, arms reaching for him.

They kiss again, and she spreads her legs. His fingers move against her sex, stroking, rubbing, squeezing and flicking her labia and clitoris, making her gasp. She clings to him, willing him to penetrate her, yet enjoying every moment of his attention. Her tongue flicks inside his mouth while she grinds herself against his hand, and as their passion builds, the noises they make become more frantic.

When his fingers finally plunge deep inside her, she opens her eyes, smiles and squeezes his bottom lip between her teeth.

'Fuck me,' she whispers.

His hand withdraws and is replaced by the warm, firm pressure of his cock between her thighs, then he is inside, pushing deeper, filling her, pulling out and plunging within again and again and again. His heartbeat matches hers, and their souls reach for one another, communicating joy, gratitude and a world beyond the confines of Earth and physics.

Shuddering, Star screams out in ecstasy. She digs her fingernails into his shoulders and tightens her thighs around his hips. His moans grow more frantic, his eyes roll and sweat washes his brow while he pants, grunts and matches her shudder.

He kisses her forehead before rolling onto his side. She places her cheek on his chest, and his heartbeat vibrates against her eardrum. With his arms around her waist, she falls into a deep sleep.

The room is dark when she wakes, screaming.

Ivan sits up and holds her shaking body. 'What is it?'

'A dream, I think.' She shakes her head trying to clear the images.

'What did you dream?'

'It was horrible. Satori was there. He was frightened and angry. I was…' She stares at the wall, unwilling to say more.

Ivan tries to coax her from her silence. 'It's okay. You can tell me.'

Her breath is ragged. Tears gather in her eyes as she stares at Ivan. She looks away from him before speaking. 'I was being fucked. He was watching.'

'Was he watching us?' He glances around the room as if expecting an audience.

'You weren't there. I didn't recognise any of them. They fucked me while Satori watched. It felt too real to be a guilt induced dream.'

'Do you think he's in trouble?' Ivan asks.

Star shakes her head. 'I'm not sure.'

'Call him.'

'It's late and he never answers his mobile, even after all these years. Let's go back to sleep. I'll call him tomorrow.'

Ivan lies back, and Star rests her head on his chest again, but she does not close her eyes. Instead, she watches his stomach rise and fall. Each time she attempts to push the images of the dream aside, they force themselves into her consciousness.

Thoughts spiral inwards, condensing and settling in the

centre of her mind. The weight of them puts pressure on her skull and makes her ears hiss like a boiling kettle. Ivan sleeps beside her. She could wake him, but she doubts he can help. Her thoughts reach out to Satori. Black hair obscures a face until Star's fingers push the silky veil aside, then milky eyes open, Raven grins, and Star pulls away, shivering in Ivan's loose embrace. Her eyes sting, but tears do not fill them. Her soul has been scooped from her body, and she is empty.

CHAPTER EIGHT

SATORI FALLS through darkness, arms and limbs flailing as his body panics. Terrified, he stares upwards while his mind tumbles with him, grasping at memories as though they are straws to a drowning man — the mirror, the voice, the fall. *I'm dreaming.* He tries to wake up, but the pull downwards is irresistible. Burying his fear, he concentrates on his breath and the process calms him, allowing his panic to subside. When his body is still, he straightens his limbs, placing his hands palms down, on either side of his hips then opens his eyes to search for meaning in the darkness. *What is the dream showing me? What must I understand?* When his eyes adjust, he sees bright specks, like dust motes, fall around him, becoming brighter as he studies them, until he fears they will burn his retinas — thousands of stars, falling with him through the impenetrable darkness. Like Alice, tumbling down the rabbit hole.

His progress is gentle, and the air doesn't rush past his body as he falls or floats. Something damp hits his hand. The brightness of stars fades. Millions of bubbles, some as small as the pupils of his eyes and others as large as his entire head, float upwards as he falls, popping against his skin or passing him to merge with the darkness above.

A black circle, so dark that it contrasts with the surrounding darkness as though one is black and the other white, imposes itself on the gloom above. A corona of red flames appears and grows brighter — a solar eclipse, a black sun with a crimson halo that moves around it like water, expanding and contracting. Molten flakes drip downwards, changing shape as they race towards Satori, becoming perfect spheres, bean-shapes or splatters, colliding with bubbles in violent-pink explosions or hitting Satori's skin — his face, his hands, a sudden sting before viscous warmth spreads outwards. Blood from the black sun coats him. It seeps between his lips, bitter and metallic as it crawls across his tongue and into his throat, too thick to swallow, making him cough. Spasms bend his body and air whistles past his ears as he plunges faster, leaving the blood behind to light the sky above like fireflies. He resembles an embryo in the womb.

He coughs and gags until a crimson sphere emerges from his throat onto his tongue. When he spits it out, it explodes like a firework, lighting the sky. The flash reveals a ladder bolted to the wall. He kicks his legs and swims against the air. As he flattens his body, his descent slows, and the blood drops gain on him again. His kicks propel him toward the wall, hoping the ladder is still there. His fingers stretch.

Bubbles pop against his back and legs and blood drips onto his face and chest, but he keeps kicking and pushing himself to where he hopes the ladder hangs. Finally, his hand touches something cold and smooth and another fierce kick allows his fingers to grasp the metal bar. He clings on as his legs slam against metal and stone. He hangs there, spine and shoulders pressed painfully against the rungs, clinging desperately, shaking his head, blinking and peering through the crimson film which covers his eyes.

The vicious rain ceases. One moment it is as heavy as ever, drenching him, and the next it stops falling. He looks up and can no longer see the ring of blood-fire. Bubbles glow as they drift upwards through starlight, reflecting silver as they float towards an unknown destination.

His heel finds a rung. Wary of the blood-slick iron, gripping with one fist while moving the other hand; biceps and shoulders burn as he turns his body to face the wall. Fingers wrapped tightly around the rung, he wonders whether he should climb up or down. Continuing downwards is a passive gesture, accepting what will be. If that was the only option, the ladder would not exist. To find this here, to reach it and be able to cling to it despite the slippery deluge, must mean he should climb.

Satori follows the bubbles upwards until he reaches the top of the ladder and crawls from the pit. Laughter to his left, its source unseen in the dark. He tries to ignore it and keeps crawling away from the pit. The sound follows him as he shuffles on hands and knees. Now the blood that soaks his hands is his own, skin shredded on jagged rock, but he continues, slipping and sliding, blinded by darkness, hopelessness heavy in his chest, doubting he will ever find his way.

He pauses, mentally chastising his foolishness. *I can make my own light.*

Unfurling his body to stand proud, breathing deeply to calm his mind, he reminds himself that this reality can be altered, but when he tries to draw light and energy into his body, only darkness penetrates his open chakras.

So, he concentrates on building a light inside him using his love. It burns in his stomach and chest — love for his mother, Ivan, Donna, Gabriel, Raven, and his eternal if doomed love for Star. It warms him. He blows on the embers until light fills him.

In its glow, he detects shapes in the gloom. The ground seems solid. It is safe to walk within his self-made spotlight. His vision adjusts until he is barely aware of the viscous, pulsing darkness that surrounds him, held at bay by his love.

Satori is in a large, wide tunnel, hewn by water or a giant worm. Silhouettes shift against the walls; they appear sentient but do not approach, and he has no desire to study them closer.

The air ahead glows red. As he rounds a sharp bend, he gasps. Two great obelisks reach beyond the limits of the tunnel, one pillar is white, the other black, and between them hovers a crimson sun.

He checks left and right, but there are no alternative routes, so he strides toward the twin towers — dark and light in balance, framing the setting sun.

Hot air stifles him. Satori pulls at the t-shirt around his neck, his face and body dripping sweat. A dog howls then something low and heavy approaches him from behind. Afraid to turn and face his pursuer, Satori sprints between the pillars. Energy hits him and every molecule in his body spasms. New connections form in his brain and nervous system, and a wide grin spreads across his face. The balance between his spirit and his body has never felt more intact. Reluctantly, he leaves the obelisks behind. The dying sun falls below the tunnel floor, revealing a chamber beyond.

The walls sweep upwards, creating a wide arch, the apex of which is too high for Satori to glimpse. An outcrop of rock makes a huge altar. Fresh water flows from a fissure onto and over it like a moving altar-cloth. On a ledge above the waterfall, two vultures crouch; one stretches its wings while the other follows Satori's movements with its head.

Satori strides towards the altar. An emerald-green frog leaps through the waterfall and hops between his feet toward the opposite wall where a trio of nakedness dances slowly, gyrating against each other, thirty metres away. Satori creeps closer. Stopping, the moment he recognises Star. Her hand is between her thighs, masturbating. Her throat emits bestial grunts.

The other two figures are male. A blond Adonis wraps his arms around Star's body, tugging and squeezing her breasts. The back of her head rests against the man's chest. Satori watches open-mouthed as the man penetrates Star, and his jeans strain to accommodate his excitement.

The second man has deep bronze skin. Jet-black hair moves around the nape of his neck. Star kisses him while he squeezes her ass cheeks, cock pressed against her stomach. He bends his back and angles his hips to slide between her legs and pushes inside. The three beauties grope, kiss and fuck each other. Star's body bounces between the two men as she rides them both with a grotesque look of ecstasy on her face. Her eyes, glazed with lust, face Satori, although she seems oblivious to his presence.

The blonde man squeezes her breasts until they redden and bruise. Her nipples swell beneath the pressure and milk sprays from them, hitting the other man's face.

Mark approaches the group. He acknowledges Satori's presence with a polite nod before joining the orgy. He grabs the men's buttocks and opens his mouth to catch the spray of breast milk.

Satori cannot move. He watches, aroused and horrified, punching his temples but opening his jeans to free his erect penis, hating himself for his excitement. The blows to his face do nothing to dull his lust. He squeezes his cock in his right fist and tugs until he explodes in blessed relief.

The cathedral breathes life into each droplet of sperm that Satori spurts into the air. He gazes mesmerised as his ejaculate creates shapes — a bloated female form, an angry male face, a wolf, a gargoyle with a long tongue and twisted horns. The images merge and a translucent face grows in the air. Its eyes are huge, its nose flat and wide. It opens its toothless mouth in a soundless scream and insects drop from its lolling tongue onto Satori's hair and shoulders. He brushes them off and steps back, shaking.

A female form with a solitary leg, which twists like witch hazel, grows from the ground. Her body sways as she reaches toward him with claws as twisted and misshapen as her leg.

An albino wolf shakes itself and splashes of the semen that created it scatter on the ground. Each puddle grows into a new wolf until hundreds of lupines snarl at Satori. They squat on their haunches, ready to pounce; their hungry eyes fill his vision, making his head spin.

Pain spreads from his frontal lobe to the back of his skull, pulsing with the rhythm of his heart. He covers his eyes with his hands, trying to shut out the light. The eyes get closer. He sees them through his lashes and the cracks between his fingers. They press against him. Their moisture seeps into his ears and nose. He tries in vain to beat them away before falling to his knees. The horrors change again. Eyeballs become rats which grow tattered wings like bats with rope tails. The world splits before him, and horrors crawl up from the bowels of hell to consume his soul.

Mark grabs Satori's hand and leads him away from the

spectres. Growling when they try to follow, making the terrors shrink back in fear. The boy's lips are soft and generous above his jutting jaw; his skin has a warm olive glow, and his eyes are the brightest green Satori has ever seen. They remind him of Lilith's. Hand in hand, Mark and Satori walk toward a low archway. As Satori's head and shoulders emerge into an anti-chamber, he hears the whoosh of a bird in flight then black wings beat against his face. He waves his free arm to scare the raven away. It croaks at Satori before flying out of reach.

'She's waiting for you.' The teenager squeezes then releases Satori's hand.

A sleeping woman lies on an outcrop of rock. Black chiffon rests over mountainous breasts. Ebony hair obscures the face, but Satori recognises the body; he knows it well, has stroked those generous curves. He kissed them, held them, admired them, long ago, before she died.

'Raven.' Satori strokes her hair away from her face.

Her eyes are closed, but her mouth hangs open. Her jaw smashed, bloody and bruised from the violence which killed her. He searches the youth's face for an answer.

'You must wake her with your wand. The necromancer must place their wand inside the corpse's mouth.'

'I don't have a wand.'

Mark's voice is faint. 'You used it before to summon Lilith.'

Angry hisses fill the room. Satori turns around. The kid has vanished and two snakes writhe on the ground, their bodies intertwined — one white, the other black. Satori backs away. His hand touches the ledge on which Raven rests, waiting for him to wake her. He scans the room for something, anything he could use to chase away the serpents, but there is nothing.

As he stares at his trembling hands, black letters rise across his pale skin like tattoos. The black letters he used in Binah to kill the wyrm. Memories of its terrible wail and the stench of burning flesh fill his mind, as the snakes slither toward him. *I have no choice.*

He utters magical sounds, directing the storm toward the

snakes. Lightning rips through the air, pinning them to the ground. They jerk and twist in pain as scales melt and meld together, becoming a single mass of disintegrating puss. Satori shields his ears from the sounds of their agony. When the storm burns itself out, the fused bodies fizzle and pop. With a blinding flash, the melted mound implodes, and a pebble of black glass, smaller than the palm of Satori's hand, clatters to the floor.

Satori's body shakes with energy and fear as he studies Raven. *The wand I used to summon Lilith.* He summoned the goddess twice, once to his bedroom to negotiate Star's release and once into Chaos.

I stood within a circle and called "Lilith, succubus, serpent, temptress of Eve, first wife of Adam, dark mother." I jerked off. My semen was the tribute, and she answered... my cock is my wand.

Raven's lips are drawn back, exposing blood covered stumps where teeth have been severed from their roots. Her jaw is a strange triangle, almost normal on one side, stretching into a wide leer on the other where it hangs, disconnected from her skull. Satori shudders at the thought of what he must do.

'We could have been good together. You flirted with me from the moment we met. How bold and dominant you seemed. I never looked beyond your armour. Never realised, until I slept beside your cooling body, that I could love you. I was so wrapped up in my obsession, my desire to save Star. I chased her and left you behind. I'm sorry, Raven. Do you want me to wake you? Star said she couldn't. Maybe she wasn't lying. Can I bring you back? Can I put my cock inside your broken mouth? I'm terrified. Why am I so afraid?'

He tries to look beyond her wounds, but his eyes return to her crushed cheek and smashed jaw.

'I don't think I can do this.'

He leans toward her face. A fairy tale kiss to wake the dark princess, but the congealed blood in her mouth smells sour and rotten, and his stomach churns, forcing him back. He paces the room like an expectant father, deathly afraid yet excited about the prospect of new life. *Coward! You owe this to her. Stick it in her fucking mouth. You weren't too proud to do it before.*

He picks up the glass pebble and turns it over. A fault line twists and moves at the centre. He recalls every book he has read, studies afresh every page, looking for an answer. *Is the stone important?*

'Yes, but only after you wake her.' Mark leans against the archway wearing a treacherous grin.

'I thought you'd gone.'

'I came back.'

'Are you really Mark?' Satori asks.

'Are you really Satori?' Mark replies.

Satori shrugs.

'Will you wake your sleeping beauty?'

'Yes. It's my fault she's here. My selfish obsession cost me everything.'

'It cost you less than it cost her.' The boy points at Raven's corpse.

Satori sighs. 'Don't watch.'

'I'll be outside if you need me.' Mark ducks through the archway.

'Raven...' Satori stares at her broken face. 'Oh god, I'm sorry... W-what I'm about to do...' He unzips his jeans and drags his flaccid penis into the stagnant air of the tomb. 'I guess I don't have to be hard for this.'

Gently, he turns Raven's head. There is a chasm where her ear used to be. He wipes his fingers and tries to control his nausea while holding his cock between forefinger and thumb, directing it towards Raven's gaping mouth. Swallowing hard, he bends his knees and shuffles forwards until he holds that small yet dominant part of himself between her withered lips.

She opens her eyes.

He jumps back, startled, pushing himself into his jeans and zipping them. 'Raven.'

'Satori.'

Her wounds heal. Those soft and generous lips smile at him.

Her cheek bone reknits, filling out her perfectly pale face.

'I think you might need this.' He passes the black pebble to her.

She swallows the stone. Her throat swells as it is forced downwards, then she looks normal again, beautiful.

She stands up and grasps Satori's hand. 'Let's go home.'

A single step takes them to the spare room in Paul's house. Satori lies above the covers while Raven moves around the room.

For a moment, she is perfect. She is everything. A fresh start.

Then she fades. Raven's skin, her hair, her dress become translucent. A narrow halo of light traces the edges of her body. Tears fill her eyes. 'I'm not real. I'm still dead.'

She strokes his face. Her fingers are deliciously cool. He reaches for her hand and draws it to his mouth, kissing each finger in turn.

'At least we can be together, as we always should have been.' She slides beside him on the single bed and wraps her arms around his body.

Her breasts press against his chest, and his penis, so shy before, hardens in response.

'I love you,' she tells him.

He replies with a kiss.

Satori's hands trace the lines of Raven's body, and he remembers the time she came to him in his room. Star had run off with Lilith, and Raven offered to comfort him. Her passion for him was real then, is it real now? Her face blurs as she kisses his mouth. Her hair shields them, a safe place in which they can hide from the world. Even if she is not real, her love is.

She rides him. Her breasts bounce above him as she moves. Being inside her feels cold, but her muscles embrace him, and the sensation is wonderful. He does not imagine she is Star; he imagines she is alive, that they never separated after that glorious day in his bedroom, that they are home, and the world is good and filled with love. He will never be lonely or unwanted again.

Beyond her beautiful face and thick black hair, a strange shadow moves across the wall. Satori's body tenses, but she does not seem to notice the change in him.

He focuses his vision on the wall. A strip of wallpaper hangs away from the plaster. As he stares, strips of wallpaper on either side curl and peel away from the wall. Flesh-pink plaster puckers into boils which grow larger and angrier until they burst and darkness flows from them, consuming the plaster, the wallpaper, and the wall. The room vanishes into darkness and all that remains is his single bed and, on it, his body ridden unceasingly by his dead lover.

With a strangled cry, he ejaculates.

CHAPTER NINE

AVALINE'S FRANTIC crying jolts Freya from her dreams. It takes her a moment to remember where she is and what has happened.

Freya pushes back the blankets and presses her eyelids with her fingertips. 'It's okay. Mummy's coming.' Eyes hooded; she pads across the bedroom floor to the cot. 'Okay, okay.'

Avaline's face is beetroot. Freya picks her up and rocks her, but the baby refuses to calm down. 'Shush.' Freya hums a melody while Ava's tiny fist tugs her pyjama top. 'Okay, I get it.'

Snuggled with her daughter, t-shirt pulled up to her collarbone, Freya falls asleep.

'Good morning, Freya.' Her mother's wide smile welcomes her into the kitchen. 'Did you sleep well? How's that beautiful little granddaughter of mine? Yes, you are beautiful.' Lorraine holds her arms open wide in the international symbol of let me have a cuddle and a sniff of those gorgeous head pheromones, please.

Freya passes Avaline across the narrow space between them, no longer an unbreachable gulf. She sits at the breakfast table, watching her mother rock Avaline. Coos of pleasure are vocalised by both grandmother and granddaughter. A new start. All it took was a baby.

'How's Rob?' Lorraine asks, looking across at Freya.

Freya swallows hard. 'We split up, Mum.'

Lorraine gasps. 'Oh, darling. I'm sorry.'

Freya bows her head and nests her forehead between her

arms to weep.

Lorraine sits opposite Freya, still rocking Ava. 'Do you want to talk about what happened?'

Freya lifts her face and shakes her head.

'Well, whenever you do…'

Lorraine stands up, leans forward and kisses Freya on the forehead. Avaline grabs a fist full of Freya's hair and pulls it as Lorraine rises. Silently, Freya touches the baby's hand and un-hooks her hair. Ava reaches for her mother and makes a noise somewhere between a cry and a hiccup.

'Do you want her back?' Lorraine asks.

'It's fine, Mum, enjoy.'

'Babies are wonderful. So full of potential, but too easily damaged when all you want to do is love them.' Tears sparkle in Lorraine's eyes. 'This little angel is lucky to have you for a mother. You'll do a better job than I did.'

'We were fine until Tanya died. I understand what you did, how you felt, I do. You did your best to protect me, and I love you.'

'Here, you take her. I'll be back in a minute.' Lorraine purses her lips to hold back her sobs and rushes out of the kitchen.

Freya rocks Ava in her arms, smiling at the look of peaceful oblivion on the infant's face. 'You are lucky,' she whispers.

Lorraine returns ten minutes later, composed again. 'Do you want breakfast?'

'I can sort myself out. I remember where everything is. Where are Dad and Ivan?'

'Mike's working, and Ivan's with Sarah.'

'Sarah? As in Star?'

Lorraine's lips tremble behind the smile. Her eyes darken. 'That's right.'

'Why?'

Lorraine plants a kiss on Avaline's forehead. 'It might be better if he told you. It's complicated.'

'Complicated in what way?' Freya's stomach churns.

Lorraine stares at the baby while she speaks. 'They are sort of dating.'

'But… Satori?' Freya scratches her forearm and frowns.

'They've been having problems for a while. Satori moved out.'

'She's a murderer!' Freya stares at her hands, remembering Dave and the way she punctured his chest with her ambition; Rob and the gaping wounds in his corpse.

'All that nonsense was dropped years ago. Can you imagine that tiny girl killing anyone? I mean really, Freya, it's like saying you're a murderer. It's nonsense.'

Freya nods. 'And Ivan's with her now?'

'He's staying there for a couple of days while she gets herself sorted.'

Freya stands up. 'I should go over there. Maybe I can help.'

Ava whimpers.

Freya sits back down, lifts her t-shirt and lets the baby latch on greedily.

'She reminds me of you,' Lorraine says.

Freya studies the baby in her arms, trying to see Rob in the pale blue eyes, shell-like ears, puffy cheeks and button nose, but recognises only herself. The wispy hair is platinum like Freya's, not strawberry like Rob's. She strokes the baby's downy cheek and sings softly while Lorraine watches from the other side of the room. Ava reaches a tiny hand towards Freya's face and Freya bends to kiss her fingers. The baby takes its mouth from Freya's breast and smiles.

When Avaline falls asleep, Freya looks at Lorraine. 'Want her back?'

Lorraine grins. 'Yes, please. Are you going somewhere?'

'Just the garden.'

Lorraine cradles the baby. Her face is peaceful. 'It's cold. Wrap up warm.'

Drab rags hang from the branches of Ivan's tree. Once vibrant colours have faded, and nothing new has been attached. *When did Ivan lose his faith? Was it when Raven died?*

She touches a damp ribbon the shade of mother-of-pearl and

tries to imagine what the original colour would have been. *Ivan and Star! How the fuck did that happen?*

She digs her heel into the soft earth and kicks. A clump of earth and grass bounces across the lawn away from her. *Fucking Star! Privileged Princess! Everyone's favourite, even Lilith's.*

Donna burnt herself when the heat of her passion was unanswered. Raven's body was broken and buried after she dared to touch Star's cast-offs.

Satori rejected Freya, telling her he loved Star, would always love Star. *Why did he leave?*

Did Star break his heart when she slept with MY fucking brother?

She'll destroy Ivan like she destroyed Donna and Raven and Satori.

She's poison.

I have to stop her.

CHAPTER TEN

EDENSUN RETURNS to Satori's bedroom. It takes him a moment to register the change.

Satori lies peacefully on his left side, and between his naked body and the wall is a woman. She glares at Edensun as she rises from the bed. Her snow-white hair dazzles him; her fragile-looking dress barely covers her ebony skin. As he returns her cold stare, her body loses its solidity. Edensun can see the pattern of the wallpaper through her skin. Satori failed. His will was not strong enough.

The woman snarls and balls her fists.

Satori shifts onto his back, his eyes flick open and stare at the corner of the room. A vein near his eye twitches. His mouth trembles. 'Raven,' he says. 'The walls are wrong.'

Edensun stares at his father in silence then glances at the woman. Hair floats around her face, and her mouth is open in a scream of silent fury. She leaps at Edensun and rakes his face with her nails.

Satori tumbles from the bed with a heavy thud, distracting the spectre. She rushes to the magician and sits beside him, stroking his hair.

'Can you see it too?' Satori's wide eyes focus on Raven's face.

'See what?' Edensun asks.

Satori's eyes search the room and eventually settle on Edensun. 'The darkness in the walls?'

Edensun shakes his head.

'There.' Satori points to the corner of the room.

Edensun looks and notices a faint speckle of mildew on the

wallpaper.

Satori scratches his arms before standing toe-to-toe with Edensun. Raven floats in circles around them, caressing Satori's shoulders, glaring at Edensun.

Raven traces Edensun's lips with cool fingertips, then returns to Satori and whispers into his ear.

'Mark, are you my son?' Satori asks.

Edensun swallows hard. 'Yes.'

Tears gather in Satori's eyes. 'You're much older than I expected.'

'Where's Mum?' Edensun asks.

'You're Lilith's. A demon. That's why those people were chasing you.'

'They want to steal my power,' Edensun says.

Satori sneers. His back straightens, making him seem taller. 'Your power? What power do you have?'

Edensun lowers his eyes.

'You were in the cave. You promised I would bring her back to life. Liar!'

'It should have worked. I hoped the two of you would live happily ever after.'

'Then you would have Star to yourself?' Satori growls.

'You don't love her, not like I love her, but you stole her from me. I want her back.'

'Go home to Binah and tell Lilith… tell her I said fuck off.'

'Don't push me away. I'm your son.'

'Fuck off!' Satori shouts. 'We won. You lost. I'm staying here, and so is Star.'

'I don't want to hurt you. You got Raven back. Why aren't you content with what you have?'

Satori presses his hands against his temples. His eyes drift from Edensun to the wall and the darkness he claims to see there. He whispers ancient words and draws energy from the room.

A ball of flame grows in the palm of Edensun's hand. 'You know who I am. You can't win this fight.'

Satori draws his hands apart, and energy crackles between

his palms. Raven floats between the challengers, scratching Edensun's face and caressing Satori's arm.

'Dad, I don't want to hurt you. Give up Star and live happily ever after with your ghost…'

Lightning bolts send Edensun tumbling through the air. The boy hits a wall and falls to the floor. He jumps back up. Face dark with shadows, Edensun breathes into the palm of his hand then launches a sphere of fire.

Satori's hair catches first, burning like a halo around his face. He screams until the flames rush downwards, ravaging his windpipe and lungs, burning through his flesh. Satori's body blackens as the inferno engulfs him. Within seconds, his father is a twisted and withered jumble of charred remains.

The fire spreads from the corpse, consuming furniture, curtains and wallpaper. When it reaches Edensun, it splits and moves around him, burning out as it reaches the door. Raven drapes her body over Satori's corpse and weeps.

'What a waste,' Edensun says. 'I'll find her anyway. Why must you always play the role of her protector?'

White hair floats around Raven's black shoulders. Her eyes narrow at the edges and bulge in the centre. Her nose flattens near the bridge and widens at the nostrils. Her mouth opens wide enough to swallow Edensun's head, revealing dagger-like fangs as she screams a silent yet terrible battle cry. She pounces; claws tear into his skin while her angry tears scald him.

Her violence sends Edensun running from the room. Her wails, as she chases him, wake other restless spirits. Dead children, mutilated by the previous owner in his quest to hoard power, sur- round Edensun eager to wreak revenge. Their suffering poisons their sleep; they cannot rest, must make others suffer the way they suffered.

While Raven pulls his hair, scratches his face and bites chunks from his cheek, the children gather around him, prodding him, punching him, kicking him, ripping his clothes, using their fists, their arms to debase him in the many ways they were debased before they died.

Pain and anger confuse his senses, making it impossible for Edensun to think. Their humiliation and rage infect him, and he sways from the impact of their blows, covers his ears against their screams. Raven has surrendered any shred of sanity to her rage. He empathises and tears of regret for the harm he has caused flood from his eyes and pores. His tattered clothing is soaked in misery.

'I'm sorry,' he says.

The ghosts step back and study him. Bruises bloom purple and green. Tears and sweat puddle around his feet, and his face hangs with sadness and shame. The ghosts cry too, sharing his guilt, pitying him.

Edensun leaves the house of death. As he strides along the curved driveway his soul is already repairing the damage, preventing the infection from spreading.

A cold hand on his shoulder makes him jump. Raven's skin is white now, and her hair is black; her features while strong and unique, no longer terrify him.

'Well done.' Her voice pours into him like freezing mercury, gripping his heart and lungs.

'I'm sorry.' He tries in vain to mimic the genuine shame and sadness which affected the ghosts so profoundly.

'You killed the man I love after he saved me from death. We were going to spend his life together.'

'Technically, you did…'

Raven screams. 'I will be avenged,' she says.

'You can't hurt me.'

'Wait and see.' Raven laughs then disappears.

Her plan is clear — Freya and a knife, but Freya will not kill Star. She will try and fail, completing the plan Lilith set in motion when she brought Freya back to the city.

CHAPTER ELEVEN

AFTER SHE prepares Avaline for the great outdoors, Lorraine gives Freya a peck on the cheek and wheels her granddaughter out of the house.

Freya sits on the settee with her head between her hands. She cannot get the image of Ivan and Star out of her head. The temperature plummets. Wondering whether she left a door open, Freya checks the front and kitchen doors. The latter is ajar.

'Star will take him from you.'

Ribbons jostle in the branches of Ivan's tree.

'You can stop her.'

Blinds rattle against the kitchen window; cupboard doors open and close, and the light flickers.

'Who are you?' Freya asks.

The voice sounds familiar. 'She has hurt us both. If you want to save Ivan, you must stop her. Kill her… kill Star… save Ivan…'

Freya shakes her head. 'Ivan isn't in danger.'

'Satori was killed because of Star.'

Freya closes her eyes against the rush of freezing air. 'Satori's dead?'

'Ivan will be next if you don't save him.'

'Who are you? Where are they?' Freya asks.

'An old friend. Now grab a pen and paper.'

Freya's hands shake as she transcribes the address. She imagines walking in on the couple as they make love and bile rises in her throat. Her mind recalls another time she watched Ivan with a woman.

'Raven?'

Laughter fills the room.

Freya spins around, searching for evidence that she isn't hallucinating. 'Is it you?'

'Star is a worthless slut! She's damaged and vulnerable.' The voice grows stronger as if rage gives it power. 'Men flock to her, wanting to be her knight in shining armour — the one to save her. A boy killed Satori to reach Star, and he'll kill Ivan too.'

Freya shrugs into her coat and places the scribbled address and a knife in her pocket. She remembers her own knight and the way Rob held her coat for her. *If I can kill the man I love, ending Star's pathetic existence should be easy.*

She arrives at the cottage and knocks.

Ivan's warm voice calls out, 'Star, someone's at the door.'

Freya cannot hear Star's reply.

The door opens, and her brother greets her with a smile. 'It's Freya,' he shouts over his shoulder.

Freya sits on the sofa. The hidden blade scratches her thigh.

'Hi Freya.' Star appears behind Ivan. She cocks her head then steps forward. 'Are you okay?'

Ivan grasps Star's arm, pulling her away. 'Something's wrong.'

Star wrestles free and strides towards the settee. 'Freya?'

The moment Star is close enough, Freya pounces.

Ivan rushes between them, grunts and falls. Crimson spreads across the carpet.

Freya screams and drops to her knees. 'Why?'

When she looks up, Star has gone, abandoning Ivan to save herself. Freya sprints to the kitchen, grabs a towel and presses it against the abdominal wound. 'You dickhead. Why did you get in the way? I'm here to save you. Satori's dead. She would have killed you next.' She puts his hand on the towel. 'Keep pressure on the wound. I'll find the phone.'

There is no phone in the cradle. Freya strides towards the bedroom.

Star's voice scratches against the other side of the door. 'The attacker's still in my house.'

The door judders as Freya hits her shoulder against it. Star has blocked it with something.

'Freya,' Star says. 'Is Ivan okay?'

Freya kicks the door.

'The police are on their way, Freya,' Star shouts.

Wood cracks and splits beneath the knife. Freya peers through a narrow hole at Star, legs pulled tight against her chest, perching on a pillow, trembling like a terrified sparrow, making the headboard rattle. Freya thrusts the blade into the crack and rotates it, trying to carve a hole large enough to reach the wide-eyed woman on the crumpled covers, so that she can save her brother from this succubus.

The knife is pulled free. Freya grunts with effort and slams the blade into the door panel.

'Freya. Go home. The police are on their way. Let me check on Ivan.'

Freya laughs darkly. 'I won't let you take him from me.'

'I'm not trying to,' Star shouts back.

The knife hacks through the panel again. Freya pushes her fingers through the jagged gap and drags out a large splinter. Sirens wail in the distance. Freya slams the knife into the slit and forces the blade left and right, trying to prise the panel apart.

'Freya,' Star says. 'Is Ivan still alive?'

Freya withdraws the knife again. The sirens are close. She places her eye next to the gap. 'Star.'

'Yes, Freya.'

'Raven says fuck you! She wants you to know Satori is dead.'

As Freya sprints past Ivan, his eyelids flutter. His skin is pale, but he's still holding the towel against his stomach. She flings open the kitchen door, emerges into the garden and uses the knotted stems of ivy to clamber over the wall.

Freya wriggles on the mattress and pulls against the restraints that hold her wrists and ankles to the bed. She's alone in the small room. Her mouth is dry, her mind heavy with sedatives.

'What happened?' Freya asks.

We stabbed our brother.

'Why?'

It was an accident. We were trying to protect him from her.

'From Star?'

Yes. The bitch enchanted him. She was going to take him away. We would have lost him.

'Is Ivan dead? Did we kill Rob too?' She weeps. 'What's going to happen to Ava… to Dad? He'll never forgive us.'

Avaline will be fine. Mum and Dad will take care of her until we're well.

'We'll never be well, Deya.'

We will, sister. Let go. I'll take over.

'No.'

When you decide you can't cope with what you've done, you'll leave and expect me to clean up your mess. Like before.

Freya tugs harder at her restraints. 'Leave me alone.'

You killed them all — Dave, Rob and Ivan — just to hold onto something that was never yours. When did you unravel, Freya?

'I don't remember.'

Was it when your sister died?

Later, I think.'

When you found the book? We shouldn't have gone into that cave. We brought Lilith here, didn't we?

CHAPTER TWELVE

STAR REACHES Ivan's body moments before police swarm into the room. Someone grabs her arm and pulls her back.

'Let the paramedics do their jobs.'

'Is he alive?' Star asks.

'I need a statement from you,' the officer says, turning Star away from Ivan's body.

Star and the police officer sit at the foot of her bed.

The officer removes her hat. 'What happened?'

'It was his sister. I think she was trying to stab me.' Star feels numb. Her body shakes, and her muscles are beyond her power to control, distant and alien. She tries to stand up.

The officer guides her back to a seated position. 'Why?'

Star shakes her head. Although Freya has thousands of reasons to want her dead, she had no reason to murder her brother. Perhaps she could explain that to the officer, but Star has remained under the police's radar for four years and cannot risk sharing too much.

'We'll need you to come to the station.'

Star rubs tears from her eyes. Her lips tingle, and her tongue is too large for her mouth. She swallows metallic saliva and coughs. 'Of course. Let me grab a few things.'

'I'll give you a moment.'

When the officer has left, Star dials Ivan's landline number.

Lorraine answers, 'Hello?'

Star sobs.

'Freya, is that you? Where are you?'

'Mrs Chaple, it's Sarah.'

Silence. The phone feels heavy.

'Ivan?' Lorraine's breath hitches. 'Is he okay?'

'I'm sorry.'

Lorraine's scream rips through the ether into Star's head, and she hears a sharp clatter as the receiver hits the floor. The scream continues, quieter now. Star hangs up. She grabs handfuls of hair, tugging at her scalp, staring blankly at the knife wound in her door. Minutes or hours later, she grabs her coat and bag. Fat tears drip from her chin as she bows her head and staggers out of the room, trying to drag her gaze away from the bloodstained carpet.

On the backseat of the police car, Star rests her forehead on her knees. She ignores the call that makes her pocket vibrate until it eventually rings off.

She sleepwalks through the police interview, feeling as though her mind and body are miles apart. She has no idea what she tells them, but at least they don't drag her to a cell or call the men in whitecoats to escort her to the nearest mental hospital.

Two hours later, she escapes into daylight. Fingernails digging into her arm drag her mind back to her body. She pulls away and vomits on the steps.

'Sarah?' a male voice.

Angling her head to peer at the pale face of Ivan's father, she wipes her lips on her sleeve.

'Where is Steve?'

She narrows her eyes. Steve? No, she must have heard it wrong. Mike would be asking about Ivan, not Satori.

'Ivan… Freya.' Her legs crumple beneath her.

Mike catches her before she collapses into a puddle of her own vomit. He guides her gently but firmly toward a metal bench, pressing her shoulder, until her ass meets the chilly seat, then he cups Star's chin, raising her gaze to his watery eyes.

'Steve is in trouble.' Mike's words are slow and clear, leaving no doubt in Star's roiling mind that for some reason Satori's safety is paramount. 'Where would he go?'

She stares at him while neurons spark only to fizzle out again. Her mind is too full of Ivan to think about Satori.

'Did Ivan…'

Mike lets go of her face. 'He's in surgery.'

'Freya...'

'They caught her. We need to find Steve,' Mike says, reaching for Star's hand, gripping her fingers. His hands are rough and calloused. Ivan's were soft, like silk.

'I don't...' There are a thousand things she wants to say, but the words stick in her throat. Lungs and heart sink toward her churning stomach. None of it makes sense. Why does Mike give a shit about Satori when his own son is barely clinging to life? Freya said something about Satori while she was trying to break down Star's door. *Raven says fuck you! She wants you to know Satori is dead.* Star decides not to share Freya's crazed ravings with Mike. His burden is already too heavy.

Star sits there, hugging herself, long after Mike gives up and leaves. There is one place Satori might hide. The house they used when they first returned from Binah.

Her phone vibrates again. This time she answers.

'Have you seen Steve?' Marian asks.

'I thought he was with you.'

'A young boy... He took my son... I'm worried, Sarah. Where could he be?'

'Leave it with me, Marian. I'll find out what's happened to Satori.'

Remembering the last time she fled from a police station, naked, hand in hand with Satori, Star races to the bus stop and catches the first one heading in the right direction. She will check Paul's house. It feels better to do something than nothing. It's a long walk from where the bus drops her, alone and afraid, but her body refuses to stay still and wait for another one.

Tears blur her sight as she jogs toward Snuff Mills, ignoring the stares of strangers. She reaches the suburbs where houses are larger and further from the quiet streets. Exhaustion drags on her shoulders and limbs, but she keeps going. *Not much further.*

She turns a corner and strides along Paul's street. His gates stand ajar, and she slips through them onto his drive, remembering when she came here before. The first time, Satori was excited to introduce her to his friend. Star shudders as she remembers Paul's coldness. He hated her. Was it because she was his rival? Or did he sense something inside her, something terrible? The last time she trudged along this driveway was when they returned from Binah and hid here. Paul was already dead, killed by Lilith.

The house glares at her, a looming bulk. She stops short and stares at lifeless windows, pulling her coat around herself to ward off the freezing air as cooling sweat prickles her skin. A movement catches the corner of her eye, a dark figure that vanishes when she focuses on the spot. She strides along the drive, rationalising away her fear. Nothing can be worse than what she has already faced, or so she hopes. The front door is locked, and she heads around the house while frightened dogs whine and growl beyond a dividing wall. As she enters the back garden the scent of smoke fills her nostrils. A hooded figure darts behind Paul's summerhouse. *Is it him? No, the shape was much too short to be Satori.*

'Who's there?' she calls.

No reply. She strides towards the glorified shed but stops short when she senses someone watching her from the house. She spins on her heels and stares at the blackened pane of an upstairs window. Something tells her she'll find Satori there.

She enters the kitchen via the broken French doors. The stench of smoke is stronger here. Shards of glass crack beneath her boots as she crosses the tiled floor. The walls are covered in graffiti. One painted image draws her attention, a curvaceous red-haired woman, snake draped around her throat like a scarf — Lilith. It's small, no larger than Star's hand, but she is drawn to it. She moves closer, noticing a pair of green eyes peering between the goddess's calves. Star clutches her chest as she stands there, staring, hoping the image will reveal its truth. Those eyes, could they… is it possible? Has someone painted an image of Star's abandoned son on the kitchen wall?

The ceiling creaks. Someone is in the room above. She drags her attention from the drawing and resumes her journey across the tiles, trying to avoid the piles of rubbish and broken glass. In the distance, the whines of terrified dogs. Below her the sorrowful cries of children. And above the footsteps of at least two people. Marian did say something about a young boy. Star glances back at the image of Lilith. Their son? That would be too much to hope for, and the disappointment might crush her.

In the hallway, footprints make a chaotic pattern across the dusty floor, at least four different sets, and all are too big to belong to a four-year-old. She tiptoes to the foot of the stairs. Three steps from the bottom, sits a teenage boy. He raises his chin as she approaches. His bright green eyes shine when he smiles.

'Hi,' he says.

She opens and closes her mouth.

When she imagines her son growing up, this is the face she sees. Satori's sharp features, Lilith's emerald eyes, her own delicate frame — angelic, almost. But only four years have passed. Still, the boy draws her toward him.

'Have you seen Satori?'

The boy's smile falls, and he shuffles on the step.

'It's okay. You aren't in any trouble. I just need to speak to him.'

'I'm sorry.' Moisture makes his eyes shine even brighter.

Raven wants you to know Satori is dead.

Star needs to see where it happened, learn whether she's responsible. 'How did he…?'

'There was a fire. My friends are up there.'

'Your friends?'

'Bodyguards. You're Star.' His face glows, and the corners of his mouth rise in a smile.

She welcomes his adoration, feasting on it like a starving vagrant at a banquet. Energy pulses through her mind and body, enough to climb twenty mountains, swim an ocean, or raise the dead.

He reaches for her. 'I'm your son. You left me in Binah with Lilith. I came here to find you.'

'My son? Mark? Did… did you kill Satori? Did Ivan die

because of you? Why would you destroy everything I… I don't understand. Do you hate me?' She steps closer, fingers pressed against her lips. Slowly, as if approaching a dangerous animal, she extends her arm and touches his cheek. 'You're my son?'

He nods. They stare at each other. Star's eyes widen to absorb the longed-for presence.

'I shouldn't have left you. I couldn't find my way back. Do you plan to kill me too?' Star notices movement on the other side of the hallway. A female figure steps out from the shadows. 'Marian? What are you doing here?'

Four black-robed figures and one in red step through the kitchen door behind Marian.

'We'll take it from here,' the woman in red says.

'Mum.' The boy grabs Star's hand. 'Come on.' He drags her behind him as he sprints up the stairs.

The robed figures swarm through the hallway, reaching the bottom of the staircase as Star and her son reach the top.

'Kevin, Simon,' he calls.

Men rush through a doorway. Star presses her spine against a wall as the skinheads dart past them. She is pulled into an empty room with no alternative exits. The small skylight in the ceiling is too high to reach. Her son tugs Star through a rip in the air. The moving darkness reminds Star of Satori's prison cell. Dead. All dead.

'Where are we?'

'Inbetween,' he says.

Star turns slowly, trying to grasp the enormity of nothingness.

'We're safe here. We can return to your world whenever we wish. I thought we should talk and then…' He holds his hands out to Star, and she grasps them. 'It's good to see you again, Mum. Tell me all about yourself, about when I was born, and why you left.'

Star punches his chest, exhausting herself with the flurry of blows. He wraps his arms around her and pulls her close until the fight drips from her limbs. 'They loved me, and you killed them both, didn't you?'

'It was self-defence.'

'I don't believe you. You were jealous, angry. Take me back.'

'Satori raised Raven from the dead then he attacked me. I didn't want to hurt him. I begged him not to fight me.'

'And Ivan?'

'Raven sent Freya to kill you. Ivan sacrificed himself.'

'Their deaths are my fault.'

'No, that's not what I meant.'

'I don't understand. You could have escaped. You didn't have to kill him.'

'I'm sorry. I can put it all right if that's what you want. I can change the past, so you never met Lilith. It would mean sacrificing myself. I will not exist. Tell me that's what you want, and I'll do it.'

Star drags on his arms until he lets her fall to her knees. She hugs herself and rocks back and forth, opening her mouth to release a bestial moan of despair.

He sits beside her, legs crossed, his hand on her shoulder. 'Hush. Let's talk a while.'

Hot tears spill from her eyes.

'I need to know where I came from. Tell me everything. Time doesn't exist here. We literally have all the time in the world. Tell me about your childhood.'

Star rubs her eyes and exhales. This won't be easy, but he deserves the truth. At first her words are choked with tears, but as her tale continues, she becomes calmer, more articulate. New pain fades, joining the background noise of old wounds. 'I was… I was an only child. My… parents were… older… religious. Dad… Dad was a preacher, and Mum never… she never questioned a thing he said. They were used to being childless, and I… I… I think they resented having to take care of me. Is this what you want to hear?'

'Anything. Everything.'

'Okay. I loved art, still do. I would paint and sculpt with whatever materials I could find, creating from my imagination, but my parents were afraid of the things I imagined, and Dad punished me. They sent me to therapists, psychiatrists and even tried to exorcise me. Have you met God?'

Edensun coughs. 'Which one?'

'The Abrahamic one. The God my father worships.'

'God doesn't exist, not in the way you and I do. Not even in the way the sky exists or trees. Everything originates from God but it, he, she has no mass, no molecules, no kinetic energy; God is pure thought. Everything that exists is God, and yet God is nothing. Everything is one and everything is nothing.'

'I don't understand.'

'The first step is to understand that everything is one. Even that might take several lifetimes.' Edensun laughs. 'Your eyes are glazed. I've lost you. Do you still care what your parents think?'

'More than I should. I left home at eighteen and escaped to university. I met Donna, and she introduced me to the others — your father, Raven and Freya. I fell in love with Satori.

'He brought things out in me, stuff I'd buried, things that scared me. I started to think Dad might be right. Maybe I was evil. I hid it from everyone including myself, but it always resurfaced, so in the end, I left Satori.

'That's when he brought Lilith here. He believed he owned me and couldn't stand the thought that I could walk away. Your father wasn't a bad man, but he was self-centred. He believed the world owed him everything he craved.

'Lilith enchanted me. I thought I loved her. Between the three of us you were conceived.'

He nods. 'How did you feel when you found out you were pregnant?'

'You need to understand what was going on... I killed my friend. When I discovered I was pregnant, I blamed you for my violence. I murdered Raven in a nightclub bathroom then ran away with Lilith. I thought she was human. I was trapped in a nightmare — terrified. When she told me... when she said I was carrying her baby... I thought I was going mad. Before I could process what was happening, Lilith was gone, and Satori was dragging me back to civilisation. I couldn't cope. And I...' Star pauses.

The boy squeezes her hand. Tears sparkle in the emeralds of his eyes.

'I stabbed myself. I was trying to kill us both. Forgive me.'

He swallows hard, pulls her trembling hand towards his lips and kisses her fingers. 'I understand. The world, your world, terrifies me too.'

'But you came anyway…'

'To find you.' He brushes the tears from Star's cheeks. 'What happened after you stabbed yourself?'

'When I woke up, I was in Binah, and you'd already been born. I don't remember your birth.'

'Did you love me?'

Star wrings her hands. 'You didn't look human.'

'I scared you. This…' He grins and passes a theatrical sweep of his hand in front of him. 'I had to learn, over time, to… pass.'

'Pass?' Star asks.

'As human.'

'How do you really look?'

'Are you sure you want to know?'

Star sighs. 'I've seen more things than a mind should be able to process, and I'm still here. Yes, I want to know how my son really looks.'

The change happens slowly and gradually. His eyes become brighter; they stretch and bulge from his face. He grows taller, until he towers above Star, almost twice her height. His hair thins then disappears, and his ears shrink until they are simply holes in either side of his elongated face. His nose widens and flattens; his warm, brown skin fades to a pale grey and splits into small, rough scales.

Clothes no longer cover him. Star's eyes glide across the grey scales that decorate his gaunt torso and protruding ribs. His upper arms are huge and powerful, tapering below the elbows and ending in vicious sting-like claws. A third slightly larger claw extends from his single, tail-like lower appendage, and framing this horrifying magnificence, huge black, leathery wings unfold from his shoulder blades and spread behind him.

Star trembles.

Tears stream from saucer-like eyes. He opens his mouth to speak, revealing razor-sharp teeth, then closes it again.

'Mark, my son.'

He reverts to his human form, steps forward and wraps his arms around her. 'My name is Edensun. That's what Lilith named me.'

Star's arms encircle his waist. She hugs him tightly. 'Edensun. You are beautiful.'

'Why did you leave me?' His tears soak her shoulder.

'Satori came,' she says. 'Every day I regret leaving you. I should have stayed or brought you with me. I'm sorry.'

'You thought of me?'

'Always.'

'We can be together now, if that's what you want, but there are rules. I can change the past, return you to any point in your life. You could have a better relationship with your parents or attend a different university and never meet Donna or Satori. Or you could stay with Satori, so he never opens the door for Lilith.'

'If those things changed, you wouldn't exist.'

'But Ivan, Raven and Satori would still be alive. That is the choice you must make.'

'Between you and the others?'

'Yes.'

Star sits down. 'You're asking me to decide whether my friends live or die?'

'I can't make the choice for you. It's yours and yours alone.'

'Why?'

'It's a delicate balance: death and life. One cannot exist without the other.'

'But why is it my choice?'

'It simply is.'

'It isn't fair. It sounds like the sort of bullshit Lilith would say.' Star considers her life, the choices she has made and the others she has avoided making while life swept her along on its current. Light fills her, despite her grief. Edensun's love energises her, making her light burn and her power sizzle. Far stronger than Satori's or Ivan's love, pure, uncomplicated. Of course, this choice is hers. Who else could make it? She nods. 'What if I return to Binah and don't leave with Satori?'

'He would stay too, and Lilith would kill him, or he would kill me. Satori and I cannot co-exist.'

'If I choose you, how do we prevent Marian and her friends hurting you?'

'I want to show you something. Can I take you to Binah?'

'You can take me anywhere you want.'

Edensun guides Star out of the darkness. They stand at the shore of a red lake. 'This is where Satori entered Binah,' Edensun says.

'Why is it red? It looks like blood.'

'It isn't blood or water. It's the Lake of Sorrows.'

Star approaches the lake and reaches down.

'I wouldn't…' Edensun says too late.

She blows on her fingers. 'It's freezing. How does it work, this Lake of Sorrows? What does it have to do with Marian?'

'The sufferings of humans are stored here when they're done with them. Energy cannot be destroyed blah, blah, blah. It has to go somewhere, so it comes here.'

'It's pain?'

'Pain, anger, guilt…'

'There's so much of it.'

'And it keeps growing.'

'What happens to the people who created it?' Star asks.

'They heal and forget.'

'How much of it is mine?'

Edensun places his hand against her jaw and rubs her cheek with his thumb. 'Best not to think about that.'

Star plants a warm kiss on his cheek. 'I thought you'd be younger. Now I think about it, I should have realised time is different here. Can you tell me what it was like growing up, or is it too painful to talk about?'

'I remember curling up to sleep between your arm and your

chest. You warmed me as your body lay still beside me. When you woke, you pulled away. I didn't understand, but it hurt. I also remember the first day you held me in your arms. I can still feel your arm supporting my tiny body. When you left, I tried to follow but couldn't. Violet, Magenta and Sapphire took care of me. I slept against their bodies instead of yours.'

Star's eyes darken, and she shivers.

'Are you jealous?' Edensun asks.

'A little.'

'I never forgot you. I grew quickly and wandered ceaselessly. Lilith promised that when I was big and strong enough, she would let me search for you. I made a plan. A way to bring you back to me. I was strong, full of energy. I had as much physical affection as anyone could need, and I had friends and advisors — Lilith and Siloth. I was happy, but I wasn't content. Does that make sense?'

Star nods. 'I have never felt content; you might have inherited that from me.'

'Are you content now?'

Star breathes deeply. 'Almost.'

'You carry too much sorrow. Maybe you should let it go. We're in the right place.'

Star stares at the lake. 'Without my memories… who would I be?'

Edensun touches her arm. 'Trauma doesn't make you who you are… it only limits what you can become.'

'If the lake absorbs our guilt, is that why we keep doing terrible things to each other?' Energy prickles her skin and sends sparks along her limbs. Her head itches as her hair stands on end. 'If we return their pain, will they behave differently? Is that how we stop Marian and her friends hunting us? Is that how we stop everything that's wrong in the world?'

Edensun shrugs. 'Maybe.'

'Can you do it?' Star asks. 'Return the waters of the lake to Earth?'

'Yes. I could create a funnel between the two worlds and

make it rain,' Edensun says. 'But that doesn't mean we should.'

'Will it teach people to be kind?' Star asks.

'It might,' Edensun answers. His expression is unreadable. 'We could ask Lilith.'

Star nods.

Lilith, Star and Edensun stand under the giant, pink flag of the Langham Hotel in the City of London. Silk crackles above them as agitated air whips the flags decorating the hotel's grand façade. Behind them, sandstone glows like sunlight while mulberry clouds gather above.

'Ready?' Edensun asks.

'I think so,' Star answers.

Star stands between the gods. Lilith squeezes Star's hands. Red rain falls, hitting paving stones and pedestrians.

Someone screams; another scream joins the first, and another, creating a blood-curdling cacophony. A man, two metres from where Star stands, covers his eyes with stained hands and falls to his knees, emitting a strangled wail. Shoulders hunched over his knees, he removes his hands from his face and punches the ground. Red rain soaks his clothes, matting his hair.

Others fall beside him. Some bend over the ground as if in prayer, hitting their foreheads against paving stones until they lose consciousness; some dig fingernails into their cheeks and tear skin from their faces, and others use bags or umbrellas to thrash their backs like penitents.

'What's happening?' Star asks. 'Why aren't they using their pain to change things? They aren't supposed to die.'

A woman kneels beside a pram, takes her baby from under its covers and shakes it by the arms.

Star steps out from under the shelter.

'Mum,' Edensun warns.

'I have to do something,' she says.

Star strides toward the mother. 'What's wrong?'

The woman doesn't answer. Instead, she lifts the baby over her head and slams it with all her strength onto the pavement. The baby's head opens like an eggshell and its blood splatters Star's shins.

Star shakes her head until the motion makes her dizzy. 'What have you done?'

The woman doesn't seem to hear. Fingers rake her scalp, tearing bleached-blonde hair out in clumps and tossing them to the ground. Star stares at the dead baby before switching her attention to the distraught woman. Grabbing the woman's arms, she tries to stop her. Finally, the woman's eyes focus on Star who pleads with her to stop her madness. The woman growls, bares her teeth and bites Star's wrist. Star screams and releases the woman who continues scalping herself.

People run blindly as red liquid covers their faces, screaming in terror, agony and rage. Insanity reigns as people rip open their stomachs to eviscerate themselves. Bodies fall. Only a few remain standing, stronger than the rest. The survivors stare at the dead and dying. The young fare better than the old.

Star scrambles over bodies to hug weeping children while rain soaks her skin.

Lilith places a hand on her trembling shoulder.

'This isn't what I wanted.' Star's lips tremble. 'Take me to Parliament Square. It might be different there.'

The Houses of Parliament look black beyond the curtain of red. Crowds of people surge into the broken building while fires burn all around them. Cars and buildings blacken in the heat. Anger fills the air with the potential for change.

'The people will take back the power that was stolen from them and each will live out their lives in the ways that feel natural, no longer cogs in a huge machine, but people. Not merely existing but living,' Star prophesizes.

'You see all that potential in this violent mob?' Lilith asks.

'Their violence is focused and has purpose. They're over-throwing the old to bring in something new, something fairer.' Star's fanaticism borders on madness.

Helicopters buzz overhead like angry wasps. Missiles hit the ground. The crowd screams but continues to swarm into the iconic building.

'Will they win?' Star asks. 'Will they overthrow the exploitative system? Will it be worth it?'

'Evolution, revolution; change is always worthwhile,' Lilith says.

'So much death.' Star gazes across Parliament Square at the charred and bloody remains. 'Just so one regime can fall, and another can rise. What the fuck have we done?'

'We're changing the world, Mum,' Edensun says.

Explosion after explosion. Star's head vibrates with the deafening sounds of bombs, helicopters and screams. Bodies tumble. Electricity tugs her hair and her skin prickles. A helicopter's weapons flare before missiles pummel the insurrection.

Star focuses her energy, and energy from the deities beside her, upward and imagines the rotary blades folding inwards. The helicopter jerks and splutters before falling like a boulder, hitting the lawn in front of Parliament, and bursting into flame. Citizens race from the wreckage, then their voices rise in celebration.

Star concentrates on a second helicopter. As that too falls to the earth, the other pilots flee with their cargoes of soldiers, turning their warbirds around and heading for safety.

Songs of freedom resound while men in suits are dragged from buildings, some torn to pieces by the crowd, while others are thrown, screaming, into fires.

'At least they have a chance now,' Star mutters.

The aroma of blood and burned flesh fills her nostrils. The final result, harmony or escalating violence, will not be decided in the coming hours. *Will people cling to old ways or embrace their new freedom? How many will survive?*

Star embraces Edensun. 'I love you.'

Careful to avoid the dead and injured, scattered across concrete and grass, Star strides to the centre of the square. The broken helicopter is a pyre. Flames warm her. Their fingers beckon her to join them. *All is nothing.*

A figure wrestles with the flames, reminding her of Raven, drunk and uncoordinated, stomping clumsily in platform boots. The world around Star fades and she imagines she is on the dancefloor at Club Midian with her friends. Lifting her arms, Star steps into their midst. Spinning through the flames, she laughs until her throat crisps. She dances while her flesh becomes ash which rises from the fire towards the stars.

CHAPTER THIRTEEN

Freya hears screams outside her cell and complaints that all is lost. Wails of despair. She recognises a nurse's voice and wonders what has happened to cause such grief. Her door is locked, so she paces around the room like a caged tiger while her eyes drift across the walls she has decorated with her hate.

Freya knocks on her cell door and someone on the other side knocks back.

'Who's in there?' the nurse asks between sobs.

'It's Freya. What's wrong? If you open the door, I could help.'

'No one can help me.'

'Let me try.'

A key turns in the lock, and her door is pushed inwards. The pink uniform is filthy, and mascara runs in streaks down the ashen cheeks of the mental health nurse. Freya holds her arms open, and the woman falls into her embrace, sobbing.

'Let's get you a cup of tea, then you can tell me what's happened.' Freya leads the nurse towards the cafeteria.

As they shuffle along the corridor, the nurse shivers, spewing the details of every harm she has caused in her thirty-odd years of existence. 'I'm a terrible person. I should be dead.'

Freya nods. 'Me too, I guess, but life goes on.'

The nurse grips Freya's shoulders. 'Humanity is a disease. I'll burn it down. The fire will cleanse us.'

'Cleanse who? Burn what?' Freya asks.

'The hospital and, if that doesn't work, the world.'

Freya untangles herself from the nurse's grip and steps back a few paces. 'I'll look for something to start a fire.'

'You'll help me?' A wide smile lifts the woman's features, and her wet eyes shine in excitement.

'Sure. Wait here. I'll be back in a minute.'

'Thank you.' The nurse sniffs loudly and rubs her face with her forearm.

Freya sprints towards the front door. None of the connecting doors are locked. It makes no sense, but after all the bad luck in her life, she deserves a break.

Are we going to help her? Deya asks.

'Of course not. The nurse is a lunatic.'

Aren't we too?

'No, we might be the only sane ones left. We're getting out of this mad house.'

As Freya flees the hospital, the madness she hoped to leave behind increases in intensity. Ambulance lights dance in the rain to the cacophony of sirens and screams. Deepening puddles at the bottom of the asylum steps glisten like pools of blood.

'Are we hallucinating?' Freya asks.

No, this is magic, Deya replies. *We should go back inside.*

'Only if we want to burn. You heard the nurse. She's going to cleanse the hospital with fire.'

Then we should go home. Make sure Ava is safe.

Freya is not dressed for the inclement weather, but instead of looking for a jacket, she descends. Her hair sticks to her face as rain drips from the tip of her nose and down her chin. It tastes bitter and weighs her down. Her nightdress reddens, reminding her of the wounds in Rob's chest. Her poor husband. He was innocent. All he ever wanted was to love his wife and daughter and keep them safe.

'It hurts!' she cries.

I am with you, Freya, hurry!

Freya runs from the madhouse and the shrieking ambulances, avoiding bundles of soiled clothing in the gutters, too bulky to be empty. People have fallen here, and they are never getting up.

The viscous rain draws Freya's grief to the surface. She beats her fists against her brow to dispel the insidious horrors.

Her sister beaten to a pulp, her brother and husband stabbed, her daughter torn from her breast while she was locked away to rot. She moans as despair rocks her. Her legs are weak, and she lurches on, blindly. One thing keeps her moving — a baby she must protect.

'Ava!' Freya cries, clinging to the thought of her daughter like a lifeline in this churning crimson ocean.

This part of the city is unfamiliar. Labyrinthine streets twist left and right. Trees line the edges, sheltering cars from the downpour, their leaves heavy, ready to purge. Freya carries her burden with her.

'We killed Ivan,' she wails.

It was an accident. Keep moving.

'Everyone around her dies, yet she endures. Fucking Star.'

We were trying to save him. Forgive yourself, Freya, and keep moving.

Puddles suck her bare soles each time she lifts her feet, reminding her of the cave where she met her goddess, Lilith — the betrayer. The rain is the colour of the rose petals that fell onto her brother's bed as she claimed his body and invoked the mother of demons.

Gravity weighs on Freya's limbs, but Deya refuses to let her fall, urging her onwards, pumping blood to her muscles, keeping despair at arms' length.

We can do this, Freya. We have to.

Freya runs for hours as the sun rises behind the clouds, and the rain continues to fall. Occasionally, she spots someone alive. Mostly, she passes corpses. Blood from broken bodies mixes with the rain. At last, she reaches a street she recognises. Nearly home. Fear of her parents' reaction slows her steps. She killed their son, and they stole her daughter. An eye for an eye, a child for a child.

It'll be okay. Daddy loves us.

'We're all he has left.'

Once there were three children. The eldest, Tanya, was murdered by boys in the park. Her parents never recovered from the loss and huddled around their remaining children, especially Freya, in whose face they saw both daughters and their failure to protect the first. They tried to keep Freya safe by locking her up, but Freya fought to be free. Kept separate from other boys, she fell in love with her brother. Excluded from life, she journeyed through books and, one fateful day, brought home a book that would change her life forever: *The Book of Lilith.*

The front door is locked. Freya rings the bell and knocks, but there is no reply. She skirts around the brick house to the back garden and stares at the familiar apple tree. Before the tree became a place of worship for Ivan, her brother and sister would help Freya climb to the upper branches so she could leap fearlessly into her brother's waiting arms. The vibrant ribbons he tied to its branches have faded. The rain stains them a uniform red, tatters of viscera torn from the heart of her family.

She recoils and concentrates on a strawberry bed where the siblings picked fruit each summer, and Freya crammed as many as possible into her small mouth before their mother could stop her. The juice of those crushed berries stained every dress she owned and earned her the reputation of impossible child, yet they are joyful memories.

Her family had been happy.

Before Tanya died.

Freya tries the back door. It is not locked. She half expects the alarm to wail as she enters, but only silence greets her.

The downstairs rooms have not changed. The same stair creaks as Freya climbs. She checks her parents' room first. A floral-patterned satin dressing gown lies discarded on the bedspread. The room smells of her father. His exhaled breath hangs in the air with hints of untreated gingivitis and beer. There is no one here. She checks her bedroom next.

A mobile with farm animals hangs above a wooden cot. The pastel pink pig honks when Freya squeezes it. A nappy changing station sits under the window where Freya's bookcase used to be. The walls are lemon and the carpet a soft blue. Nothing of Freya remains, except what she passed to her daughter. The cot is empty except for a lilac blanket and a chewed bear.

She searches the bedrooms of her dead siblings. Ivan's room remains as he left it. His MP3 player sits on his chest of drawers embraced by neat coils of headphone cable. She opens his wardrobe and finds his clothes hanging from the rail, awaiting his return.

She swallows a lump in her throat as she hesitates outside Tanya's room. Blinking tears from her eyes, she opens the door. What she imagined as she stood outside her sister's room is rubbed cruelly in her face and lodges in her throat, making it hard to breathe.

There are a few subtle changes to the room. Freya's dismantled bed frame rests against a wall beside Tanya's single bed. Her mattress is stacked on top of Tanya's, reminding her of a childhood fairy tale *The Princess and the Pea*. Beneath the bed, piles of Freya's books, CDs and a suitcase of her clothes have been stashed, hidden from sight. There is no sign of the dressing table where Freya sat watching her reflection, weaving ribbons into her hair.

'Fuck! Fuck! Fuck!' Freya wheezes.

Deya rises, but Freya pushes back. Her parents have expelled her from their lives. Happier to wallow in the pain of Tanya's and Ivan's memories than in Freya's continued flawed existence. Her knees buckle. She clings to Tanya's bedspread, and it follows her down, covering her with the scent of mothballs and dust. She fights the fabric which tears easily in her hands. Too easily. She gains no satisfaction from the destruction. Hurling herself towards the window, she bites and pulls the curtains, dragging them from the pole with satisfying rips and clouds of dust, then wraps a shred of the cotton brocade around her fist and lurches at Tanya's wardrobe. The mirror reflects her despair before she punches it, cracking the glass and splintering the wooden frame.

Deya tries to take control, but Freya refuses to submit. She wrenches the buckled door open and pulls dresses from wire hangers, watching shredded lace float like feathers around her trembling body.

'Why do they hate me?'

Deya does not answer.

Exhausted, Freya shuffles from the bedroom. Deya closes the door behind them.

The strange storm is not letting up. Corpulent red raindrops hammer against the kitchen windows and door, casting an eldritch glow around the room.

'Where are they?'

They are safe, sister. I can feel it. Have a shower. Wash off the rain. Warm yourself.

Freya fills her stomach with bread and cheese before allowing Deya to guide her to the bathroom. It will be a relief to change into her own clothes; the nightdress belonged in the bin even before it was stained red.

The silence of the house seems unnatural. The hospital was never quiet, and sleep was almost impossible with the constant din of screaming and singing. Now only the percussion of rainfall punctures the suffocating stillness. Freya lies on her brother's bed, pops his earphones in her ears, and selects a Nirvana tune from his collection, allowing mournful vocals and screaming guitar to drown out the sound of the rain.

She prays little Ava is safe. Her heart aches for her baby, forgetting the exhaustion and resentment of motherhood and remembering only cuddles and smiles. When the rain stops, her parents will come home, or she will go out and search for them.

When the rain stops.

She idly flicks through *The Book of Lilith*, retrieved from Tanya's room along with ten other books she has piled onto Ivan's bedside table. Anger and hatred have replaced the devout love she once offered the goddess.

She remembers when she discovered the book. In a restrictive world, full of arbitrary rules, the bookseller represented freedom, but he was a fisherman and *The Book of Lilith* his bait. The world he opened to Freya rotted her soul until she no longer recognised right from wrong. These are thoughts she has never considered before. Perhaps the rain that batters against the bedroom window is part of her now? Is it making her see things she never dared acknowledge? In her sacred space, beneath the willow tree, she felt free, but it was another prison. She had been losing pieces of herself in exchange for this fake freedom years before the wyrm bit off her arm.

Deya tries to console her, realising the danger of this train of thought. *Be strong for Ava. You can't change your past, but we can survive it. We can be better.*

A yawn breaks free of Freya's lungs, and she drags the duvet across her body like a cocoon.

In Freya's dream, she is her sister, Tanya, dressed in flowing fabrics and wafting around the house. Every surface warms beneath her fingers, and mouths curl up at the corners as she passes. Parents cease arguing; siblings trot behind her like puppies. The apple tree is full of white blossoms that speckle the grass like snowflakes.

She drifts from safety and out into the world. It is a glorious evening. The few soft clouds have salmon underbellies, and her nostrils catch the fresh fragrance of recently cut grass.

She meets a friend in the park. He passes a brown paper bag across the chilly metal bench, and Tanya grips the neck of the bottle contained within.

'Happy birthday, Aaron,' she says as she lifts the bottle to her mouth and takes a tiny sip. The liquid makes her lips tingle and burns her throat. She blinks tears from her eyes and crystals speckle her pale cheeks.

The friend laughs and pats Tanya's thigh, then swigs from the bottle, his Adam's apple bobbing as he swallows. He attempts without success to hide a grimace, and Tanya tries with more success not to laugh at the boy playing a man on his sixteenth birthday.

CHAPTER FOURTEEN

STAR GLIDES among mulberry clouds. Far below, Edensun shouts at Star's blackening corpse, but she cannot hear his words. She tries to dive towards him, wishing to comfort her grieving son, but her spirit rises until the boy and her vacated body disappear. She is one speck in a sky bright with ancient stars whose lights pulse, relaying tales of long-dead worlds.

She is huge. Her body fills the sky, swallowing galaxies; yet somehow, she is also tiny enough to traverse the landscape of her skin where pale hairs tower like redwoods between the chasms of her pores. An insignificant speck of dust incapable of unleashing Hell, yet also a Titan able to crush humans like insects. These two states of being alternate so rapidly Star becomes both at the same time — inconsequential and cataclysmic. It's dizzying, but intensely pleasurable, to be simultaneously large and small enough to fall into any one of her five million pores.

Her experience belongs outside of time. This reshaping of self might last for seconds or years, but it makes no difference. She can only enjoy and accept it. Having suffered her own rigid permanence and the immutable consequences of every action she takes, the fluidity of her form and presence in the universe allows her a sense of freedom she has never felt before. Nothing matters. Every action or inaction is meaningless, erased by her shifting perception of self. To believe she has changed the world, for better or worse, is an inconceivable arrogance when she is both the universe and an inconsequential mote within it. She could no more end the reign of Man than a flea could flood a valley or a mountain could crush a flea.

She wanders through the forest of her hairs and gazes into the shadowy chasms of her pores with no desire to climb or fall. Her contentment is absolute and the love she offers the body beneath her feet is a cornucopia that overflows, adding to her sense of peace. No joy or sadness. No desire or fear. She floats in the womb of the universe, marvelling at the intricacy of her skin.

The flesh beneath her feet warms until she has to hop on one foot then the other; she remembers the same ritual on hot summer sand as she raced, with a child's excitement, towards the sea, but there is no sea here. She leaps with both feet and floats while the surface blackens around veins of molten red, bright enough to burn her eyes. Strips of skin curl and break away, turning silver as they rise — ash from her cremated corpse. Flakes of it stick to her as she levitates, her pale skin hidden beneath growing patches of grey. When she looks down, the redwood forest and chasms are gone, and she is floating among stars and ash.

A tunnel of air rushes downwards. She focuses her energy on pushing against the pressure and remaining airborne, like salmon swimming upstream. When the wind stops, the ash has been blasted from her skin.

Electrical current darts through her veins, and her body tingles in ways that resemble excitement or sexual desire, reminding her of how Lilith made her feel when the goddess knelt in front of Star and dried her skin with a soft towel, teasing the hairs on her body until each one stood erect, only to moisten it again with kisses. She trembles as energy builds in her stomach, sending tendrils of pleasure from between her thighs to her chest and mind. She is acutely aware of her flesh and the way it stretches and aches, begging for release from the intensity of the experience. Another human paradox. Intense pleasure is painful, and pain can be pleasurable. A razorblade's bite unleashes the same chemicals as a lover's kiss.

Her mind is full of dazzling white light flecked with gold. Pressure pushes against her eyeballs and squeezes her throat, bruising her ribs and threatening to shatter her skeleton. She senses a primordial force ready to explode outwards and create a new universe where she will be the divine progenitor, a god. The levee breaks through her skull. The anterior fontanelle widens and softens as she reverts to the vulnerability of infancy. The membrane splits and energy races upward, emptying her of all other sensations. At first the feeling is intensely pleasurable, the release of an orgasm, but as it continues, it becomes a hollowing out.

In that moment she is remade.

She floats above the mouth of an abyss. Bubbles drift above and around her, blown from a golden circle held by a creature with downward curved horns, one red and one black, tipped with silver balls that chime softly as it moves. It grins even as it blows air through the ring. Its expression is manic, like those she has glimpsed on the faces of some of her friends — Satori and Freya; even Raven wore such smiles at times.

Star focuses on the bubbles and the movements within them. She plays a central role in each scene, but they are not memories. *What magic is this? What are the bubbles trying to show me?* She reaches towards them full of hope.

Star's index finger pierces the membrane of a bubble. Soap suds scatter, covering her skin, glistening franticly. Beside her hovers a young woman with an identical face, whose hair is Star's natural colour, a pumpkin orange that evokes images of Halloween. Manic curls are pulled back from the freckled sun-kissed face and held securely with a turquoise bow. The strange doppelgänger wears a navy and pastel pink floral dress; a modest gold cross hangs from a chain around her throat. Star shakes her head. The figure is the antipathy of Gothic elegance — neat, prim, submissive and chaste. The vision widens, and Star glimpses parkland. Star's mother is with her, pushing a pram and beaming with a grandmother's pride.

Rhythmic knocking fills Star's ears, drowning out the conversation between mother and Stepford daughter, but it's obvious there's a loving bond between the women; a stark contrast to the tense and toxic relationship between Star and her real parents. The knocking emanates from the other Sarah's chest; that name suits the devout figure better than it ever suited Star. She focuses on the third button down of the modest shirtdress and wills herself to move closer. Focusing her eyes beyond the floral pattern and pink flesh, she finds a black box lodged deep within the solar plexus. Nails have been hammered along the edges of its square lid and chains have been twisted around the cube to imprison whatever is inside, but the trapped and hidden aspect of this woman rails against its incarceration and pounds on the ebony prison from within. Star understands the sacrifice this version of herself has made to capture her mother's love and live up to the expectations of her parents. She pulls back and gazes at the pretty face, the gentle, patient smile that doesn't reach the eyes. Those soft, unfocused blue orbs bulge with unfathomable sadness and incalculable pain.

A child shouts. 'Mummy, mummy, did you see how high I soared?' The little boy races across grass to reach Sarah. Arms wide, he tries to make a circle around her legs and prevent her from walking away. She ruffles his blonde head and smiles.

'You are so brave, Mark.'

Star has seen enough of this life to realise it is a choke collar. Traces of the scene tickle her flesh and play out across the iridescence which clings to her body while she chases another bubble. What other truths might be revealed? Are these the alternate lives she might have led if she'd made different choices? She's relieved she did not live this life of lies, sacrificing parts of herself to gain parental approval.

She pops another quivering membrane and stands before a canvas, paint brush in one hand and pallet in the other. Her hair is a dull shade of copper, tangled and matted, starting to dreadlock, and she wears an oversized black shirt and leggings spotted with paint. Her skin looks sallow and, as the scene widens, she notices a bottle of absinthe and an ashtray among tubes of acrylic paint on top of a trestle table. She hopes this other is careful to avoid the flammable paint-fumes when lighting her nicotine sticks.

The two vertical walls are exposed brick. A small velux window in the pitched ceiling is open, and street noises fill the space — the constant roar of car engines and frequent blaring of horns indicate a busy city.

The shimmering soap from this second bubble mingles with the first, and her skin glistens with rainbows. The simple honesty of the second vision softens the affected façade of the first. Could her parents love her this way as well? She doubts it, but she respects the unpretentious figure, the artist for whom work is everything, and who cares little about personal appearance or her surroundings unless they directly feed into the paintings she produces. There's a double bed, and the covers are in disarray. She wonders how often this woman shares that bed with others or whether work forms the entirety of her life. She seems focused not lonely, but Star suspects many disappointments led her to this point. What else would explain the presence of alcohol and cigarettes?

There must be an ideal world, somewhere. She kicks her legs and moves towards another bubble, shattering it with her nail and coating her body with glycerine. A kiss. This time Star's face is pressed against Donna's, and the heat of the moment, the passion, makes her see her friend in a new light. Feeling strangely voyeuristic, she watches herself embrace a woman who has always loved her, always caught her when she threatened to fall too far, always defended and protected her. The scene widens, and Star realises they are sitting in the back row of a cinema; from the monochrome lights that flicker around them, she imagines they are half-watching a classic black and white movie. Fingers tangle in each other's hair, and their kiss tells her that she has missed out on the great love of her life. Pain fills her chest, and her vision blurs with tears of regret.

Blindly, she pops another bubble while the residue of her and Donna's great love story joins the other potential lives that coat her skin.

She's alone again. Ginger roots suggest six months of growth since she last dyed it, and she's wrapped in white. Her shoulders are rounded, and her unfocused eyes dwell within crimson rings of exhaustion. The scene widens. The straps of a straitjacket pin her arms in place. Scars cover this pitiful creature's cheeks, perhaps from self-inflicted wounds. The room is almost bare, and only the bed and the padding on floor and walls offer any concession to comfort. In this barren space, like a tundra of the soul, everything has been directed inward until self-hatred and grief spill out in the foam that speckles her chin.

She recoils. Such a fate has always been within her reach. Is this pathetic figure her real self? Are her adventures with Edensun and Lilith pure delusion? Is it more likely that she's psychotic or a goddess who became the sun?

This vision too, spreads across her body and becomes part of her, but not the only part, she reminds herself. She stretches her hand, pricks a nearby bubble and licks her lips as another aspect of her sexuality plays out.

It feels strangely familiar, as if she dreamed it once. In the vision, her doppelgänger is bent at the waist, her hand moving franticly between her thighs while her stretched throat emits bestial grunts, and when the scene widens, rock walls are revealed — a cave perhaps, naturally hewn. A naked man, a blond Adonis, moves behind this version of Star and wraps his arms around her body, tugging and squeezing her breasts. She leans her head back against his chest, sighing in pleasure. Star gazes entranced at the couple as the man penetrates a woman who looks exactly like her, who might be her. She cannot feel the bulk of him push inside her eager body but imagines the sweet pressure.

A second man with bronze skin and jet-black hair joins them. He crushes her breasts with his chest and squeezes her ass cheeks while his erect penis presses against her stomach. He bends his back and angles his hips until it slides between her legs and pushes deep inside. The woman's body glistens with sweat and bounces between the two men as she rides them both, and those blue eyes, glazed with lust, turn away from Star. When she follows the direction of her doppelgänger's gaze, Star spots a familiar figure.

At the centre of the cave, about twenty metres from the ménage à trois, stands Satori. Is it his fault that she has reached this place between life and death, witnessing other lives that she might have lived were it not for her ex-lover's jealousy and magic, or would she have reached this point with or without his influence, just as her father predicted? It hurts to remember Satori. She loved him and he loved her, but it was a destructive love that eventually killed them both. Seeing him in that great cavern, afraid and vulnerable, is too much to bear, and she reaches for another bubble.

A toilet seat and black curls gripped by a pale fist. A scene she remembers from her own history but reversed. This time, it is Star's face that is pummelled into shards of broken bone against the porcelain while Raven towers above her, mouth twisted in bitter hatred.

'You stole Satori from me,' Raven shrieks and slams Star's head down again.

Star tastes blood, smells urine, feels fear. She's no longer a spectator; she is the victim, murdered by a flat mate she once considered a friend, yet she cannot wrap her broken head around why this is happening. She tries to push back against the violence, but her friend is too strong and determined, and Star is already weak from shock and blood loss. She prays that her death comes swiftly.

A bubble rises from the bowl, and she pops it with the tip of her tongue. The violence clings to her skin; lust and love, inspiration and the costly admiration of her mother all become one. The bathroom disappears, and she's racing through a forest, chased by the ghosts of her victims, while trees hasten her steps, shouting how brave and selfless she is, how her sacrifice will not be made in vain.

A bubble rises from the coarse grass, popping under her bare toes, then she's slumped in a doorway with a black hood to hide her unhealthy skin, while her right hand holds a paper bag weighted with a bottle of liquid which will warm her and make her forget how she got there. The feet of club goers skip past, oblivious to her presence, while she drinks, remembering happier days, dancing in Club Midian with her friends, before she lost everything in the bottom of a bottle.

Bubbles and lives — some happy but most troubled. She enters and leaves, taking with her the strength and determination, sorrow and despair of all those other selves, while remembering the life she really lived, unless that was a fabrication she created to escape some other reality. The abuse from her parents who hated her preoccupation with darkness and unearthly music; the therapy they tried after an exorcism made no difference to their daughter's temperament; her escape to university where she concentrated on reproducing her thoughts onto canvas before meeting Donna then Satori and Raven and Freya and of course Lilith; washing blood spatters from her face in the club toilets after murdering Raven, and the journey north with Lilith to escape arrest; Satori finding her and trying to reach beyond Star's trauma to some part of her who wanted to survive, but never managing to do so because she was lost by then; she killed herself and awoke in Binah, nursing a demonic infant — Edensun; she became the sun to Lilith's moon before returning to Earth with Satori, but she left part of herself on Binah — her son, and couldn't find peace until the boy found her. She chose Edensun when a choice had to be made, sacrificing her friends and Satori in the process, but contentment remained out of reach. In a desperate attempt to heal the world, purge it of greed and selfishness, she asked her son to bring the terrible red rain and watched as people tore each other to pieces.

The bubbles show Star what might have been, but she suspects each and every journey would have led to her oblivion. She's not strong enough for the world. She never was. The strengths and weaknesses of lives both lived and not-lived create layer upon layer of iridescence that form wings of such beauty that Star stops to admire them for a moment before they carry her away from the bottomless pit and its bubble-blowing jester. She soars across alien landscapes, through the violet roiling sky of Yesod, the chartreuse landscape of Netzach, the azure pyramids of Chesod, until she floats over the pure blue mist of Chokmah, and her wings become a robe of many colours, covering her body and pooling around her ankles when she lands in shallow water.

CHAPTER FIFTEEN

THE RUM bar seems a cosy setting to wait out the apocalypse. Other than the ruby smears down the ersatz leaded windows and the occasional battered body stumbling against them before lurching away, Marian can almost pretend it is an ordinary day. Of course, ordinary is a relative term. Marian's ordinary days can be compared to many people's worst nightmares, and it amazes her she is here at all. Only her connection to higher forces keeps her functioning; she has responsibilities she cannot avoid.

Marian Michaels, even in her fifties, is an attractive woman. Her long black hair is pulled back from her shield-shaped face in a messy bun. The people she trusts more than any living beings dominate the room. A few faces are unfamiliar, parents and children of the Morrigu worshippers, she suspects. They have gathered in this haven, summoned by their leader, the Oracle, and her granddaughter Jessica. A comfortable lounge with low lighting and warm drinks where they will face whatever comes.

Marian concentrates on Jessica who brought her here — a young woman with long black hair, prominent cheek bones and a sensual face that radiates power. She is coleader of the group and greets Marian warmly when she arrives, leaving her blind grandmother, the Oracle, at the table where two Doberman Pinschers guard the old woman's feet.

'What is it? Why are we all here?' Marian asks.

Jessica pulls her into a tight embrace, squeezing Marian's grief to the surface until she is incapable of doing anything other than sob on the younger woman's shoulder; wrapped in each other's arms and the tense atmosphere of the room, two raven-haired, pale skinned women, one in her prime and the other still in her youth. They could pass as mother and daughter. Only their eyes and mouths are different; Jessica's eyes are larger and darker and her lips fuller, although they share a similar shaped sneer when their features are at rest.

Marian understands that she was not called here on a whim. Something terrible is happening outside, and it has everything to do with that strange red rain.

Jessica leads Marian to her grandmother. Marian perches on a stool, and one of the dogs nudges her thigh with its damp nose. She pets its bony head, eliciting a low, contented growl.

Bill brings Marian a glass of syrupy amber liquid, which warms her throat and chest while she waits patiently. When the Oracle speaks, everyone listens. Her voice is harsh like tobacco, but her ancient lungs have lost their power and, although Marian sits only a metre away, she leans across the table, trying to drag the drawling vowels and rolling consonants to her ears.

'They are three,' the Oracle says. 'They bring the Lake of Sorrows with them. The red waters will soak through every skin and rip open souls. Regrets shall be laid bare until the pain becomes unbearable. Many will not survive this day, and those who do will be changed. Psychopaths shall inherit the Earth. We shelter here together, each other's strength, each other's shield, and thank Morrigan for her wisdom and forewarning.'

Marian nods respectfully at the old woman, takes her drink and withdraws across the room to where Bill waits on a faux-leather couch. A diamond panelled window dominates the wall behind them. Marian swivels her neck to watch the rain as it forms a red river in the gutter. Her brow creases as she tries to process the Oracle's words. Shivering, her mind drifts, and she remembers her beautiful boy. Her golden child who she refused to tame or bring to heel. Steve had power, more perhaps than the Oracle, however blasphemous that might sound. Now, he is dead, murdered in an Oedipal nightmare, and if today is Marian's last day on Earth, she will die without vengeance, with only memories and alcohol to warm her bosom.

Marian's gunmetal-grey eyes soften as she downs the dregs of her fourth rum and Frangelico cocktail in a half-hearted attempt to drown her self-pity. Bill stands up, eager to fetch her another, but she lunges gracelessly and grabs his sleeve, pulling him back. Bill has been a constant in her life since they buried her husband. His toned physique suggests he is built for war with his tight stomach muscles and bulky, tattooed arms, but he wears the gentle face of an adoring puppy under his short chestnut hair.

Her head spins and her stomach churns while her heart is a boulder that weighs her down. It would be too easy to drink herself into oblivion; she has shut herself away from these friends for months, but they never complain; they understand her suffering, many have shared in it, and they know what it costs her to answer Jessica's summons. She belongs with these people, and the only way she will heal is with the soothing balm of their love, but if she drinks much more, she will empty her gut over the table. She shakes her head, and the room lurches.

Against the far wall, under paintings of debauched saints and half hidden by shadows that muted amber lamps cannot dispel, her double vision suggests two oracles and two Jessicas. None of their shifting features carry the slightest accusation, but Marian still feels personally responsible for the carnage unfolding around the city and beyond. The Oracle says this is not the end. Marian finds that hard to believe despite years of devout faith. Her only son is dead, and her grandson is out there somewhere, holding open the gates of Hell.

Jessica helps her grandmother rise to her feet. The old woman's face seems weary. They have been sitting in this room for hours but, beyond the windows, the rain still falls. Bill rushes to take the Oracle's other arm.

'She needs to sleep,' Jessica says. 'Will you help me take her upstairs, Brother Bill?'

In Bill's absence, Marian approaches Mike and his family. The baby is beautiful with feathery white hair and Freya's ice-blue eyes. It is the first time Marian has met the child and the first time in years she's seen Lorraine, Mike's wife — Freya and Ivan's mother.

'What's her name?' Marian asks.

Lorraine smiles serenely. 'Avaline.'

'She's beautiful.'

Lorraine nods and strokes the sleeping girl's brow. The calmness radiating from Lorraine is fragile. She has a temper that Freya inherited. Marian does not ask after Ivan or Freya; she already knows the family's heartache. Instead, she offers to get drinks.

Julio sits in front of the bar, reading. He glances up as Marian approaches.

'Do you have family?' Marian asks, acutely aware that this is the first time she has conversed with the man beyond ordering cocktails.

'Jessica and her grandmother are my family,' he answers.

His eloquent English is enhanced by a rich Mediterranean accent that matches the tanned skin he reveals between the open buttons of his canary yellow silk shirt. She wants to hear his history: where he comes from, how he met the Oracle, why he works here. After she delivers drinks to Mike's table, she makes her way back to the bar and sits beside Julio, nursing her Salvation.

He faces her, inviting questions, but first asks one of his own.

'Is it true the Bringer of Chaos is your grandson?'

Marian is not surprised by Julio's insider knowledge. 'Yes.'

He exhales with a whistle.

'How long have you known Jessica and the Oracle?' she asks.

'Fifteen years. I came to England for love. When that ended, Grandma took me in.'

'But you aren't a worshipper?'

He shakes his head. 'I respect the Oracle and love her. They are my family, but family doesn't have to follow the same path.'

She nods. Steve did not follow her path either. 'What do you believe?'

'I suppose I'm agnostic. I've seen miracles, but I am not convinced they originate from an external source, and they are common to all religions, as far as I can tell.'

'What's your theory?' Marian asks.

'That we're accessing forces inside ourselves. Morrigan, God, Satan, Buddha, and the rest are the same thing with different names. The Oracle draws wisdom from deep inside herself when she communes with her deity. That's my theory.'

'In that case, why the décor?' Marian asks. 'It looks Satanist.'

'Ambience. The Lucifernum is a theme pub. No one complains… How did you join the Morrigu?'

'My mother and the Oracle were at school together in Pontypridd. When the Oracle moved, Mum followed. She brought me up in the old religion. Morrigan was always part of my life. I guess it's like being brought up Catholic, except we actually commune with our deity.'

He grins. 'I was brought up Catholic, and we have our share of people who commune with their deity, as you say.'

'Do you have any aspirin,' Marian asks. 'I can't shift the pain in my head.'

Julio passes her a box of painkillers and a tumbler of water.

'I introduced my son to our ways a long time ago, but he felt suffocated by them and slipped away from the Morrigu and me into obsession. He was a headstrong boy, so I gave him a lot of rope; sadly, it was enough for him to hang himself. Sometimes I thought he might be mad, but he knew and saw more than I did. I'm not sure what I could have done differently. Perhaps, some things are meant to be.' Marian attempts an unconvincing smile. *Why is it easier to tell strangers the truth than admit it to oneself?* 'It was good talking to you, Julio.'

'It was good talking with you as well,' Julio replies.

Marian stands up, intending to return to Mike's table, but her head spins. 'Can you help me?' she asks.

Julio takes her arm and escorts her to the table. No longer trusting herself on a stool, Marian sinks onto the couch beside Lorraine and offers a lopsided smile to the baby.

The oak door vibrates as someone pounds on the other side of the barrier. No one moves to answer it. Upstairs, the dogs bark. A shadow crouches beyond the leaded windows, then glass explodes inwards, and a fist fills the jagged hole. When it withdraws and the silhouette staggers away, rain rushes through the broken pane and streams down the inside of the glass, soaking the couch that she and Bill recently vacated.

'Mierda!' Julio yells. His eyes dart around the room as if searching for something to block the hole.

'Table?' Mike asks.

Julio nods and the two rush upstairs to retrieve one from the kitchen.

Marian stares at the broken window. If it had smashed while she and Bill were sitting there, what would have happened? Would she and Bill, soaked in misery, kill the rest of the worshippers then each other? The Oracle warned them that the rain rips open souls. How much sorrow does Marian's contain? Far too much. What-ifs smother her even without the influence of the red rain, and it is all she can do to hold her regrets in check and keep living. Living? Is that what she has been doing? No, she has been hiding and clinging to the memory of her son. What of Bill's sorrow? A sunny disposition masks his sadness, but he has lost people too.

The last time Marian felt this close to death was when her husband was beating her for the crime of feminising their son. She holds back a scream of fury. Let them come for her. She will fight them until her final breath to avoid feeling that powerless again.

Lorraine adjusts her hold on Avaline, shifting the peaceful sleeper from one arm to the other, and stares at Marian who shudders in anticipation. Lorraine's expression is expectant; she wants something, but Marian cannot guess what. Mike's absence makes his wife seem jumpy. Marian and Lorraine have never been friends. In fact, Marian has often been the sympathetic ear to Mike's complaints about his wife. If she were sober and more coordinated, Marian would get up and move to another seat, however rude that might appear, but she has no confidence in her balance and doesn't want to draw attention as she abandons Lorraine. Better to sit still and try to brush off any questions, although her mind is too fuzzy to be trusted.

'Can I ask you a question?' Lorraine asks.

Here we go! Marian tries to hold down a burp, part nerves part inebriation, that she is worried might morph into something more violent. Trapped, she carefully nods her head.

'If our children had joined this cult of yours, do you think things would have been different?'

Acid bubbles and burns Marian's oesophagus. It is a question she has asked many times since Steve's death and before, when he was arrested for Sarah's murder, but how can she answer this woman who has also lost everything? The aggression behind the word "yours" is not lost on Marian, and Lorraine's mournful eyes refuse to be denied, begging for peace and solace, desperate to hear that the deaths of her children are not her fault. She deserves an honest answer. Would Tanya and Ivan be dead, would Freya be a murderer, if they had been protected by the Oracle? Would Steve still be alive?

As Marian opens her mouth, the suppressed burp rips through her throat, and Lorraine's face softens. A narrow smile flashes across her face, before disappearing, but it happens so quickly that Marian suspects she imagined it.

'I'm so sorry,' Marian says, covering her mouth. 'I'm ridiculously drunk.'

'But the children,' Lorraine insists, wrinkling her nose.

'Why didn't Mike bring them to us?' Marian asks, deflecting.

Lorraine stares at her lap. 'I was afraid of the cult, so I begged him not to, but they were all strange anyway. I guess they got that from their father.'

Marian doubts it. Lorraine is stranger than all of them, but she pushes that thought aside and tries to form another. 'Steve's father wouldn't hear of it either. By the time Carl was… out of our lives, my son was already lost. I tried bringing him into the fold, but he felt suffocated, and I feared the goddess might kill him for some reason I couldn't understand until now. Would it have been different? Maybe for Ivan, maybe for Freya, but what happened to Tanya, well that was terrible, and maybe the Oracle

might have foreseen, but she doesn't see everything. Some trag-
edies are unavoidable.'

'I miss them so much.' Lorraine's eyes shine with tears.
'Would you hold Avaline for a moment?'

Avaline stirs as she is transferred but settles when Marian
brings her to her chest, calmed by her heartbeat or perhaps the
gurgling of her digestive system. Avaline reminds Marian of
Steve when he was a baby. Her pride and joy. The marriage had
been difficult, but her husband gave her the love of her life, a
son. She will always be thankful for the twenty-eight years she
spent with Steve, watching him grow into a man. At times she
thought her son mad, but his brilliance fills her with pride, and
she aches with his loss; a hole she can never fill. At least Lorraine
has Avaline, the chance of a new beginning.

'Ivan was the sweetest boy, but I never understood Freya. She
was a rebel. Ivan was always so easy, so content. You remember
that tree in our garden, the one with the ribbons. He tied those
scraps of fabric to its branches and said each one was a prayer
that had been answered. He never took anything for granted. Not
like Freya who was always acting out and claimed we trapped
her, smothered her, but we were only trying to protect her. After
Tanya, we were terrified we might lose Freya too. Girls are
fragile. You worry about them more.

'Tanya was beautiful. When they took her from us, it broke
her daddy's heart. The police never caught the boys who did it.
All that evidence and the killers somehow disappeared. I need
to know, Marian. It might not matter now, but if you can tell me
they were punished, those filthy murderers and rapists, I will be
in your debt. Did he kill them? Did Mike find them and make
them pay for what they did to our daughter? I've been married
to him for over thirty years, but you know him better than I do.
You know what happened, right? I need you to tell me.'

Marian focuses on the tiny brow and pale fluttering lashes
of the sleeping baby. Yes, she knows. More than that, she helped.
Mike and Bill caught the boys and brought them to the basement
of The Lucifernum. They tortured the teens for days, ensuring

the boys relived every wound they inflicted and more, until they wept blood. Lorraine is right, but it is not Marian's place to tell her. Thankfully, she does not have time to answer. Julio and Mike re-emerge, grunting with the effort of carrying a heavy kitchen table.

When the broken pane is blocked, there is a sigh of relief. The room is darker than ever, and Marian is glad when Julio lights a fire. She appreciates the light more than the warmth. Mike joins them, sweating profusely, and seems surprised that Lorraine has released her hold on Avaline. He stares at the women before noticing his wife's distress. His face creases, and he sits beside Lorraine, pulling her close to his musky body. Lorraine seems comforted by his stench. Before Marian can make her excuses and hand over the baby, Bill pens her in on the other side.

'How is the Oracle?' Mike asks.

'She's sleeping,' Bill answers. 'Jessica plans to sit with her a while. What happened to the window?'

'Some cunt smashed the glass, and the rain was getting in,' Mike answers. 'Did she say how long she thinks it will last?'

Bill shrugs.

'Want another drink, anyone?' Mike asks.

Only Marian shakes her head. The others eagerly accept.

'Can I have her back?' Lorraine asks, grabbing Avaline.

Lorraine recovers her serenity, as if the child insulates her from her pain. Marian's skin itches, feeling trapped between Bill and Lorraine. She makes her excuses and rushes to the bathroom.

The air is chilly beyond the warmth of the fire. Marian stares at the mirror. Age has altered her face, and there are lines across her forehead she never noticed before, and strands of grey pepper her dark hair. Her mouth tastes as though something crawled in and died there. She gargles under the tap. The water is frosty and makes her teeth ache.

Marian enters a stall and locks the door, glad to be alone. Lorraine has sapped her strength. She wants to go home, sleep on Steve's sheets, hear his soft breath in the air of his bedroom. Incorporeal perhaps, but his presence fills her home, their home.

He has not abandoned her.

When Steve was a baby, he was every bit as sweet and beautiful as Avaline. He chose the name Satori later, but he would always be Steve to Marian, much to her son's frustration. "Names have power," he would say. *Not enough to save you though, my love.*

When Steve was little his father, Carl, doted on him but, by the time Steve turned seven, he was too sensitive, too feminine, and it enraged Carl to see his son gaze longingly at his mother's soft fabrics. Carl refused to understand why Steve would choose to read a book instead of kicking a football around in the park with his father.

Confused and angry, Carl blamed the boy's mother for being too indulgent, and their home became a battleground. Marian's friends, her work, her appearance, even the food she prepared for them were blamed. The first time Carl struck Marian was the evening after Steve's eighth birthday party. All the guests were girls, and the cake had lilac icing. After shaving the boy's head and sending him to bed, he picked up Steve's purple glitter scooter and threw it at Marian. Steve sneaked downstairs and witnessed it all. The boy's scream was the final straw. Carl stormed out of the house only to return drunk the following night. Marian planned to leave many times but feared losing her son if she fled. Their final separation was nothing she could have planned, and thankfully something Steve does not remember.

One night, when Steve was ten years old, the boy saw his father slap Marian so hard that she fell back onto the sofa. Her son might have been small, but the way he jumped seemed more like levitation, and the lamp he wielded struck his father with such force that the back of the man's head crumpled inwards with a sickening crunch. Carl fell face first into their coffee table, smashing the glass top, and Steve rushed to his mother's arms to comfort her.

Mike and Bill helped clean up the mess, and they pretended Carl had left. Steve accepted the lie without question. Christmas and birthday presents were sent by proxy until at thirteen Steve admitted he was glad his father had gone and no longer wanted his stupid gifts.

It was just the two of them — closer than mother and son; them against the world. Despite girlfriends and the occasional male admirer, they remained inseparable. Sarah changed everything, and Marian had to come to terms with letting go.

She never understood her son's obsession with the delicate, pale girl. The Oracle warned that the relationship was destructive, but nothing Marian said made any difference. Steve gnawed the umbilical cord like an ungrateful pup, but she still loved him. She will always love him.

Marian checks her watch. It is well past midnight. Her ass cheeks have bonded with the toilet seat, and she struggles to stand up. She stares at the pitted glass of the mirror as she washes her hands then her face and swills out her mouth. Her tongue tastes like rank milk, an echo of too many cocktails. She wishes she had brought a toothbrush or mouthwash, but she never expected to stay this long. She wants to curl up in Steve's bed, not snatch a couple of hours sleep on a narrow pleather couch in the bar. The rain beats a steady rhythm on the skylight.

When Marian emerges from the bathroom, couples are curled up together, trying to grab some sleep. No one appears comfortable and, despite the roaring fire, the room is cold and damp. Bill sits with Mike. Avaline is strapped into a car seat, and Lorraine lies on the couch with one arm draped over the edge so that her hand rests on the baby's chest.

'Why don't you try to get some sleep?' Bill asks when Marian returns.

Bill wraps a protective arm around her shoulder. Without over-thinking, she rests her cheek against his chest and closes her eyes. His warmth comforts her, and it is not long before she drifts into unconsciousness.

The world looks very different now. The rain has stopped at

last, but the silent streets are strewn with corpses. Marian drives and Bill sits beside her on the passenger seat. Neither comment on the number of bodies they swerve to avoid nor the smashed windows and burned-out buildings that line each street. Thirty minutes ago, the Oracle asked Marian to retrieve an item from her home. Her quest is to recover Steve's athame and deliver it to The Lucifernum.

The thudding of fists against wood reminds Marian of a tribal drum. She slows the car and stares at a desperate man pounding on a locked door. Blood flows freely from a head wound above his left ear.

'Should we stop and help?' Bill asks.

'Help who, the man at the door or the family cowering within?'

'I suppose you're right. We don't know why he wants to get inside.'

They pull up outside Marian's house. The front door is cracked as though someone kicked it and left a grimacing mouth in their wake.

As Marian gets closer, she sees the navy paint is decorated with insults, and her eyes dart around the street. *Which of them hates me?* she asks herself.

Bill scratches at the black letters with a blunt fingernail. 'What the fuck? Who did this?'

Marian is empty of tears, but her lips tremble.

'Someone you rejected, perhaps?' Bill suggests.

'I don't speak to anyone.'

'Sorry, Sister Marian, I'm not saying you did anything to deserve this. It's probably some nasty piece of work who thinks because you're beautiful you owe him your attention. Ignore it.' Bill seems unable to heed his own words and rubs his elbow against the black graffiti declaring *SLUT*.

'Let's just get inside,' Marian says.

The rooms are as she left them. Dirty glasses crowd the kitchen surfaces, and a damp towel hangs over the back of the sofa. She resists the urge to tidy for her guest and climbs the stairs to Steve's bedroom. Bill follows.

A voice yells, 'It's your fault. You're making him soft. Mummy's boy.'

She stops climbing, heart hammering in her chest. 'What did you say?' she whispers.

'Nothing,' Bill says.

His warm breath teases the air on her forearm. *Did Bill hear the voice too, or is it in my head?*

'I heard a voice,' she says.

'You think someone's upstairs? Let me go first.'

He grabs her waist gently as he squeezes past on the narrow staircase. She does not try to match his pace, and before she reaches the final tread, he is calling from the door to her bedroom.

'No one here,' he says.

He is wrong. Carl's ghost is everywhere, even if Bill cannot feel it.

She takes off her shoes and tiptoes across the landing to Steve's door. The painted planks scratch her soles. She remembers the charcoal sigils Satori scrawled over the bare floorboards. That must have been four or five years ago. She scrubbed in vain for days, attempting to remove them. In the end it was the choice of fitted carpet or painting the floor. Together, Marian and her son settled on paint, and he promised to use chalk if he felt the need to decorate the floor again.

She reaches the rug. Its soft fibres tickle her splayed toes as she steps across. Bill is beside her when the door slams behind them, making them both leap into the air.

'It must have been the wind. Maybe you left a window open.'

Marian does not argue even though the cruel laughter of Carl fills her head.

The bookcase is only two steps away. When she stops trembling, she will be able to reach it and recover the knife from behind the paperbacks on the middle shelf, then they can leave. She prays Carl has not returned, and this is merely a psychotic break from stress and grief. She cannot share her home with that jealous, possessive, violent man again. If it is a ghost and not psychosis, maybe he reappeared only because she arrived with another man. That would make sense. Her husband hated Marian having male friends when he was alive. She silently promises to never bring a man within these walls again as long as Carl leaves her the fuck alone. It is a promise she will find easy to keep.

'Maybe you should leave?' she says to Bill.

'Leave you alone.' Incredulity widens his mouth and eyes.

'Okay, let's just get the dagger, and we'll both leave. The house doesn't want us here.' *Carl doesn't want* you *here.*

She takes a tentative step toward the bookcase, acutely aware of all the shadows in the room. Her legs shake beneath her, muscle spasms jolting her thighs.

Bill grips her elbow. The ghost responds with a fury that rips books from the shelves. Marian ducks as paperbacks, their soft covers like wings, fling themselves at her face. Bill yelps as one smashes into his nose. She drags him to the floor and covers her face with her arms, her lips kissing the carpet. Books bounce against her spine and the back of her skull, making her thankful that none of Satori's heavy magical volumes are stacked on those shelves. Even so, her body is bruised by the impact.

She plans to wait out the hurricane of pulp fiction, protecting herself the best she can until she remembers what she hid behind the books on the middle shelf and glances up. 'The dagger!'

As if summoned by her memory, the metal quivers. She screams as it hurtles, blade first, towards her face. With reflexes faster than Marian imagines possible, Bill reaches out to deflect the knife. It slices the flesh between his thumb and forefinger and hits the mattress with such force that the blade disappears into the bedding and only the jewelled hilt is visible.

Bill pinches the loose skin of his hand to stop the bleeding.

'Let's get that bandaged up,' Marian says when she can speak again. 'Thank you.'

'Any time,' Bill says, managing to sound heroic despite the pain he must feel.

Blood drops mark their journey to the bathroom where Marian cleans and dresses his wound.

'What happened in there?' he asks as he tries to flex his bound hand. At least the bleeding seems to have stopped.

'I don't think Carl is happy I brought a man home.' She bites her lip, awaiting ridicule that does not come.

Bill strokes her cheek with his bandaged hand, and the touch is abrasive but reassuring.

'I'll get the knife,' he says. 'I'll meet you in the car. Make sure you lock the doors. It isn't safe out there either.'

His warning insults her intelligence, but if it weren't for his heroics, she would be bleeding out on her son's rug, so she forgives his patronising concern.

CHAPTER SIXTEEN

THE BEDROOM is dark, thanks to blackout linings, but a pool of sunlight blanches the grey carpet directly below Donna's window. She yawns and checks the clock — eleven. After five hours of bizarre dreams, her head threatens to burst open.

Donna rotates her stiff shoulders until the muscles click then massages the tendons in her neck. Finally, some gentle leg stretches. She is only twenty-six, but her body demands regular maintenance. With all the stupid, crazy stuff she has done, she is lucky her body functions at all. Donna pulls on a t-shirt, skinny jeans, and an over-sized striped sweater then drags a brush through her hair without checking her reflection. It is time to open the curtains and greet the dazzling morning.

The post has arrived. She flicks through the envelopes, searching for Sarah's familiar handwriting. It has been over a month with no word from Bristol, but no one could call Sarah reliable, and it is pointless to worry. Donna places her mother's letters on the hall table beside the phone. She tosses the one addressed to herself in the kitchen bin before switching the kettle on.

Donna moved into her mother's house four years ago. Occasionally, Donna feels a nostalgic ache for the busy city but suspects what she really misses are the dizzying chemicals that flooded her brain when she was near Sarah.

She opens the back door and breathes deeply, filling her lungs with fresh, chilly air before lighting a cigarette. 'It won't kill me,' she says with a sardonic chuckle.

Burgundy clouds gather in the pale sky, jostling together,

expanding and thickening until sunlight cannot penetrate the dark crowd. Donna shivers and steps inside, discarding her half-smoked cigarette as the first red raindrop falls.

After a bowl of granola sweetened with honey, Donna takes her second cup of tea into the living room. Wails from screeching tyres and crunching metal. Donna peers through the net curtains. Two cars are nose to nose — a collision? Heavy rain hammers on the heads of two men as they emerge from their vehicles and attack each other with fists.

Returning to the sofa, she turns on the television.

Breaking News. Images of Parliament Square, London. Chaos as people assault each other. Smoke rises from the Houses of Parliament and pyres dotted across the lawn. The reporter at the scene, bulbous microphone in fist, shouts to be heard above the roar of helicopters and screams. His black umbrella shelters him from the red rain.

'*Unexplained eruptions of violence have been reported across London and beyond. Here in Parliament Square, people are rioting. Politicians are being dragged outside and set alight. So far, we cannot confirm or deny that the conflict we are witnessing, and the red rain are connected, but people are warned to stay inside and lock their doors until peace is restored. The prime minister declared a state of emergency shortly before he was kicked to death by an angry mob and doused in kerosene. We understand that the royal family have been evacuated to an undisclosed location.*'

The camera zooms out and pans to the left. Among a group of angry strangers, Donna sees a familiar figure. 'What the fuck?' It cannot be Sarah. Why would Sarah be in London in the middle of a riot? She approaches the screen as the camera arcs back to the reporter.

'*We repeat, all citizens are advised to stay indoors until we confirm that the danger has passed.*'

The screen flickers. White specks dance in darkness. Donna changes channel, but it remains the same. The signal must be down. She grabs her mobile and tries to call her mum but gets a network busy message. The landline is dead.

'What the hell is going on?'

The old banger Mum bought so Donna could get to and from work sits on the driveway. Donna grabs the keys and an umbrella. She parks in front of the clinic and rushes to the door, forgetting to retrieve the umbrella from the back seat. Before she reaches the entrance, her hair becomes a heavy shroud blocking her vision.

The door is locked. She beats on it with her fists, but no one comes. Despair, the debilitating madness that made her set fire to her flat, grips her mind like a vice and squeezes.

She shudders. 'Mum!'

The lights are on, but no one answers.

Donna grabs her umbrella and walks a complete circuit around the single-storey building. All the blinds are closed. She taps on each window, bleating 'Mum,' then 'Linda,' hoping her mother will respond.

No signs of life. Without forcing entry, breaking a window, and leaving the doctors, nurses, and patients vulnerable, Donna cannot be certain her mother is inside. If Linda is hiding in the clinic, she should be safe at least, unlike the poor souls Donna passed on the way. She tried not to stare at the shuffling figures or their potentially fatal wounds. The tiny town has morphed, within a single hour, into something that resembles the setting of a horror movie.

'What is happening?' she mumbles as she heads to her car. She locks the doors and places the folded umbrella on the back seat, shivering as a few drops of rain drip on her hand. *We cannot confirm or deny that the conflict and the red rain are connected. Really? I am pretty fucking certain they are,* Donna thinks, rubbing her hand on the passenger's seat to dry it.

Donna glances toward the clinic-cum-fortress where she hopes her mother is safe then fires up the engine. She heads to the motorway, but the slip road is choked with what might best be described as zombies. Figures whose faces gape with terror stagger down the slope unable to escape others who wield make-shift weapons: tyre irons and hub caps. A more ambitious monster drags a signpost behind him. Donna chooses a different route north, hoping for the best, fearing the worst.

Her conviction that Steve and Sarah will know why the rain is falling grows more compelling with each mile Donna covers. She recalls the letters Sarah wrote about the son she left behind and missed desperately, the goddess she forgave, and the fairies she painted. If anyone can explain the magical storm, it will be Sarah. *I just have to reach her.*

Donna flicks through radio stations without taking her eyes off the road. Most are white noise, but one repeats a message in a clipped Edinburgh accent: 'Stay inside. Lock your doors and await further instructions.'

She glances at the fuel gauge, hoping there is enough in the tank to complete her journey.

Although the roads are less congested than the motorway, she frequently encounters streets blocked by "the crazies" and their abandoned vehicles. After driving for well over an hour, she finds herself on the wrong side of the Quantock Hills and tries to navigate around farmland and forests, hamlets and small villages until she finally reaches a junction beside a reservoir and spots a signpost to Bridgwater. As she approaches the old industrial town, road signs are unnecessary. An enduring stench of sulphur points the way. The cellophane factory closed in 2005, and yet the unholy smell has embedded itself in the concrete of the town. It reminds Donna of her journey with Steve through a nightmare world. A towering citadel of skulls, a stinking yellow river, and the dragon circling in the air above them. She will never forget that dragon.

The car runs out of petrol as Donna reaches the southern limits of Bristol. She cruises past a golf course on fumes and pulls onto a grass verge to avoid blocking the road. If she finds no abandoned cars with keys in the ignition and a conveniently full tank, she will walk to Sarah's cottage, assuming she isn't murdered en route.

It is four in the afternoon, although the berry-coloured clouds block most of the sunlight, there are at least three hours until sunset. The rain is still falling, but her umbrella is on the seat behind her. Donna tries to call Star's number, but the network remains jammed. The same result when she tries her mother again. There is an atlas in the glove compartment. She takes it out and studies a map of the city.

She considers her options and decides to avoid the heavily populated city centre. The simplest route seems to be to walk towards Clifton then head north. It will take at least four hours, but the only alternative is to sit in the car and pray that the rain will stop, and the world will recover some sanity. Walking, even in the dark, seems preferable to that.

An hour into her walk, Donna realises she has made a good choice. She regularly encounters abandoned cars and vans, even one ambulance, but no crazies. Her umbrella groans beneath the unrelenting rain, but it holds out and keeps most of her dry. Her boots leak, and her toes feel like ice blocks, but the stabbing pain in her extremities has eased. Now they are numb. This might be worse in the long run; she imagines frostbite and amputation.

Another hour of marching on autopilot and she reaches the gates of Ashton Court Estate. She hikes across the lawn, but the ground is too soft, and mud rises over her soles, coating her boots. Muscles ache as she lifts the weight of her dirt-encased feet time and time again. When she sees a path, she changes direction and joins it.

The last time she was here was a hot summer afternoon. Sarah, Steve, Raven, Freya, and Ivan were with her. Others too, people from Club Midian whose names she has long forgotten or never learned. The music festival was an excuse to get wasted. They stayed cool under parasols and drank strong cider while batting curious wasps away. The music was background noise. They were there for the sense of camaraderie, a change of scene from the dark tables and sticky floors of their usual drinking haunts. An island of black in an ocean of pastels and tie dye, attracting stares from the "normies". Despite her aching limbs and numb toes, Donna is warmed by the memory.

Brunel's bridge rises before her. Its festooned lights seem festive against the bruised sky. The dark river reflects it back and calls to Donna. She is too high up, the current whispers. She should jump and restore the balance. Submerge herself in the romantic, watery depths. It is a seductive suggestion, but one she walks away from.

The narrow bridge stretches ahead across the breach from one cliff to another. There is nowhere to run and hide if she commits to crossing here, but what choice does she have? The central section resembles a car park. *How many living souls are sheltering in the metal cages?* On either side are footpaths and of course the river far below, whispering to her.

She sticks to the centre, weaving between cars. Most are abandoned while others contain sleepers or barely conscious people with blank stares. Donna's already half-way across when she hears the groan of a car door opening behind her. *Fuck!* They might want her help. They might only need company, but she does not think so. Her hairs bristle as adrenaline rushes into her muscles. Her legs will hate her for it; she anticipates a painful burning of nerve endings, her punishment when the adrenaline declines, but she sprints ahead.

'Hey!' The voice is female, but Donna keeps running.

Women kill too.

She sees Raven's hair tangled around Sarah's fist, and Raven's cheek smashing against white porcelain. Donna's pounding heartbeat and the sharp sounds of her friend's cheek-bone cracking align as the inexplicable murder chases Donna across the bridge. When she reaches the other side, she follows a path, carved into the grass, and hides behind a tree to catch her breath.

Donna's legs tremble beneath her when she risks continuing her journey. She tells herself she is over half-way there, but that still means at least two more hours of trudging. She grips a lamp post when her knees buckle. Paint crumbles beneath her fingers, her back bends, and she vomits bile onto her muddy boots. Painful stomach cramps remind her that, like her car, she cannot keep going without fuel.

The public toilets are open. Cautiously, she steps inside. Finding it empty, she gulps water from a tap before huddling in a relatively dry spot and listening to the steady beat of rain against the roof and high windows. Eventually, the rhythm lulls Donna to sleep.

Donna's back and neck ache, and her arm tingles. All the stall doors were open when she fell asleep. Now one of them is closed.

'Hello,' she calls.

A gentle whimper pushes her to her feet, and pain darts through her limbs and along her spine. Keeping an eye on the closed door, she shuffles across to the sink and takes a long drink of oddly metallic water. No one emerges from the stall, and she has no desire to add their troubles to her own, so she leaves.

The light is hazy, but bright enough to hurt her eyes. The rain has stopped, and red puddles reflect sunlight like rubies around a wealthy woman's throat.

She uses her umbrella as a walking stick at first, hobbling cautiously. By the time she is half-way across the grass, she has stretched most of the pain out of her muscles and rests the brolly on her right shoulder like a miner's pickaxe, hoping she does not have to find out whether it makes an effective weapon.

Three-storey town houses overlook the green. She is in a wealthy part of the city where slave traders and tobacco merchants built their homes. Most have been converted into hotels and expensive apartments.

Her route is strangely quiet, and there are plenty of trees and high walls to hide behind when she occasionally spots another walker. She checks her phone to see what time it is, but the battery must have died overnight. Her nerves are stretched so tight it feels as though they are waiting to snap.

An eastern pinpoint of brightness, low in the misty sky, suggests it is still early. The birds survived the night, and their gentle chirps warm Donna's heart, giving her the strength to keep moving.

She passes a sign for the zoo and hopes the animals will not starve. Maybe activists will set them free, and Bristol can be repopulated by all kinds of exotic mammals and reptiles.

A black and white dog, with its lead trailing behind it like a broken tail, bounds across the grass, barking at her. She holds her ground, afraid to run. It is friendly when it reaches her, optimistically sniffing her empty left hand, hoping to be fed. She rubs the dog's ears and unhooks its lead, and it follows her until she crosses the road and enters a tangle of houses at the edge of a vast residential area. She keeps the sun to her right and strides northward, hoping her luck will hold.

The houses become smaller and huddle closer together the further she walks. When she hears voices, she freezes. The way the sounds echo between the buildings makes it impossible to pinpoint direction, but they are getting louder. She hurdles a garden wall and crouches behind the grubby bricks. The grass is wet, and her splayed fingers chill as they touch the ground. Her body shivers, and she sees the newspaper headline *Goth bitch-fight blood bath.* She should have sensed something was wrong before that fateful night. A good friend would have helped Sarah escape Lilith's clutches. Donna had been a terrible friend, consumed by her own jealousy. Fat tears roll down her cheeks as she forces herself to stay low rather than spring back up, away from the damp grass and the painful memories it evokes. She squeezes her eyes shut and is back in her apartment while flames dance around her, licking her skin.

In the real world, footsteps clatter close by, and she hears cruel laughter and the bassy voices of men approaching her hiding place.

She crouches lower. Blades of grass tickle her cheek and the same trembling lips that Sarah kissed to heal her. How did Donna repay her friend's kindness? She left. Freya was right when she said Donna was empty, hollow, and what else? Yes, a crazy cunt. She should have found a way into the clinic and helped her mother. *Sarah cannot fill my emptiness. No one can.* She pulls the umbrella against her chest until the metal point bruises her jaw. The pain quiets her thoughts.

Glass shatters nearby, and Donna is transported further back in time, celebrating her promotion, having triumphed over a colleague who thought the team manager position was hers for the asking. In the too warm, too crowded bar, it felt as though anything was possible, standing side-by-side with the woman of her dreams and downing cocktails, while surrounded by girls in thin summer dresses and men in polo shirts. Donna and Star stuck out like bruised thumbs in purple and black.

'Watch out!' Donna yelled as a drunk twenty-something lad with gelled hair crashed into her shoulder.

She recovered her footing and squared up to him. His watery eyes narrowed as he considered her with a malevolence she could taste, then brought his bottle of continental lager to his mouth and gulped. His thin lips twisted into a sneer and time sped up. He smashed the bottle on the edge of a table and thrust the jagged remnants into her face. The world turned red. No pain at first, but she couldn't see him or anyone through the oozing crimson filter blurring her vision. Arms reached for her, gripping her shoulders as her knees buckled. Sarah kept assuring her that she would be okay. Donna heard screams. She wobbled at the epicentre of a dervish as bodies rushed around her. She knew she should be afraid, but Sarah was there, holding her up, pressing something against her eye, telling her she would be fine.

Donna touches her face. There is no scar. Sarah kissed it away. Her body trembles as she resists the urge to get to her feet and run. It is safer to hide. Sarah isn't here to save her.

The voices move on, and after minutes of silence, so does Donna. Houses block the sun from view, but she is certain she is walking the right way. How much farther? A couple of hours, maybe three. She will need to find something to eat soon.

A trifecta of circular towers rises above Donna as she climbs the hill; a landmark that tells her she has almost reached the cottage. Sarah brought her here last summer, while Donna was visiting. Long grass tickles Donna's hand. It was here that they found a five-pound note, waving like a flag caught on a blade of grass, and spent it on ice cream.

That weekend, Sarah finally told Donna about the child she abandoned on Binah. The woman had been an emotional fortress, and Donna remembers how good it felt to be let in after hammering on the drawbridge for years. The privilege of sharing the burden of her friend's pain was sweeter than any ice cream.

Donna is surprised how well she remembers the route from Blaise Castle to the cottage. She has been travelling for more than twenty-four hours with minimal sleep and no food, but the knowledge that she is close to her destination spurs her on.

The gate squeaks as she opens it. The garden is overgrown, and abundant weeds reach feathered stems towards her. She knocks on the door, waits, then opens the letter box and sees an empty hallway. She peers through the window. Someone has torn the sofa apart and smashed picture frames. Donna imagines the worst. Did Satori find out about Sarah's lover? If so, he is probably at his mother's house, licking his wounds.

The green door at the far end of the garden hangs open. The park is Sarah's favourite spot to sit and paint. Donna rushes across the uncut grass and flings the door wide. There is someone there, in her usual spot, but it is not Sarah.

CHAPTER SEVENTEEN

CAT SITS by the window, scanning the city below. Although the rain stopped half an hour ago, blood-red rivers race down the gutters on either side of her street. She spots David Garlow's black BMW draw up outside and makes her way down the communal staircase to greet him at the main entrance. Neither speak as they climb the stairs. David likes privacy, and they have perfected this ritual over the years. He is one of very few visitors who doesn't seem to notice the mess or the smell of her flat, which she finds refreshing. They sit on either side of the crowded coffee table, mugs in hands.

'Thank you for your warning. I got Louisa and the kids indoors before the rain fell,' David says.

Cat nods. 'It was the boy you sent to me, the one who killed his father.'

'Mark?'

Cat nods again, then pauses to sip her tea. There are few benefits to having a human body, and Hecate takes none of them for granted. Now, she enjoys the vibrant response of her taste buds to the smoky flavour and the euphoric rush of dopamine that follows.

'Why?' David asks.

'His mother wanted to change the world.'

'They certainly did that,' David says. 'I preferred it the old way.'

Cat glares at him. At least part of David Garlow believes his assertion.

'The world was no better last week, last month or last year;

murder and war have always gnawed at the core of humanity. The old regime has fallen. You've been bending my ear for months, telling me how you'd do a better job of running the country. Here's your chance.'

Catherine's thoughts fill the shared mind — *have we become Macbeth's witches, urging David towards his own destruction?*

'I could take my boys to London; find out what remains of the capital city. Terrified people turn to strong leaders and religion. I will reach out to them in the churches where they seek sanctuary… Would you lead me astray?' David asks.

'We would never do anything to hurt Louisa or her family. You know me better than that.'

'Where is Mark?'

'Mark is the name his human mother whispered in his ear before she abandoned him, but his true name, the one you will need if you wish to summon him, is Edensun. He can be found at his mother's cottage, grieving.'

'Will he help me?' David asks.

'If I tell him to. Catherine and Helen have expressed deep reservations; I don't share them. What must happen will happen. You will taste the nectar of power.'

He stands up, ready to leave. He will find his own way out of the tower block and the maze of streets. David Garlow spent his childhood in a flat like this, brought up by working-class parents with nothing of value to aid their son's ambition. Everything he owns he has worked for — if you consider lying, cheating, violence and extortion to be work. He thinks he can lift England out of the extreme violence the red rain brought, but he hasn't washed the blood from his own hands.

Hecate waves goodbye to David as he slips out of her door. The coming hours will be filled with arguments and complaints from her cohabitants. Sitting cross-legged on the armchair, she welcomes their comments.

Helen begins. 'He's evil. We hate him. How dare you help him?'

'Hecate,' Catherine says. 'Why are we urging him toward a

power grab? People could fix this mess themselves through peace and co-operation rather than further oppression and violence.'

'What about the boy? Where does he fit into this scheme? All he wants is to find his mother. Why do you think he'll help this lunatic?' Helen asks.

'Because we'll tell him it's the quickest route to finding her. Don't you trust me?' Hecate asks.

'It's about sacrifice, isn't it?' Catherine says.

The three understand sacrifice. Soon after Louisa and David were married, Helen and Catherine were taken to a cellar beneath an ostentatious faux-Tudor manor house. Each remember vivid snippets of events. Together they see the big picture. That's the beauty of three minds, three souls in one. Each benefit from the arrangement even if it was forced upon them violently and without their consent. The sacrifice troubles them less and less as years pass. They are eternal, omniscient.

Helen was a bridesmaid at her mother's wedding, and Catherine the maid of honour. Louisa's mother didn't attend, and her father wasn't invited, so Louisa gave herself to David, something she's been doing ever since. Two months later, David collected Catherine and Helen from the flat, promising them a grand party. Helen thought he was planning to adopt her and bring her to live with her mother in their new home.

David pulled up outside a beautiful house that Helen assumed was their new home. The door was opened by a thin, blonde man who introduced himself as Paul. Helen and Catherine were given sweet drinks that made it hard to focus. Colours shone brightly and the faces in the paintings moved.

They were carried to the cellar and placed on cubes of black stone that stank of blood. Their clothes were removed. A voice in Catherine's head begged her to fight or run, but she could do neither. Instead of the molestation she anticipated, she and Helen were dressed in long white gowns and gold slippers.

Between the black cubes, gulloi stones Paul called them, was a throne. Red carpet runners created a cruciform on which throne, cubes and torches rested, and around that a white circle had been drawn with salt, flour or chalk.

The men removed their shirts. Paul wore a pendant, a black stone, which hung from a leather cord around his throat. As he came closer, Catherine noticed an image carved into the talisman — the body of a woman with three heads, one young and female, another a dog and the third a goat. David and Paul knelt before the stones to self-flagellate, while Paul recited poetry. Catherine didn't understand most of the words, but she picked up a couple of phrases — 'crowned demon', 'shining veil', and the name Hecate.

The men cast the whips aside and spun the strange wheels hanging from the ceiling. The weird music they made reminded Catherine of wind roaring through a tunnel. David and Paul grabbed either end of a shimmering yellow veil, covered the throne with the iridescent material, and draped the ends over Catherine's and Helen's heads. The scene took on a golden shimmer as the men rotated the musical wheels, and Paul repeated the verse.

One torch ignited with a roar, although no one stood close enough to light it, and the veil lifted slightly. Catherine glanced to her right and watched as the veil on the throne rose to accommodate a sitting figure. Catherine's essence, her mind and soul, pushed through her scalp and into the veil. A tickle as she seeped through silk to join the woman in the throne.

'Why have you summoned me and tied me to these two humans?' Hecate's voice was rich and smoky.

The men kneeled when she spoke. David answered. 'Great Hecate, triple-form goddess, crowned demon, maiden, mother, crone. I bind you to these lives, to these women whom I love and have sacrificed only for your strength, comfort and nourishment, and to the home where they have lived so that I may call on your wisdom as all-knowing oracle. Accept my offering of blood and honour me with your friendship and guidance.'

Hecate attempted to rise, but the insubstantial organza veil weighed her down. She saw before her two power-hungry men. One would die at Lilith's hand within six years and the other, after a decade of wealth acquisition, would crown himself king only to be crushed by greed.

'Goddess, we require a sign of your agreement, then we will gladly release you from the veil,' Paul said, pretending supplication.

She smelled the blood of children on the gulloi stones and knew this blonde man had drained a young boy's veins three hours before. She sensed the sorrow of a dozen children beneath the flagstones; their angry spirits filled the room, impatient for vengeance. She knew the vacated flesh of the two mortal women whose spirits were inside her would be added to the dirt and covered in lye and water to hasten decomposition. Their souls and consciousness would accompany her when she left this funeral place.

She nodded, and the veil was removed. David brought her to the tiny flat, and her newly created body had remained there for almost ten years.

Edensun believed the rain would bring his mother closer, help her see that he would make all her wishes come true. Instead, Star ran into a fire. *Why? Why did she do it?*

Lilith heads home after they pull Star's corpse from the flames. Edensun stays in Malkuth. When the rain stops falling and the sky clears, Edensun heads to the cottage Star shared with his father, hoping to understand her better, learn where he went wrong so he can do things differently next time. As he stands outside her front door, he hears car engines approach and hides himself in the garden.

Two cars pull up outside his mother's cottage. Men's voices bounce off walls and windows into the backyard, reaching Edensun's ears intact. Edensun peers through the kitchen window, ducking as a face he recognises enters the room. It is Kevin, one of Garlow's crew. Briefly, Edensun wonders why they are here, before he realises, they are looking for him.

'No one's home, Mr Garlow.'

Edensun is certain they will check the garden next. He wants to be left in peace with his mother's belongings, but if they find him cowering like a mouse in the shadows it will put him at a severe disadvantage. He straightens his back, puffs up his chest, and after a final glance through the window, strides around the cottage.

Garlow does not seem surprised to see him. 'Mark!' he exclaims. 'How have you been, son? You found your mum! Glad to have helped. We need to talk. We'll bring you back later.'

'I have things to do first,' Edensun says. 'I can meet you at the social club in a couple of hours.'

Garlow shakes his head. His face is a vision of faux sympathy. 'I'm afraid I must insist. You owe me. Don't force me to summon you.'

Edensun gulps spit. *Summon?* Invisible cords wrap around his wrists. Garlow would need to know his real name.

Garlow's smile grows wider. 'Edensun, get in the car please.'

'It's a ghost town,' Garlow says, as the car rolls slowly away from the kerb. 'The whole country is in a state of panic. The government can't be reached for comment. You brought the rain, right?'

Edensun gazes out of the window. The streets are lined with corpses. Only a few shuffling scraps of humanity remain standing. A net curtain twitches as they pass a red brick house. Where there's life, there's hope. Not in this car, but in flats and houses, hiding and waiting for a sign that it is safe to emerge.

Edensun does not take his eyes from the car window. He scans the fronts of houses for other signs of life. 'How did you know where to find me?'

'I promised we'd find your mum. Tell me about the rain. What does it mean? What will happen next?'

'Do you ever think the world is messed up?'

'Every day,' Garlow answers. 'There's no room to be kind or gentle anymore.'

'My mum thought that too. She, we, thought the rain might

be a… a palette cleanser. A fresh start.'

'Did you know people would attack each other?'

Edensun shakes his head. 'We didn't know anything. We had naive optimism.'

'People are frightened. I see the curtains twitching too. They need guidance. A lighthouse to navigate the rocks. Me and the lads are heading up to the capital tomorrow. We'll roll our sleeves up and get stuck in. This country used to be something special, something worth fighting for. Will the madness continue, or will it stop now the storm is over?'

The car heads towards the sun. The longer the journey takes without reaching a destination, the more frustrated Edensun feels. When Satori summoned Lilith, she went to him. Now Garlow wields the same power over him — the God of Inbetween, but he has no intention of becoming Garlow's familiar.

The car stops outside a modern mansion.

Louisa Garlow stands alone in the master bedroom. The large room dominates the upper floor of the east wing. She peers out of their bay window, using the curtain to hide herself, and checks the driveway. An ornate pair of antique opera glasses inlaid with mother-of-pearl are within easy reach in case she wants a close-up view. Every twenty minutes or so, she breaks her vigil to judge beauty contests between her children before sending them away to experiment further. A little over an hour later, her patience is rewarded, and the convoy of vehicles crawls towards the front door.

David steps out of the back of the first car. He circles to the other side and waits while the driver opens the door for his guest. A scrawny looking lad with shoulder-length dark hair emerges. She magnifies his face with the glasses. He is not what Louisa expected. David seemed afraid of his guest when he called him unpredictable, but only the boy's strange eyes mark his difference, a subtle hint at danger. They resemble emeralds held in front of flames.

She withdraws into the shadows when the boy glances up and spots her. Caught for a moment in his cold stare, Louisa remembers the crazed eyes of their rain-drenched cat as he scratched the glass door with bloodied claws, trying to force his way into the sun lounge and tear them to pieces like the decapitated robin at his feet. Her stomach cramps, and her heart races as she flees along the hall to check on her daughters. They are safe in Bree's room, painting brightness on their cheeks and eyelids. She checks the nursery and finds David Jr sleeping peacefully. She hopes she is wrong, but she senses disaster. She hears the men and boy enter David's study then close the door, but she dares not go downstairs to listen.

Politics did not interest David until recently. Unless he saw a potential for profit, he refused to spend energy pursuing things, but something changed after his son was born. Maybe he was building an empire, a legacy for David Jr. One way or another his interests evolved and became less about making easy money and more about accumulating power.

The boy downstairs, the one with the bright green eyes, is part of her husband's plan to build a new empire on English soil. She cannot fit all the pieces together but sees enough of the final picture to predict it will be a violent and hellish tableau.

She misses the man she married. The romantic low-level gangster who made money to enjoy life, spending as much time as possible with Louisa and the kids.

The visit does not last long, perhaps only half an hour. The slamming of car doors alerts Louisa to the boy's departure, and she is near the curtain with the opera glasses held in front of her eyes when David joins her in their bedroom.

'What do you think?' he asks, making her jump.

Her cheeks flush as she tries to hide the glasses, even though she knows she has been caught. He is not upset; his smile reminds her of happier times.

'About the boy?' she asks.

'How does he seem to you?'

'He has strange eyes,' Louisa says. 'Is he going to help you?'

David nods. 'I'm not sure he wants to, but Cat assures me he will, and she hasn't been wrong yet. I'm leaving for London tomorrow. I don't know what sort of state the capital is in, but I'm going to help them rebuild. The old politicians are gone, and a strong leader must replace them.'

'I will always be by your side in everything you do, but perhaps the children and I should wait here until you know it's safe.'

He kisses her. 'You're a good wife. The best a man could wish for.' He wraps his arms around her waist and kisses her again. 'Are the children distracted?'

'I'm waiting for the next interruption. It won't be long.'

He brushes her hair from her face. 'To be continued,' he whispers. 'You don't need to hide upstairs anymore.'

CHAPTER EIGHTEEN

By morning, the rain has slowed to a gentle shower. The water is clear now, and Freya's tempted to go out but fears she will miss her parents' arrival if she does.

Deya cleans the kitchen before and after breakfast. Freya observes passively, no longer having the energy to care. Deya drags the hoover over carpets and washes windows inside and out. They do not enter Tanya's room. The door to that room remains closed. Deya does not trust Freya to remain calm inside those walls.

No one interrupts her work. The street seems eerily quiet; the neighbours are probably asleep or dead. Freya remembers the hundreds of corpses she encountered on the way home, but she also saw a few still living. Some survived.

Indecision traps Freya in the house just as she was trapped here as a teenager by her parents' obsessive over-protection, as securely as she was locked in the psych-hospital until the homicidal nurse set her free.

The familiar mantra, 'It isn't fair,' rises to her lips, but she tamps it down. Life is not fair. Fate is cruel and sly. She must endure this new trial like the others. She must wait for her baby, or some sign of where to search for her family. They are probably waiting to make sure the rain has stopped for good. They will be home soon. She is sure of that at least.

Freya is in Ivan's bed when she hears a key scrape in the front door. Bodies move softly into the hall as if afraid of what they might find. Her daughter whimpers. Freya hears the scrubbing of soles on the doormat. They are home.

She waits until they move into the kitchen and fill the kettle before she creeps downstairs. Avaline's car seat dangles from the crook of her father's arm while he watches Lorraine drop three teabags into their vintage pot. They have not spotted Freya yet, and she does not want to startle them in case Mike drops the baby, but she would like to join them for tea. They could sit around the kitchen table and discuss why they removed all memory of her from their home.

Not a good idea. Not yet, Deya warns.

Okay, just tea. The accusations can wait. She yearns to sniff her baby's head, get high from the pheromones, pretend that everything is good with the world, and that she is loved, both as mother and daughter. A childish fantasy of course. It is more likely that she will be greeted with screams than hugs. Moisture gathers in her eyes as she keeps to the shadows, summoning courage.

Perhaps her father senses a presence in the house, because the car seat is placed carefully on the kitchen table, and his shoes squeak softly as he creeps to the door. She imagines a weapon in his fist, a knife maybe or a rolling pin. She steps back, giving herself room to flee.

'Hi, Dad, Mum,' she says.

Metal clatters on the floor. A knife.

'Freya?' Her father's voice sounds too high. He rushes to her, giving her no chance to escape. His arms wrap around her, and his tears wash her hair. 'Thank Morrigan you're alive! Lorraine, Freya's here. She's safe.'

'Has she come to hurt us?' Lorraine asks.

Freya stifles a bitter laugh. 'No, Mum. I don't want to hurt anyone.'

Freya enters the kitchen, hurries to the table, and inhales Avaline's scent. The baby gazes up at her, gurgling with delight, Cupid's bow lips moving as if trying to say hello. Freya kisses the silky forehead. 'I've missed you so much. How big you've grown.'

'Don't take her away,' Lorraine whispers.

A second chance. Daughter displaced by Granddaughter. *Fuck you, Mum!*

Freya picks up her daughter and faces her mother. 'She's mine. I gave birth to her, but I'm willing to share.'

Lorraine's eyes are huge, and her hands shake as she holds them in front of her, silently begging for the baby to be passed. Freya shakes her head.

'Mummy needs cuddles first,' Freya says. 'Where were you? You were out all night.'

Mike answers. 'There's a lot we need to tell you, Freya. It's time you learn the truth.'

Freya sits at the table, clinging to Avaline. Her eyes communicate her refusal to give her child up for any reason. Lorraine brings cups of hot tea to the table.

'Watch out, you don't want to spill it on Avaline,' Lorraine says.

'I know, Mum.' Freya scowls. They are behaving as though she didn't take care of the baby herself for months. She pushes down her anger. It would not do to frighten them. Avaline is in her arms and that is all that matters. 'What do you need to tell me, Dad?'

'I'm a member of a group called the Morrigu. Remember Bill? You met him in York. He's one of us. Marian, Satori's mother, is too. We got a call yesterday, before the rain fell, telling us to hurry. We stayed with them last night, but we popped back this morning when the rain stopped to gather clothes and nappies and things.'

'The Morrigu?' Freya asks. 'Who are they?'

'We support each other. The Oracle tells us what to do, and we follow her orders.'

'Is it a cult?' Freya doesn't mean to say the word with quite the venom she feels, but Mike flinches.

'A religion,' he says. 'I know you didn't kill Rob, Freya.'

'You do? How?'

'The Oracle. Rob was killed to bring you here. Something about gathering people together — you, Star and Satori. The Oracle explained it to me. She says I shouldn't blame you for Ivan's death.'

'I want to meet her,' Freya says.

'She wants to meet you too. She told me you'd be here.'

'You didn't tell me,' Lorraine snaps.

'I didn't want to worry you,' Mike replies.

Lorraine picks up her cup and leaves the kitchen.

Freya suppresses a laugh. Same old Mum, unable to control her temper. The guilt Freya has been carrying falls from her shoulders. She did not kill Rob, and her brother's death was not her fault. It is news to her, but very welcome news that she will work on incorporating into her personal history.

'How long have you been part of this Morrigu? Why didn't you tell me about them before?'

'Now, you mustn't blame your mother...'

Freya trembles. 'You realise how different my life might have been if you'd let me in, right? I was alone. I was used.' Blaming exterior forces is an old habit, and Freya embraces the opportunity to pick at the unhealed scab of her parents' guilt.

Mike nods. 'I know. I'm sorry.' He reaches for her hand and squeezes.

Freya glances down at Avaline. The baby is wide awake and perfectly content. Freya sees a smile. Could it be Avaline's first? She beams back and strokes the baby's button nose, making Avaline blink.

'Tell me everything,' Freya says.

Mike sucks his lips, studies his daughter's face silently for a while, and eventually nods. 'I'll try to summarise, but the Oracle will be better at explaining it all. We'll go to her soon. There's only twelve of us in this city, but more around the country, especially in Wales. We follow the Celtic tradition. You and your brother aren't the only ones in this family who have a talent for ritual magic. You'll meet everyone soon. There's the Oracle and her granddaughter, Jessica, who pretty much run everything. There's

Marian, Bill, and me. You've met the others in passing, though you might not remember — Sophie, Grace, Clementine, Tara, Penelope, Nick and Aaron. Four men and eight women. We protect each other, avenge each other. I suspect I only coped with losing Tanya, Ivan, and you because of their support. The Oracle warned us the destroyer was coming. We tried to stop him, more than once, but each time we got close, someone protected that demon. Now the world is dying, and we failed to prevent it. The Oracle has asked Morrigan for guidance, and we will do what it takes to make things right. If you want to join us, your mother won't try to stop you, not this time.'

The streets are far worse now than when Freya escaped the hospital. Mike steers the car around broken bodies every hundred metres or so, and many of the homes they pass are burnt out. Smashed shop windows and flashing lights of car alarms demand their attention, their sirens long since silenced. At the edges of the streets, drains overflow with what might well be blood.

A few people wander through the carnage on foot, but not many. Freya counts fewer than twenty living souls. Those she spots seem to shuffle aimlessly. Although perhaps others wait behind closed doors until they can be certain it is over.

Avaline is strapped into her car seat at the back. Her tiny, dimpled chin brushes against her chest each time the car swerves, but she sleeps peacefully. Mike and Freya sit up front. Lorraine stayed at the house. Mike tried to get her to join them, and Lorraine tried to convince Freya to leave the baby at home, but both stubbornly refused. Like mother like daughter.

The car radio repeats a warning on a loop, pre-recorded in preparation for any disaster. It tells people to stay indoors and await further guidance. The voice is female and has a soft Scottish accent.

'What does it mean?' Freya asks.

'It means this isn't only local,' Mike replies.

'Worldwide?'

'I don't know. Perhaps just Britain. I haven't heard any news other than what the Oracle says, but if the government's gone, our electricity and water will follow, so we have to prepare in case this is a long-term emergency.'

'Can you switch it off?' Freya asks. 'That voice is making my head hurt.'

'We should keep it on in case there's news,' Mike says, but he reduces the volume until it hums softly in the background.

'Do you hate me?' Freya asks.

Mike hits the brake, and the car shudders to a stop. 'No, of course not.'

'Mum?'

'No.'

Freya hears insincerity in the single syllable and narrows her eyes.

'She has never hated you, baby.'

'Then why did you clear out my room? Ivan and Tanya still have bedrooms in your house.'

'We needed somewhere for Avaline.'

'Bullshit.'

'What do you want from me, Freya?'

'The truth, Dad.'

'We were angry, but we never hated you. Never!'

'You and Mum expected too much. I couldn't replace Tanya.'

'I know, love.'

'You shouldn't have locked me up like a princess in a tower.'

'I'm sorry.'

'I'm rotten. My heart rotted in that prison.'

'You aren't rotten, Freya.'

'Yes, I am, and you still refuse to listen. Daddy, hear me now, I'm your daughter and you threw me out of your home. Why?'

Mike does not reply.

'Daddy?'

'We should hurry,' he says at last, pressing the accelerator pedal, staring at the road ahead.

His ragged breath fills the car, as she presses her spine against the seat.

Forgive him, sister. Deya's plea echoes inside Freya's head.

I don't think I can.

Mike double parks. Traffic laws are a moot point with no one to enforce them. Freya has patronised this bar before — The Lucifernum. Raven took them here from time to time; the ambience amused them.

The bar is dark. Freya notices a wooden table jammed against a window, blocking out most of the daylight that might otherwise lift the funereal gloom of the crowded room. She acknowledges the flamboyant barman and gazes across faces of people she cannot name although some seem oddly familiar. She spots Marian and feels a sense of guilt for the woman's loss. Satori might have been a piece of shit, but his mother loved him. Freya still has a hard time not holding herself personally accountable for every death, a habit that began with her sister's.

A beautiful woman approaches, arms outstretched. Her long, black hair is tied in a high ponytail. Her lips are full and painted red, her cheekbones high and sharp.

'Freya,' she says. 'I'm Jessica. The Oracle is waiting to meet you.'

Freya looks to her father for guidance. He nods, assuring her that she is safe. She lets Jessica take her hand and lead her across the room to a woman with white hair and equally white cataracts. The old woman smiles as they approach. Jessica indicates a stool onto which Freya lowers herself. The dark-haired beauty skirts the table and sits beside the old woman.

Silence lingers until Freya itches with discomfort, but she refuses to say the first word. Afraid guilt will pour from her lips and make her claim culpability for all their woes. She wishes she were holding her daughter, but Avaline is with Mike and temporarily out of reach. She wants a drink and glances at the bar, but the barman does not notice, so she waits, fidgeting on the seat, twisting her hair, and biting her bottom lip.

The Oracle's smile is fixed, no longer welcoming, it morphs

into a hideous mask. Freya feels all the eyes in the room focus on the back of her head.

What do we do? she asks her sister.

Be patient, Deya says. *Find out what they want.*

She wants to be patient, but she has never learned how.

'Can somebody get me a drink?' she asks.

Jessica nods, either to Freya or someone else in the room, and a frosted glass of rum and coke is swiftly delivered to the table. Freya sips it slowly, allowing the alcohol to calm her while she studies the dogs at the old woman's feet; they appear to be sleeping, but their ears twitch constantly, alert to danger, ready to protect their mistress.

'Shall I come back later?' Freya asks Jessica.

The entire room holds its collective breath at her insolence, but Freya is bored. She waited a day for her parents to come home, months to get out of the hospital, years to be free, and now she is expected to wait for this old woman to speak to her. She grips the cold glass and moves to stand up, but a pale, skeletal hand with tissue paper skin grabs her wrist. The grip is strong like a vice and completely unanticipated from such a frail looking source.

'Please wait, Freya,' Jessica says. 'The Oracle is not ignoring you. She is communing with Morrigan, asking for guidance.'

Freya nods, and the old woman releases her wrist.

'Can I have another?' Freya asks, lifting her glass. She downs the drink. Someone will bring another to replace it. She might have only been here for a few minutes, but she is already getting a feel for the hierarchy.

At home, Mike is the head of their family, by title if little more, but here he and his friend Bill are servile, fetching and carrying for these women. Bill brings her another rum and cola.

'Freya,' the old woman croaks. The voice is husky yet quiet, sharp but blunt like rusty razorblades that drag across her senses. Despite herself Freya leans forward, directing her entire attention toward the Oracle.

For a moment, the old woman grows quiet again. Perhaps

she expects acknowledgement.

'Yes,' Freya says.

'What do you know about the rain?' the scratchy voice asks.

'It makes people crazy, desperate, violent,' Freya says.

'Do you know where it comes from?'

Freya shakes her head then reinforces the action verbally. 'No.'

'It is water from a lake at the edge of Binah.'

'Lilith's realm. I knew she was behind this.'

'Lilith's realm, yes, but she didn't bring it here,' the Oracle says.

'Who then?' Freya asks.

'The one they call Edensun. The Bringer of Chaos. Do you know him?'

'I don't,' Freya admits.

'He is the child of Lilith, Star and Marian's son, Steve.'

'Satori? How old is this Edensun?'

'Time is different on the planes of existence,' the Oracle says. 'He is almost a man. He came to find his mother. She called down the rain.'

'Fucking Star! I'm sorry, excuse me.'

'She isn't here anymore. She's gone,' the Oracle tells her.

'Back to Binah?'

'Morrigan doesn't know yet. She says you have great power, Freya.'

Freya nods. She could learn to like Morrigan.

'Morrigan believes that you could lead us in our battle against the Bringer of Chaos. He is powerful, but he is mortal. He can be defeated.'

'Won't Lilith protect him?' Freya asks.

'Morrigan says he plans to come alone to collect his mother's things. He killed Marian's son. Morrigan warns of worse to come if we don't stop him.'

'What does she want me to do?' Freya asks.

'She wants you to lead us.'

Freya glances at Jessica who seems agitated. The granddaughter has probably led this group for years, being usurped by a newcomer is unlikely to sit comfortably with her. Gleefully Freya accepts. 'I will happily lead, but does she know how we can defeat the demon?'

'I see a blade — it's wavy, and there are colourful crystals on the handle.'

'Satori's athame,' Freya whispers. 'I don't know where it is.'

'I have it,' Marian says.

'I will stab it through Edensun's ribs if he has them and penetrate his heart,' Freya promises.

The old woman gasps and moans. Her wrinkled head falls back.

'That's enough,' Jessica says. 'The Oracle needs to rest. Mike, can you help me take her upstairs?'

Hang on, Freya thinks. *I'm in charge*. Her eyes bore holes into the side of Jessica's face, but the dark-haired woman does not seem to notice. She is organising things around Freya, keeping a firm grip on the group for as long as she is able, and Freya cannot find a valid argument against any of Jessica's orders, so she withdraws from the table to bide her time rather than appear petulant. She has no intention of sharing leadership, and she will make that quite clear at the earliest opportunity.

Marian and Jessica sit side by side on the back seat of Mike's car. Mike and Bill are in the front. Marian wants to warn Jessica about the raw ambition she saw in Freya's duplicitous face but is afraid to say anything in front of Mike. Family can test people's loyalties, and it's impossible to know whose side Mike would be on in a battle for leadership.

The convoy reminds Marian of funerals. This time they are not mourning a lost life; they intend to destroy one. Her son's murderer deserves to die. She hates the Bringer of Chaos with a venom that poisons every cell in her body, but Steve's killer is her grandchild and her only living descendent. His death will cut short the immortality of her genes.

She squeezes Jessica's hand, and the younger woman returns the reassuring pressure.

Marian peers out of the rear window. The car containing Freya is directly behind them. Why isn't Mike travelling with his daughter? Is he here to monitor Jessica? Is he worried that the Oracle's granddaughter might plot against his sole surviving child? Perhaps he is right to worry. Anger and tension radiate from the woman beside her. Does Jessica feel her position is threatened by the emotionally unstable upstart?

'Jessica,' Marian says. 'Can you tell me again what the Oracle said? Why are we here? What should we expect when we reach the cottage?'

'Freya has been sent to kill Edensun. The Oracle says she is the only one powerful enough to succeed. The rest of us are here to support her. The demon wants to gather Star's things from the cottage. If he is there already, we will fight him. If he isn't, we will fill our cars with as much as we can carry and take it to The Lucifernum. In our temple we will have the upper hand, and we would prefer to battle Edensun there. Morrigan has promised to support us.'

'What will he do if we fail to stop him?' Marian asks.

'Something terrible.' Jessica shudders. 'We cannot fail.'

The cottage comes into view. Weeds choke the once vibrant flowers in the front garden, and the windows are streaked with grime. Twelve people exit the cars and crowd together at the gate. Marian senses a powerful presence and is certain that Edensun awaits them beyond the front door.

'He's here,' Freya says, approaching the gate. 'I can feel him.'

Steve's dagger glistens in Freya's fist. The crowd surges forward.

'I have a key.' Marian says, passing it to Bill.

The awkward bulk of bandages affects the mobility of his right hand, so he takes the key with his left. He opens the gate and strides toward the front of the house. His bravado cannot mask his fear, and he glances back at the group before slotting the key into the lock.

'Wait! We should check the outside first,' Jessica says.

Freya laughs. The violence of her amusement dismisses Jessica. It tells her to shut up and mind her own business.

'Open the door, Bill,' Freya says.

He controls his trembling fingers and turns the key. When the lock clicks, he pushes his elbow down on the rough wrought-iron handle and shoulders the door open.

Marian touches Jessica's shoulder. They stand back as the rest of the group swarm into the house.

'She can't be trusted,' Marian whispers.

'I know,' Jessica replies. 'But it is Morrigan's will.'

'If we succeed today, that power-hungry harlot will take over the Morrigu.'

Jessica nods.

'She poisons everything, betrays everyone. She's a murderer. You cannot let her take over.'

'What do you expect me to do?' Jessica asks.

'Something,' Marian says.

Bill approaches the two women. 'There's no one here,' he tells them.

Marian and Jessica share a meaningful look and enter the house.

Marian sprints toward the noise of something tearing at the end of the corridor. In the guest bedroom, Freya slashes Star's paintings with the magical dagger, her rage focused on destroying what her nemesis created.

'Aren't we supposed to take everything back?' Marian asks.

Freya bares her teeth. 'Morrigan didn't say those things need to be in one piece.'

Freya's jealousy pollutes the air. Marian leaves the girl to it and heads to the main bedroom where other group members are pulling out drawers, spilling the contents on the floor and bed. Satori's underwear and t-shirts are strewn across the carpet, trampled under uncaring feet. She runs away, brushing aside Jessica's hand as she flees. Outside, she veers right and skirts the house. At least the back garden is peaceful. She has space to think here. Birds squawk protests at her intrusion, but she ignores them, and eventually they leave her to her chaotic thoughts.

She senses someone standing behind her, spins around and sees Jessica.

The priestess's face is full of sympathy. 'I'm sorry, Marian. I should have realised how difficult this would be for you.'

Marian shakes her head. 'My son…' The rest of her words are swallowed as grief squeezes her throat and tears spill from her eyes.

Jessica wraps her arms around Marian's shaking shoulders. 'We'll wait here together.'

In the dappled sunlight, Jessica resembles her mother. Memories of Blodwyn, the friend Marian followed from Wales, dispel her pain for one blissful moment. Melodies of bird song and buzzing insects lighten her heart, and she forgets the destruction inside the house.

'I wish your mother was here,' Marian says.

'I do too. It's an impossible task to fill those shoes, but somehow people expect me to do it.'

It is the closest thing to a complaint Marian has heard leave those full lips, and she realises how difficult the transition from daughter to priestess must have been for the young woman. Blodwyn died too soon. Hers was not the only death the Oracle failed to prevent or predict although it was the first one to pierce Marian's heart. It happened six years after Blodwyn sent Steve away to save him from Morrigan.

Before the diagnosis, everyone believed Blodwyn was inheriting her mother's gift. Her predictions were vivid and precise and until proven erroneous they had driven the Morrigu in new and exciting directions. By the time Blodwyn knew she had a malignant brain tumour, it was too late to operate. Losing Blodwyn, shook every one of them, and some left the group in despair, replaced later by Aaron and Clementine — young blood, untainted by the false prophet.

Steve was only ten years old when he killed his father. Marian remembers that evening with all the clarity of yesterday. When Carl's face smashed the glass, a fragment was lodged in Steve's shoulder. He needed stitches, and later created wild tales as to the origin of this strange lightning-bolt-shaped scar.

Carl returned in their sleep each night to kill them. After weeks of nocturnal torment, Steve refused to go to bed; he couldn't function in school, and he stopped talking.

Marian had nowhere else to turn. The Morrigu took them in and helped Steve forget. For a while, Marian thought the boy might become part of the group.

The dreams stopped, and Carl's absence seemed complete.

Marian woke one night to find her son's face had turned blue. His hands clawed at the skin around his mouth, and he was wheezing; eyes wide open, drowning in a dream of death, a raven reflected in the black pools of his exaggerated pupils. She sat him up and held him to her bosom, hitting his back to dislodge whatever blocked his throat. He coughed up black feathers.

'She's suffocating me,' he choked. 'She wants me dead.'

Marian carried him to Blodwyn's room. Steve felt lighter in her arms than the feathers he spat up. Blodwyn stared at the distraught mother and child, the saliva-soaked feathers that clung to his t-shirt, and his gaping mouth desperate for air.

'He cannot stay,' Blodwyn said. 'Take him home.'

Back in the house, Marian expected the dreams to resume. Carl's rage was a presence she could taste as they climbed the stairs. They stayed in Steve's room that first night. He slept peacefully in his own bed and when he woke, he was her son once more. He seemed to have no recollection of the night he killed his father or of choking on Morrigan's plumage.

Marian thanked the goddess for saving her son's mind, but she never took him with her to the Morrigu again. He was too precious to lose. Too great a sacrifice to gift wrap for her faith.

Her heart was in two halves, one of which belonged to her son and the other to her goddess, never to be reunited. But Steve was safe, and the goddess was calm. Carl's death became an accident until it had not happened at all. The presents by proxy she sent her son from his absentee father, and the lies she told Steve about his father leaving them became her reality until she felt angrier at the man for abandoning them than for beating her senseless. Steve believed the same fiction, but part of him craved a father figure.

Paul's arrival on the scene seemed a blessing at first. He took them on day trips and spoiled the boy, never asking for any affection from Marian. Only later did she worry, did she wonder, whether Paul was grooming Steve. She never allowed Paul to be alone with her son and watched him like a hawk, so he had no opportunity to violate the young lad's body even if he wanted to, but the older man filled her son's head. He planted a seed that grew into a forest of magic. Steve did not need a goddess after Paul taught him that he was his own god.

The change was slow. So subtle only a mother as doting as Marian could see the alterations. Her son might have grown arrogant and strange even without Paul's influence. He was happy at least, and he forgot or buried any guilt he might have felt about his father.

Perhaps, if she had brought Steve back to the Morrigu, things would have been different, or maybe Morrigan would have killed him. Her son might have died in his sleep, suffocated by black feathers. Hindsight is not always twenty-twenty.

If Morrigan had succeeded in killing my son, would it have prevented the apocalypse?

Grief is Marian's constant companion, together with guilt, confusion, and torn loyalties. She would not exchange those years with him. Knowing this only increases her feelings of guilt.

She squeezes Jessica's hand, silently communicating love and devotion for both the priestess and her deceased mother.

Jessica's mobile phone chirps, and at first Marian thinks it is a particularly noisy blackbird, then the younger woman puts the phone to her ear and nods solemnly.

'It's Grandma,' Jessica says. 'She wants us to head back to The Lucifernum. You can wait by the cars while I round up everyone.'

Marian shakes her head. It is her turn to be strong.

The cottage is in chaos. Mirrors have been smashed and furniture shredded. Black bags stuffed with anonymous items are stacked at open doors. The two women step carefully to avoid ripping plastic as they pass.

There is no love left in this place. The cottage Steve selflessly provided for Star in a desire to protect her from the world is shattered. The hours he spent polishing wood and painting walls; the energy he spent cocooning her from all harm as he waited in vain for the reward of her love means nothing now. Photos have been pulled from all surfaces, some so roughly that the frames have smashed and glass shards glint in the carpet. Others presumably packed into the black bin liners that squat around the edges of the room.

Tables and chairs have been tipped on their sides for no reason that Marian can imagine, and curtains have been torn from the windows.

Marian pulls back. Only Jessica's presence prevents her from abandoning the group to its madness. Jessica seems just as troubled. She wrinkles her nose with distaste as she surveys the damage. Remaining strong requires a lot of effort.

The Morrigu gather in the living room. Shame and worry fog the air, but Freya has no time or energy for either. If Marian wanted to preserve her son's memory, she should have emptied the house when he died. It is not as if Marian was locked in a mental hospital.

'The Oracle called me,' Jessica says. 'We are to return to The Lucifernum. Grab what you can. We leave in five minutes.'

Freya stews in her own juices on the backseat. There are three others in the car, and there was not enough room in the boot for all the bags, so the woman beside her, Grace, has one on her lap, and another is jammed into the foot well in front of Freya.

They are the first car to pull away from the cottage. Aaron's Audi is new and sporty, and he drives recklessly, leaving the other cars to fade into the background behind them.

The driver and passengers are worried. They race towards their destination, fearful of their oracle. Freya is forgotten. Her role as de facto leader ignored as she reverts to the newbie, a hanger-on.

Grace, Aaron, and Clementine take it in turns to reassure each other. Their nervousness grates Freya's nerves. These so-called soldiers are afraid of their general. They close themselves off, build a wall to exclude Freya's influence, as if they blame her for their own actions in the cottage.

Aaron stares ahead as he drives, careless of the obstacles that litter the streets. His knuckles are pale as if the steering wheel is a lifeline he is gripping too tightly. Clementine sits beside him. Her auburn hair falls like a veil over the back of her seat. When Clementine is not staring blankly out of the window, she's checking the rear-view mirror and catching Freya's eye before looking quickly away.

Grace squeezes the bag on her lap like a teddy bear or comfort blanket, childlike in her fear, refusing to look at Freya, focusing instead on Clementine's curls. Pathetic.

The car jolts as it rolls over another corpse.

Freya notices Clementine is not forced to share her space with a black bag full of Star's shit. She tries to pull the rubbish bag out from beneath her, planning to push it into the back of Clementine's head, but plastic rips between her fingers, and Freya is left holding a fragment. She tries to throw that at Clementine's rotten-carrot-coloured head, but it falls short and flutters ineffectually to the footwell. Freya scowls.

Aaron does not stop at the junctions, although he slows the car to a crawl before they join the main road. Apart from the other Morrigu, Freya has seen no moving cars on the roads, but perhaps old habits die hard. As Aaron steps on the accelerator to pull away, something slams into the left side of the car. Clementine screams as the passenger door is wrenched open. A grey figure, dishevelled with a patchwork of scars on his cheeks, grabs her arm and tries to drag Clementine from the moving vehicle.

'Keep driving,' Clementine begs, playing tug-of-war with the sprinter.

Aaron accelerates and the junkie, if that's what he is, falls to his knees and is dragged along the concrete while Clementine slams the door repeatedly on his filthy forearm. Grace squeals and buries her head in the black plastic bag. Freya's adrenaline spikes, making her giggle. Her laughter is ignored by the others, too busy to be distracted by her hysteria.

Finally, the man gives up on his prey, and Freya watches through the rear window as he bounces twice then rolls away, stopping at the kerb. The door slams shut, and Clementine dissolves into sobs.

'Are you hurt?' Aaron asks, still hammering down the road.

She shakes her head, but her sobs grow louder.

Pathetic.

They are the first car to pull up outside the bar, but the others are close behind. The encounter with the vagrant must have given the rest time to catch up. By the time Clementine has stopped shaking enough to clamber out of the car, the other drivers and passengers are already cramming themselves into The Lucifernum.

Freya cannot see the barman or Avaline. Her vision is tunnelled on the pony-tailed priestess. If Jessica were a dog her tail would be hanging between her legs as she climbs the staircase anticipating chastisement from her grandmother. Freya waits until the others are distracted and creeps softly upstairs. The door to the bedroom is ajar, allowing Freya to discern two raised voices and the soft whimpers of dogs. By resting her head against the door frame, she glimpses Jessica's hair, shoulder, and arm through the narrow gaps between the hinges.

Jessica's voice is a plaintive whine. 'I'm sorry, Grandma. We brought Star's things here; those things we didn't destroy.'

The old woman's rasp is deeper, more powerful. 'What do you mean, destroy?'

Jessica avoids her grandmother's eyes and stares at the floor. 'Some of them got a bit carried away. Freya...'

Freya grimaces. *Bitch!* She considers interrupting to defend her actions but decides to wait and listen instead. *Better the devil you know.*

'What did they do?' the Oracle asks, her voice softer again and trembling.

'They shredded Star's paintings, trampled clothes on the floor, slashed sofa chairs, smashed mirrors and photo frames, more perhaps, while I was outside with Marian.'

'You should have guided them, Jessica.'

Jessica lifts her face and stares ahead. 'You put Freya in charge!'

The silence is heavy for a few moments before the old woman breaks it. 'Morrigan said...'

'Didn't Morrigan also say he was going to do something worse?'

'Yes.'

'But now she says something else? Let me get this straight. If she hadn't sent us to the cottage, he would have collected his mother's things and left. Our actions, following her instructions, are what causes his anger... his revenge, is that what you're telling me? How could Morrigan have been so wrong?' Jessica wails.

A thin speckled hand reaches out and pats Jessica's knee.

'I don't know, child,' the Oracle says.

'What should I tell them?'

'Who?'

An exasperated sigh. 'Everyone downstairs.' Jessica slouches forward, head in hands, like Rodin's Thinker.

'Tell them I'm still speaking to Morrigan. I'll let you know when I have an answer.'

Jessica stands up and nods. There is nowhere for Freya to hide before the other woman reaches the door, so she stands straight and proud and glares at Jessica when they come face to face.

'You were eavesdropping,' Jessica says.

'Who is it?' the Oracle inquires.

'Freya,' Jessica says.

'Let her come in.'

Jessica's face reddens, and she takes a deep breath, pushing past Freya and retreating downstairs. Freya steps into the Oracle's bedroom.

'What happened at the cottage?' the Oracle asks.

Freya inhales. 'He wasn't there when we arrived, so we did as you instructed and gathered Star's things.'

'Why did you tear the paintings?'

'They angered me. If you knew Star… what she did… to me, to Ivan, to Raven… you might understand.'

'Your brother loved her,' the Oracle says.

Freya stiffens. *How much does the crone know?* 'Yes, but that isn't all of it… You put me in charge. You said Morrigan...'

'I believe Morrigan might have overestimated you.' The white globes of the Oracle's eyes bore into Freya, as if judging her and finding her wanting.

Freya recoils in rage and indignation. 'How dare you?'

'So much hate, Freya. Your jealousy blinds you to what's important.'

'What is important, old woman?'

'Survival,' the Oracle replies.

Freya laughs. 'How many years have you got left?'

'More than you if this is how you continue to behave.'

Freya lunges but is repelled by a wall of energy that knocks her back onto the bed. The dogs leap up and pin her down, sitting on Freya's chest and legs, growling. The weight of the one on her ribcage makes breathing difficult, and the jaws of another are inches from her face. If the old woman commands it, the dog might tear out her throat.

Deya wrenches control and offers words that would stick in Freya's throat. 'I'm sorry. Can we discuss this calmly? Please ask your dogs to let me sit up.'

Without vocal commands, the dogs withdraw and return to the feet of their mistress, hackles up and vicious teeth bared, their eyes focused on Freya, following her subtle movements while growls rumble in their throats.

'I believe Morrigan was right to make me leader. I have more power than the others.'

'Power isn't everything. A leader needs wisdom.'

Freya clenches her fists. It is lucky Deya can speak for her because Freya is angry enough to storm out of the room. 'I have faced others like him.'

'And how did you deal with them?'

'I'm still breathing, aren't I?' Freya says.

The old woman smirks. 'Leave now. I need to speak to Morrigan. You can wait for me downstairs.'

Deya stops Freya from rushing at the woman again. Perhaps the dogs sense her inner turmoil because their growls grow louder and more insistent. The Oracle pets their heads, but they refuse to relax.

After leaving the room, Freya hits her forehead against a wall to clear her mind. *How can I face the others?*

Smile at them, Deya tells her. *We have a terrifying smile.*

Freya fixes her face and descends to the bar below.

Avaline wriggles in Mike's arms. Freya joins her father and takes the baby, sniffing the top of Avaline's head and feeling immediately calmer as the powerful pheromones fill her nostrils. They should bottle that smell and sell it as an antidote to almost anything.

Marian stands by the bar with Bill, but Jessica is nowhere to be seen.

'What did she tell you?' Mike asks. 'Is he coming?'

'She doesn't know,' Freya replies. 'Is she always in the dark like this?'

'Some answers take longer than others,' Mike says. 'It isn't your fault. We all got carried away. Don't blame yourself.'

'I don't,' Freya assures him.

'Good.'

Freya sniffs Avaline's head again, holding the scent in her nostrils before exhaling as much tension as she can.

Bill approaches their table, carrying a tray full of alcoholic drinks. The skin tightens around the edges of Freya's face as she offers him a smile.

A low rumble of murmuring heralds the return of Jessica and the Oracle. After escorting the old woman and the dogs to her chair, Jessica heads to the bar and speaks to Marian. The two women shoot glances towards Freya's table, then Marian follows Jessica to the centre of the room.

Jessica addresses the group with a strong melodic voice that radiates confidence. 'Morrigan warns us to expect our visitor soon. Take the items from the cottage and place them beside the altar in the cellar. When the items are arranged, send your families home. We will need to fight, but Morrigan has promised her protection.'

Freya wants to go home, but Deya convinces her to stay. Something important is about to happen, something Freya will not want to miss. *I will protect us*, Deya promises.

But what if they sacrifice us to save themselves?

Father will not let them.

Freya sits, staring at the baby in her lap. There is nowhere Avaline will be safe. Not at home with Freya's mum or here with a blind oracle and her group of hapless followers. Ava is the only thing in this goddess forsaken world that truly belongs to Freya, and she cannot lose her. No one should lose their daughter...

CHAPTER NINETEEN

THE FRONT door of the cottage is ajar when Edensun returns. He steps inside, pulling it shut behind him, and surveys the damage. The sofa is torn apart, its fillings pulled out and trodden into the carpet. Photo frames and mirrors have been smashed, and shards of glass glint between carpet fibres. Beneath the window frame, lies a dead bird staring upward as if in disbelief.

Kitchen drawers have been pulled out, and cutlery litters the vinyl. He picks up Star's knives and forks and pushes the drawers back on their runners. If Garlow had not taken him away, this would never have happened. What was the point in dragging Edensun across the city? Nothing was said that could not have been discussed here. Was it simply a show of power?

Edensun admits that there were aspects of Garlow's performance that seemed compelling, but there was darkness beneath the well-rehearsed speech about greatness, stability, and triumph, and Edensun's certain this is not what his mother wanted.

When he feels stronger, he continues his tour of the wreckage. His feet lead him to a small art studio where only a few scraps of his mother's paintings remain. The scent of urine makes his eyes water.

He heads to the bedroom where his mother's scent still lingers. Edensun falls onto Star's dishevelled bed and begs her to return. His rage wants to use him to enact vengeance, but even as the red shroud descends, he realises it is pointless.

I must be the most pathetic demon to have ever existed, he muses. *I am no man of action. Chaos is the antithesis of action. How can I choose a side or a course? Whenever I force myself to choose, it ends in disaster, like this bloody rain. My anger never lasts, too quickly replaced by empathy. If I could be more like Lilith or even Garlow… I would not be frozen by indecision.*

The rain made people violent, but many were violent before the storm. The skinheads, who broke the homeless man's skull, did not need water from the Lake of Sorrows to encourage them.

The sun has passed its apex and is sinking towards the horizon when Edensun emerges into the cottage garden, rubbing his eyes. He unbolts the green door and steps into parkland. He touches bark and feels the slow heartbeat of the tree. The fallen leaves are red and orange and crunch beneath his feet. Others, still clinging to branches, rustle and whisper above his head.

Edensun relaxes on the grass with his legs crossed, leaning back against a tree trunk, and supporting the weight of his upper body with his arms. The ground beneath him has dried and the sun gently warms his face.

His mother sat here to paint, and it takes minimal effort to see her crouched on the grass before him, her graceful hands making careful brushstrokes.

'The Morrigu took my things so you would go to them.' Her soft voice caresses his ear. 'They want to save the world from you.'

He gazes at the branches, watching fairies at work. His thoughts are focused on their labour, as his mother's had been before him. Even if Star is not actually talking to him, if her voice is only his imagination spanning the gulf between his open mind and her spirit, it feels as though he is sharing a magical moment with her.

'Satori?'

The voice is female and hesitant, exhausted. An exhaled breath that carries three tentative syllables to Edensun's ears — his father's name.

The woman has short black hair, cut in a neat bob, and wears skinny jeans speckled with grass seeds, a striped sweater and velvet jacket. An umbrella rests on her shoulder, and beads of sweat sparkle like zirconia above her arched eyebrows. Too weak to stand without support, she leans against the rough stone of the garden wall.

'Who are you?' she asks. 'You look like a friend of mine, but younger. I'm here for Sarah… Star. Do you know where she is?'

'Donna,' Edensun says, recognising her from his mother's description. 'I'm Edensun. I'm Star's…'

'Son,' Donna finishes.

Edensun nods. 'How are you?'

'Hungry.'

Edensun takes her to the kitchen. Donna retrieves a can of baked beans from a cupboard; after a bowlful and three glasses of water, colour blooms in her cheeks.

'I think I saw Sarah on TV,' Donna says.

'I'm sorry. She's…' He cannot say dead; the word is too sharp to squeeze through his oesophagus. He wonders what people say instead.

'Gone?' Donna asks. 'Back to Binah?'

Edensun shakes his head. 'She walked into a fire.'

'Typical Sarah, always killing herself. It's a bloody annoying habit. Where's Satori? He brought her back last time.'

'He tried to kill me. I had no choice.'

'Fuck!' She rubs her eyes. Dark circles bulge below the sockets like bruises.

'Why don't you get your head down for an hour?'

She shakes her head and strides toward the park, trembling.

'We could visit the witch in the tower block. She might be able to help.'

'Okay,' Donna says, glaring at him.

He grabs her hand, makes a rift in the air, and drags Donna through Chaos. They emerge in the stairwell of a decaying tower block. Donna's breathing is ragged. Edensun supports her weight as she bends forward and vomits over the grimy vinyl tiles.

'Are you okay?'

She shakes her head. 'What the fuck was that?'

'I'm sorry,' he says. 'I didn't mean to scare you.'

She coughs up bile, wheezing. Her face a portrait of pain

and horror. When she is able to drag oxygen into her lungs, the sheen of sickness abates, and her colour returns to its normal porcelain shade. She backs away from the steaming pile and disentangles herself from Edensun's protective grip. Shoulders pressed against a wall, she sinks slowly to the floor and sits there, staring up at him. Her eyes are glazed, and tears look like glitter around the edges.

When he steps toward her, she recoils, as if she would rather push herself through the disintegrating plaster than let Edensun get any closer.

'I thought you travelled The Planes with my father,' Edensun says, confused.

'It was nothing like that.' Donna's chest rises and falls rapidly as she hyperventilates. 'It felt like madness. Nothing was solid. Nothing for my mind to grasp hold of. Was it air or water? What the hell was it?'

'Chaos. It's how I move from place to place.'

Donna is in Chaos for less than a second, but what her mind manages to grasp during that moment remains with her when she steps into the litter strewn stairwell. She cowers before Edensun, unable to breathe. The cloying darkness clogs her throat and her stomach cramps. Her mouth opens, and she purges her stomach with jolting violence.

The darkness of Chaos creeps within her veins. The moving blackness that invaded her body during the micro-second she spent in that other place remains in her core. Throwing up did not help; it still feels like insects crawling beneath her skin.

She wipes her lips self-consciously then studies the fingers of the hand that was recently held by Star's overgrown son. If his accelerated age is not disturbing enough, what he became during that split-second journey between the cottage and this run-down building could drive Donna to madness. He is not human.

In her letters Star described her son as a dragon, but that

descriptor did not prepare Donna for what she saw. She attempts to reconcile the handsome youth before her with what she glimpsed. It is not a quick process, and she is still labouring at the task while she answers his questions, accepts his proffered hand, and allows him to pull her to her feet.

The woman who answers the door is not what Donna expects, and she almost laughs with relief at the mundane, working-class solidity of the short-haired blonde in dressing gown and slippers, a newly lit cigarette hanging from the corner of her chapped lips.

The grubby flocked wallpaper and brown velour furniture seems oddly familiar, like the house of infrequently visited grandparents. The woman invites Donna in, and with an understated twist of her nicotine-stained hand, offers her a seat.

'Wait here,' the woman says before Edensun can follow.

Donna stares at the boy and sees a monster.

'What? No!' Edensun yells. 'I must talk to you. I have questions that need answers. Where's Mum and where are her things?'

'You will have answers, but can't you see she needs my guidance first?'

Edensun bristles and glares at Donna. 'That isn't fair,' he growls. 'She wouldn't be here if I hadn't brought her.'

'Wait your turn,' the woman says, blocking his entry with her body.

Donna fears for her. She has seen the real Edensun, and this tiny woman will not be able to stop him doing what he wants. 'It's okay,' Donna calls. 'I can wait.'

'See!' Edensun exclaims.

The woman does not move aside.

'Don't push me away.' A dazzling spectrum of emotions gather on Edensun's face — anger, fear, hope, despair, and others Donna cannot name.

'Don't,' he says again. 'My mother died. I need to understand why.'

'I will help you, but *you* need to be patient and wait here.'

'What am I supposed to do? Just sit here? I'll go mad.'

'Take a walk and come back in an hour,' the woman says,

shutting the door in his face.

Donna trembles as she imagines Edensun pacing the narrow corridor, deciding whether to smash the door or do as he is told. He is a child, despite his terrible ancestry, a baby, and she does not want to witness the ferocity of his temper tantrum.

'Sit down, Donna,' the woman says. 'We have much to discuss. My name is Cat.'

Cat glides across the room and settles onto a threadbare armchair, motioning for Donna to make herself comfortable on the sofa opposite, seemingly unaware that it is covered in dishes holding remnants of a strange dark broth. Donna transfers the obstacles to a coffee table that lurches under the additional weight. She holds it steady with one hand and jams a folded magazine beneath the broken leg with the other. That seems to work, and she sits on the sofa with both hands in her lap.

'You are troubled,' Cat says. 'May I ask why?'

'Can I have a cigarette?' Donna asks.

Cat lights one and passes it across.

'Thanks, it's all too much — the rain, my mum, him.' Donna nods towards the door.

'He will want to talk about the rain. First, tell me about your mum.'

'I need to know she's okay, that she didn't get caught in the rain or attacked by madmen.'

Cat closes her eyes. 'I see a room with green walls — a medical facility. She's helping someone with a head injury.'

Tears swell in Donna's eyes and spill over her cheeks. The sense of relief is profound. It warms her chest and spreads to her wet cheeks. 'Thank God. Can you see my friend, Star?'

Cat purses her lips, and her eyelids wrinkle, forming lines between her eyes that spread upwards across her brow. She is silent for almost a minute before she exhales loudly, then she opens her eyes and shakes her head. 'I'm sorry. I can't find her.'

'Does that mean she's dead?'

Cat tilts her head. 'Would you like some tea?'

'No thank you,' Donna says.

'I'll brew a pot, then I'll explain what I can and cannot do. Help yourself to another cigarette.'

When Cat leaves the room, Donna takes a moment to examine her surroundings. The apartment is a dump. It seems likely the woman has not cleaned a single surface in decades; the carpet is covered in litter, clothing, loosely scrunched balls of paper and cigarette butts stained with dark lipstick. Filthy net curtains hang around dusty windows, caught in a breeze that does nothing to freshen the room. Their hems dance above the lit candles that cover a half-moon table. How can the woman live like this? Donna feels a prickle of shame, judging a stranger for her housekeeping, but it is appalling. An army of rats might make it their home and never be seen for the piles of rubbish. She grabs another cigarette.

Cat appears with a chipped mug of tea. 'I see the future, the past and the present,' Cat says, settling back onto the armchair. 'I can see your friend dancing in a bonfire on Parliament Square, but nothing after. If she still exists, she's beyond my vision.'

'In one of the other worlds?'

'It's possible.'

'Is Edensun dangerous?'

'He's an anomaly, created by god and mortals, neither one nor the other. A creature of chaos, fluid and changeable.'

'Will he hurt me?' Donna asks.

'He will do all he can to protect you. You're all he has left of his mother.'

'Should I stay with him?'

'Yes.'

The woman's face shifts, and Donna sees other beings inside her — one ancient and the other young.

'Cat?' she asks.

'I'm still me,' the hag answers.

The face shifts again and is young and fresh, pink cheeked and beautiful.

Donna tries to fix the woman's appearance in her mind but fails. It is as though three people are merged into one body, taking it in turns to appear. The waxing and waning faces are like the moon.

'The world is in flux. The old is trying to re-establish its hold on the minds and hearts of men. Eventually, it will fail, but change is often violent, and we can expect years of turmoil before a decisive victory, unless Edensun does as I ask.'

'Who are you?' Donna asks. 'A goddess?'

'If an archetype is a goddess, then so am I. I live in the mountains of Yesod. This apartment is only my place of business, my office on Earth. Perhaps you know me better as Hecate.'

A hesitant knock informs Donna that her one-to-one is at an end. It is hard to believe an hour has passed.

'Come in,' Cat says.

When Edensun steps into the room, his earlier arrogance and bravado are absent. Cat beckons for him to sit beside Donna on the sofa. Her face has settled, and she looks like a blonde woman in her thirties whose appearance and manner complement the disarrayed council flat perfectly.

'You have questions,' Cat says.

'Why did someone wreck my mother's house?' Edensun asks.

'To summon you.'

'Who are they?'

'They worship the goddess Morrigan and believe it is their duty to stop you before you destroy the world.'

Donna laughs. 'Aren't they a little late?'

'They tried before.' Edensun's response is dark and humourless.

Cat nods. 'You will find the Morrigu in a cellar under The Lucifernum.'

'If they have my mother's things, I want them back,' Edensun whines. 'My mother killed herself, and these Morrigu bastards have stolen or destroyed everything that belonged to her. I could have stopped them if Garlow hadn't summoned me and wasted an hour of my time. How did he know where to find me?'

'How does a spider know a fly has fallen into its web?'

'What does he want?'

'That's not important. Whatever is done can be undone. What do you want?'

'A second chance with my mother.'

'I believe you've had a second chance already. Wouldn't this be the third? Third time's the charm. Three is a potent number. Youth, adulthood, and old age; birth, life and death.'

'Will I get a third chance?'

'Be patient. You will find her, but your mother won't recognise you. You might think that's enough at first, just being in her presence, but you'll become frustrated — it's in your nature. The new things she's learning overwrite the old, but you'll recognise this too late even though I've told you. The key to it all can be found in your mother's paintings.'

'Can't you give me a straight answer?'

'Some things cannot be told only experienced. When you are in the middle of it, all will be clear. You'll find her and undo all the harm you, Star, Lilith, Satori, Paul and Garlow have caused or will cause. Your friends, your mother and father, they will all live again.'

'I watched my mum burn...'

'Have faith, Edensun. Good luck, both of you,' Cat says and opens her door, dismissing them.

Donna and Edensun emerge onto the hallway. Donna's head spins with everything she has heard.

'I know where The Lucifernum is. My friends and I used to drink there,' Donna says.

'We can travel there through Chaos,' Edensun replies. 'Just close your eyes.'

'I can't. We'll have to walk.'

'You're being stupid and stubborn,' Edensun says.

'I'm protecting myself.'

'No, you're not. Walking around out there, is the opposite of protecting yourself. We'll be vulnerable.'

'You're a god, right?' She glares at him before descending the stairs. Her knuckles whiten around the handrail, irrationally afraid he might shove her, out of spite. *Just follow me*, she begs, silently.

Outside, the air smells like cut grass after rain. Through a narrow gap between two blocks of flats, she glimpses a radio tower at the summit of a hill. If she is right about their location, it should be a short walk to the motorway. They pass redbrick houses with small front gardens. Abandoned cars herringbone the silent side streets, which stretch endlessly out at regular intervals. Donna and Edensun hurry past these junctions; she keeps to the pavements, more from habit than necessity.

The road flattens to cross a river, and to her right, Donna spots a retail park where she once shopped for household goods with her flatmates. They lost all sense of direction in the maze between displays, and Raven lost her temper and shouted at strangers, while Donna and Star laughed so hard, they had to lean on each other for support.

The roundabout sweeps left and right, and concrete supports grope upwards to cradle the motorway. Its bulging underbelly hides carnage from the innocent sky — hillocks of crumpled metal, the battered remains of dozens of collisions. Abandoned cars wait nose-to-tail in a frozen stream on the slip road. Donna and Edensun edge between them and the chest-high barrier, while a distant horn vents its frustration in a mournful note that will eventually expire.

When they reach the main carriageway, Donna and Edensun gaze down on rooftops. They dodge open doors and clamber over the hoods of cars that have skidded to a final halt against the barrier. Plastic bumpers are cracked in unique patterns, and shards of smashed headlamps crunch underfoot. None of the engines are ticking over, but petrol fumes hang heavy in the air, making Donna cough. The white dome of a temple or mosque rises above the barrier on their left, beyond four lanes of un-moving traffic.

Ugly industrial buildings make way for similarly unattractive red brick terraced houses, and graffiti covers their walls and boarded windows. They pass trees, blackened by pollution but still thriving, and Donna suspects that within a few years nature will reclaim all this concrete, and the roots of these trees will crack through the asphalt, reversing mankind's scarring of the world. *Will I survive to see it?*

Edensun grabs her arm a second before she hears laughter. The harsh sound communicates malevolent glee, reminding her of hyenas.

'Where are they?' she whispers.

Edensun points to what looks like a leisure centre. She spots four silhouettes, moving in circles around a central point, like hedonists who whirled around bonfires in the alcohol-fuelled parties she attended at midsummer.

One comes to an abrupt halt, making the others stumble. 'Hey!'

'Shit,' Edensun mutters, echoing her thoughts. 'Run.'

'I'm safer with you.' Her legs tremble, too weak to run far.

'Hey kids,' a man shouts. 'Want to see something cool?'

Edensun is not far ahead, but he feels further away than the stars, and he's striding towards the group of men.

'What are you doing?' Donna tries to keep up.

'Calling their bluff.'

Laughter resumes, louder now they have an audience. Are they laughing at a young boy's courage or his naivete?

Edensun stops a few metres short of the men who stare at Donna as they might a piece of meat. They stand side-by-side like a football line up, partially concealing a bundle of flesh on the ground. Donna sprints around them and sees the body of a young girl. Her hair is dark red, although it might be another colour beneath the matted blood, and bruises decorate her throat, a filigree of violence. Her glassy eyes stare accusingly, and there are deep bite marks on her wasp sting breasts and across her open thighs. However hard Donna tries, she can see no flicker around the nostrils or lips to indicate life.

'She's dead!' Impotent rage overwhelms Donna, and she screams.

The predators respond, grinning, perhaps planning a similar fate for her. The violence is aeons old, rooted in misogyny, and repeated often — Tanya, Donna, this poor, young woman.

'You're fucking animals,' Edensun says.

Donna is ignored for the moment, and she watches, shaking while adrenaline courses through her body. She wants to join the fray, snap some necks. Self-preservation urges her to run instead, but leaving Edensun would be suicide, so she stays, hating everyone including herself.

One man pulls out a knife, the others raise their fists. Edensun's face is scarlet, and his hands are clenched. The men deserve whatever punishment he delivers. She glimpses yellow between Edensun's fingers before he releases fireballs which hurtle through the silent air, spreading as they hit their targets. The men's screams sound more animal than human. It smells like a barbecue. A bearded, burly looking bastard rushes at Edensun, burnishing his knife. He stops suddenly as flames engulf him too. The last one flees for his worthless life, then Edensun approaches Donna and the dead girl, extinguishing the balls of fire in his palms.

'Should I chase the other one?' Edensun asks.

'We should get to the bar. It's not much further. Help me cover her.'

They find a roll of lino nearby and drape it across the girl. Donna offers a few prayers while Edensun's gaze prickles the back of her neck. When they have done what they can to honour this victim, while acknowledging the loss of countless millions, they continue in silence until Edensun stops short again. Donna anxiously surveys their surroundings.

'Why did they do that?' he asks.

'Because they're men. It's what men do.'

His forehead creases toward the bridge of his nose. 'Did my father… Satori?'

'No, not all men, but too many.' She feels unnaturally calm. *Will it hit me later?*

Silence blankets them. Donna keeps her own counsel, and Edensun wears a confused frown that looks natural on his teenage face. They pass a car rental warehouse with ramps that spiral between caged floors, reminding Donna of giant oil drums.

Department stores loom ahead, providing landmarks that reassure her they have almost reached their destination.

The Bear Pit is a strange name for a roundabout, and thankfully, they do not have to walk under it to reach the bar. It was a scary place before the rain, the haunt of homeless men and women, psychotic after years of abusing alcohol to make their existence bearable. Her pity never made her less frightened, but they pale into insignificance compared to the violent men who Edensun burned, and she realises her fear had been misplaced; those lost souls of the Bear Pit were victims, not aggressors, and in many ways an apt replacement for the cruel bearbaiting that probably gave the roundabout its name.

A short, narrow lane, paved with flagstones, is bordered by a park and ancient buildings. It leads to stone steps, and when they alight, the rum bar greets them.

The double doors at the entrance are not locked — *they're expecting him,* and Donna and Edensun enter a quiet room with subdued lighting. The bar is deserted, but melodic chants waft through the hall at the back of the room, mingling with stagnant air.

Donna steps toward an open door that leads to the cellar. 'Do we go downstairs?'

'I might not be able to protect you. If you want to wait for me here, it's okay.'

'After all we have seen, do you think I'm afraid? How many are down there?' Donna asks.

'A dozen, maybe, but I can feel something else — something divine. Morrigan is spoiling for war. And I can feel my father's dagger. I think they plan to kill me with it.'

'What shall we do?'

'Go down there and say hello.'

Donna strides towards the hallway.

'Maybe I should go first,' Edensun says.

'If you wish.'

The light from the doorway flickers. Candlelight, Donna presumes. Edensun stands motionless. Donna feels impatient;

she wants this finished, but she does not say anything to hurry him along.

Gulping down air as if a vacuum awaits them, Edensun descends. Donna follows.

Candlelight fills the basement, and the scent of melting wax is oppressive. Black bin bags, full to bursting, surround the altar, and a group in hooded robes gather near the edge of the room. Donna grips Edensun's hand.

She spots Freya, the only one in the group not wearing a hood. Her blonde hair is tangled with ribbons, red, purple, and green. Beating wings make Donna glance up; a raven flies over the worshippers and lands on the shoulder of a red-robed figure. A red ribbon dangles from its beak, probably from Freya's hair.

'I'm here. What do you want?' Edensun says.

Freya steps forward. Candlelight makes rainbows with the jewelled dagger in her fist. 'You murdered Rob,' Freya says.

Donna squeezes Edensun's hand then edges towards Freya, displaying her empty palms. 'It's good to see you again.'

A bulky figure in black, steps out of the group behind Freya and places a large hand on her shoulder then whispers something in her ear. Freya shakes her head, raises the dagger, and holds it flat against her chest. The wavy blade points to the floor, and her fingers grip the jewelled hilt.

Donna takes another step towards her old friend.

'This is between me and him, Donna,' Freya says.

Donna shakes her head. 'You know that isn't true. Let me help you.'

'I don't need help,' Freya spits out the last word as if it is toxic.

The hand moves from Freya's shoulder and snatches the dagger from her fist.

'Give that back!'

'It's Donna,' a masculine voice says.

Donna nods. 'Hello, Mr Chaple. How are you?'

'You look well, Donna. I thought...'

'I got better,' Donna says. 'Thanks for the flowers.'

Donna steps within arm's reach of Freya while the woman is distracted. Without missing a beat, she wraps her arms around Freya and hugs her. Freya wrestles free and reaches for the athame, but Mike holds it above his head.

The raven croaks. Edensun and the figures in red stand facing each other. It is odd, even in a week of strange things, but Edensun seems to be talking to the bird, and it moves its head, as if answering.

CHAPTER TWENTY

FREYA PUSHES Donna to the floor.

'Freya, no!' her father shouts, rushing to her side.

As Mike kneels beside her, pulling Freya's arms from Donna's head, she spots the dagger tucked inside a pocket, moves in close and pulls the blade free, hiding it inside her own robe. With his focus on Donna, he does not seem to notice.

A second figure kneels beside them, cloak folding behind it like wings, and cradles the stunned body, pulling Donna up until she is seated, unfocused, but not broken.

'She's okay,' Marian says.

Freya shifts her attention to Edensun, Jessica and the Oracle. Something interesting is happening; a raven is perched on Jessica's shoulder, and Edensun dry heaves at the feet of the women.

Mike loosens his hold, and Freya shrugs free to creep behind the worshippers and follow the shadowy walls. The dagger feels wonderfully heavy in her hand; hopefully, her father is too distracted to notice its absence.

Freya avoids tripping over the bin bags which rest in the shadow of the altar. No one faces her, but her skin prickles across her shoulders, warning her she is being observed. The sharp edges of jewels dig into Freya's palm. Once upon a time, she held this dagger in a desert and dreamed of killing Satori. Now, she has a second chance with his son. If she stops to consider her own blood lust, it might lead her to terrifying places, so she ignores it. Killing is part of who she is now; without Dave's death, she would not share this flesh with Deya. Lilith taught her that killing can be holy; one of the few truths the goddess shared with her acolyte. No one here would argue. They destroyed the boys who murdered her sister — none of their consciences is unblemished.

Pulling the hood over her head, she creeps onwards, the hem of her cloak whispering behind her. Donna is with Marian, and Edensun is on his knees, eyes locked with the raven on Jessica's shoulder — a demon humbled before a carrion bird.

'Freya!' Mike shouts.

The shadows hide her, but his shout alerts the others. Edensun takes a deep breath and rises. The raven squawks then takes wing, circling the room as Freya creeps along the outer edges. The bird's amber eye fixes on Freya's face, but before it can swoop, she leaps onto Edensun's shoulders and holds the tip of the dagger to his throat.

'Stay back!' Freya shouts.

Ice brushes across the base of Freya's skull and crawls down her right arm to the knife-wielding hand. A whisper in her ear orders her to, 'Kill him for Ivan, for Rob, for Satori.'

Mist rises from the stone floor; it shrouds Freya and her intended victim. Raven urges Freya to kill Edensun, and maybe she can rely on the ghost of her friend to delay the worshippers long enough so Freya can escape after the deed is done.

Raven is not alone. Children cling to her long skirt, wailing and hissing, tiny fists scratching and punching the chilled air that seeps from them. The Morrigu shrink away. Cowards in the face of this phantom. Mike shakes his head, reaching out impotently as Donna strides toward Edensun.

'Don't you dare hurt her!' Donna shouts.

Her? Freya's confusion does not stop her pressing the blade deeper into Edensun's flesh.

'Yesss,' Raven hisses.

Freya pushes the tooth of the blade into the boy's throat and revels in his hiss of pain. The dead children swarm towards them, their fingers like ice when they cover her hand. They are trying to squeeze his throat, but their incorporeal bodies do not have the strength. It is up to Freya to finish this.

Candles surge, brightening the room for a moment before they extinguish and darkness envelopes them all. Freya holds on tight while the demon's scent fills her nostrils, making her dizzy. She rises until her crown brushes the ceiling; the skin beneath her blade is scaly, and her arm cannot reach around him. In the dark, Edensun is growing.

When the light returns, the creature below her no longer looks human. Leathery wings stretch from its shoulders, and its skin is covered with armoured scales which she has no chance of piercing with her blade. Donna sways unsteadily as though she might faint, and the Morrigu have abandoned their Oracle and Jessica, huddling as far from the demon as they can.

The Oracle and Jessica unfreeze and pull down their hoods, then the pair merge into one figure surrounded by black feathers. A dark-haired beauty emerges from where the two women had once stood side-by-side. Adorned with feathers, she faces the dragon-like form of Edensun, and Freya feels his body stiffen beneath her. *Is he afraid?*

'Kill him!' Morrigan screams.

Freya renews her efforts, but the scales are too densely packed for the dagger to penetrate his throat. She slides from his back and lands awkwardly behind him, noticing his strange single rear leg, tipped with a vicious hooked claw. She has never seen anything like it even in her frequently surreal nightmares. *How can he balance?*

Donna rushes towards her. Her friend's head barely reaches the demon's hips while his body fills the room, bending forwards because the ceiling height cannot accommodate him.

Donna's voice penetrates the silence. 'Let her go, Edensun!'

'I don't need you to protect me,' Freya hisses.

Yes, you do, Deya warns.

Edensun stomps toward the cowering worshippers, claws scarring the rough flagstones. He turns around and glares at Freya. When Donna grabs her hand, she does not pull free. His footsteps make the cellar shake as he marches towards Freya and Donna. She releases Donna's hand as Edensun hooks her hood with one of his foreclaws and tries to lift her. The robe slides off her body, so he lifts her by her hair. She pushes back her fear and scowls at the monster, while he cocks his head, perhaps wondering whether she is a threat. She must look like a mouse dangling on a cat's claw.

Freya raises her arms and tries to untangle herself, but the pressure on her scalp brings tears to her eyes. Donna moves in and kicks one of his limbs. Freya sees him wince, though she suspects it is not from any physical pain. Either way, he lowers his claw until her feet touch the floor.

Trying to save face, she uses the same irreverent humour that worked so well with Samael. 'This new look suits you better.'

He grunts. *Can he speak in this form?*

'Why did you kill my husband?'

Raven appears by Freya's side. 'Why did you kill my lover?' the ghost asks.

The ghosts charge, covering every inch of Edensun's gigantic bulk. Raven clings to his nose, scratching his eyes with her nails. 'You vicious bastard. Satori was mine. Mine!'

Edensun shakes himself like a wet dog, shedding spectres rather than water. The children vanish as they hit the stone floor, but Raven springs back to her feet and lunges again.

'Nooo!' Donna cries. 'Stop this. Edensun, stand down. Raven, please! Freya, I won't let him hurt you. Give me the knife!'

Edensun shakes his head. Freya grips the knife tightly, unwilling to lose her only weapon against this monster. Morrigan claimed she could kill the demon with Satori's athame, although she has lost faith in the goddess's words. The room is in chaos. The worshippers too afraid to fight, and yet Morrigan is merely standing there with a cruel smirk curling her lips. *Fucking duplicitous goddesses!*

'This isn't what your mother would have wanted,' Donna tells him.

Freya remembers Star differently. She destroyed Raven for less.

'Everyone, get out of here,' Donna says, when her appeals

to Edensun seem to fall on deaf ears, but the worshippers ignore her too and squeeze closer together, looking frantically from the feathered woman to Edensun. Freya suspects their minds have been broken.

Freya's hair remains entangled around his claw, and Raven stands at her side. The feathers around Morrigan's shoulders bristle, and she widens her stance, lifting her arms above her head. Donna glares at Edensun. Two women, the ghost of a woman, and a goddess challenge the demon, while the others cower in fear.

'Do you want to die?' Edensun asks Freya. *So, he can talk!*

She shakes her head, twisting ribbons tighter around his claw.

'Then, why are you here?'

'To punish you and Lilith. You took everything from me. Lilith made me think I was special, but she never cared.' Freya feels herself pout. This is not how she wanted to sound, but at least it is honest.

'Lilith and Star,' Raven adds.

'Gods don't care,' he answers. 'Look at Morrigan. The Morrigu thought their goddess would protect them, but she's leading them to a war they cannot win.'

Morrigan spits at Edensun. Some of it lands on Freya's cheek, burning like acid. She rubs it away, but the pain lingers.

'Star isn't a god,' Raven hisses.

'If I let you go, Freya, what will you do?' Edensun asks.

Freya trembles, glancing at Edensun then Raven. *Should I surrender? At least I will live to fight again.* Donna's soft eyes beg Freya to accept mercy.

'What would you have me do?' Freya asks at last. 'I'll belong to you, right, if you spare me, is that the rule?'

'If I let you go, you must take Satori's mother and your father and leave this place. Dedicate your life to being a good mother to Avaline and a good daughter to your parents.'

'You're asking Freya to be selfless?' Raven mocks. 'You might as well kill her now.'

'Fuck off!' Freya shouts at Raven.

The ghost recoils and stares at Freya with undisguised hatred before floating through a stone wall and out of sight. Freya looks at Morrigan; the goddess shakes her head but does nothing to release Freya from Edensun's grip. *Fuck you then!* She looks at her father. His face shines with tears, but he does not peel his trembling back away from the wall.

What choice do we have? Deya asks.

'I can agree to your terms as long as you apologise.'

'Apologise?'

'For killing Rob.'

'I didn't kill him, but I'm sorry he died,' he says.

'If you didn't, who… Lilith killed him for you. Why? To bring me here? To kill Ivan?' Freya squeezes her skull between her hands. Hissing through clenched teeth, she rocks herself back and forth, trying to make sense of the senseless. 'Can you bring him back?'

Edensun shakes his head. 'The threads are too tangled. I can take you to a place where you can free his spirit. He'll be like Raven, here but not here.'

'He wouldn't want that.'

Edensun nods. 'Raven is wrong. You are selfless.'

'Nobody else thinks so.'

'I do,' Edensun says.

'So, do I,' Donna agrees.

Freya blinks back tears and wipes her nose with the back of her hand. 'I've always been used and discarded. Lilith wasn't the first or the last. I would like to protect my father, mother, daughter, and Marian, if you let me go.'

He withdraws his claw from Freya's hair, and she races into the crowd, pulling Marian and Mike away from the others and leading them to the staircase. Her body is flooded with a sense of euphoria that makes it difficult to focus on climbing the stairs.

CHAPTER TWENTY-ONE

HECATE SITS in her armchair, drinking tea and chain smoking. She will not be stuck in this flat for much longer. She knows David Garlow plans to burn the flesh she inhabits. One of his cars is already pulling up outside. Louisa — Catherine's sister, Helen's mother — will soon emerge from the back seat and beg Cat to go with her and David's four children to London. Once Hecate agrees and clambers into the car, she will have another week at most. Despite knowing this, Helen and Catherine want her to say yes. They are willing to sacrifice themselves to spend their final days with their family.

After the aborted battle in the cellar, Donna joined Freya and other disgruntled ex-members of the Morrigu, forming a small group who worked together repairing homes and helping survivors of the storm to rebuild their lives. As Hecate waits for Louisa to knock on her door, Donna and Freya are bundling soiled sheets. Freya will keep her promise to Edensun until a band of Garlow's supporters chase them down in an attempt to rid England of magic and witches.

Like many others, Donna and Freya will fear the news that will soon come out of London. Freya's great-grandfather and many others fought in the second world war against men like David Garlow, and the idea of someone using the massacres, grief and disruption that followed the terrible rain as an excuse to rebuild England in Nazi Germany's image will be anathema to many but not all of their descendants. Donna will worry about it constantly, even while stripping sheets or helping to mend doors or feed families. Her past ambivalence to politics will make her blush with shame as poverty, homelessness and violence become impossible to ignore.

Garlow's velvet voice will offer false promises of safety and new wealth, but it will be people like Freya and Donna who strive every day to make a positive difference to survivors' lives, wiping blood from bedroom walls with a sponge and bucket, while the percussion of hammering nails keeps time. Instead of rebuilding homes and people's lives, Garlow and his ilk will simply build mountains of wealth while the world is crushed.

In three days, there will be a meeting at Freya's house. Friends will gather together, have a few drinks, relax, share their experiences, and prioritise the things they still need to achieve. Many of them were in the cellar at The Lucifernum when Edensun and Donna arrived to collect Star's belongings. The evening will progress, fuelled with alcohol, laughter and the heady joints Aaron supplies. Ideas will be brought before the group: lists of children who need new families, ideas for establishing schools and reopening medical centres. Many will be long-term goals, but the protection of orphans is something Marian will start work on immediately, allowing her to heal from her great loss and gain a sense of hope.

A knock on the door will make Donna jump and a minute later two women will stand in the hallway and peer into the living room — one ancient and the other young. Aeronwen, the blind oracle, and Jessica, her granddaughter, will gate-crash the party, and Mike will not be happy about it.

'What the hell are you doing here?' Mike will growl.

Others will stand in defensive poses around the room, and Donna will rise from the sofa to secure a view.

'Morrigan has been imprisoned in London by David Garlow's soldiers. We plan to rescue our goddess and hope you will join us. This is what she trained us for. Most of you are Morrigu,' Aeronwen will say, extending her frail arms towards the gathering in a show of humility, a plea for their help.

'We shouldn't have kept the goddess's wisdom from you, Brother Mike, and we're sorry,' Jessica will add. 'But we need your help. It isn't only Morrigan who's in danger. Garlow plans to erase all magic from England. If we do not resist, each of us will be taken or killed — one by one.'

They will be told to wait outside while the group discusses whether to help, and the two women will bow their heads to Freya before they leave.

Donna will speak to the group. 'Edensun told me about Garlow. He was generally dismissive about what the man might achieve but feared his power, at least at some level. David Garlow is a credible threat. Cat, I mean Hecate, warned us that he would use Edensun to rise to power. When I met her, she was staying in a tower block in the city. We could ask her advice.'

'I don't think there's time,' Aaron will argue. 'And if this Garlow has Morrigan, he's probably taken Hecate as well.' *Aaron will be right. By the time they are having this discussion, I will be locked in a magical cage awaiting the pyre.* 'We have to leave now. I don't agree with what our leaders tried to do to Freya, but Morrigan is our goddess. She's part of us, and we swore to fight for her.'

'A vote then,' Freya will say. 'We have three options, and we'll vote on each in turn. The first is to ignore this call and continue our work with the people who need us here. The second is to gather more information on Garlow and try to speak with Hecate. The third is to drop everything and go with the Oracle and Jessica to London. Hands up who wants to stay and continue to rebuild the city.' Roughly half of the hands will rise including Mike's, Freya's and Marian's.

'Who wants to speak with Hecate?' Donna will raise a lonely hand.

'And who wants to go with the Oracle to rescue Morrigan?' The other half will raise their hands, including Aaron and Clementine.

Freya will feel the weight of leadership as she considers the options. 'The half of us who wish to stay will stay, and the half who want to leave should leave now. I understand the compulsion to follow a goddess better than most, and you will be welcomed back whenever you choose to return. Safe journey and good luck.'

Farewells will be accompanied by tears and hugs. Neither those who stay nor those who leave will be entirely confident in their choice.

Edensun will arrive at Freya's home in the early hours and warn them to leave the city. 'Garlow has captured Morrigan, and he plans to execute all witches and magic users. His plan is to purge England with fire. Maybe you can escape if you head to Scotland.'

He will ask Donna to come with him to Chokmah, where he believes he will find his mother. 'I am not sure whether the human mind can survive that realm, but if you want to come with me...'

She will choose to stay with Freya. 'It wouldn't feel right to leave Freya and her family, not now. Bring Star back to me when it's safe, Edensun.'

Afraid of losing his last connection to Star, he will offer to escort them to safety. 'I could stay — protect you and Freya, if I can. I can look for Mum when you're safe.'

'How do you plan to protect us, by killing anyone who comes too close?'

'That's not all I am, Donna. I could take all of you to one of the planes of existence — Yesod or Netzach.'

'I'm sure Yesod and Netzach are lovely this time of year, but our fight is here, Edensun,' Donna will say.

Cat pulls her thoughts back from the future and focuses on the present. She hears rubber scuff the vinyl tiles of the stairwell as Louisa fidgets nervously on the other side of Cat's door. Then a gentle knock.

'Come in,' Cat says.

'There's a car outside. We're heading to London. Will you come with us?' Louisa asks.

Cat nods. Her bag is already packed, and for the first time in years she isn't wearing a dressing gown. Instead, she is dressed in an oversized sweatshirt with wrinkled leggings that are at least one size too large for her thin limbs.

It's eight o'clock in the evening, when Cat squeezes into the back seat of a limousine crammed with toys and suitcases. She is greeted by squeals of joy from Louisa's three daughters.

The car glides expertly along the motorway. Cat barely feels the car turn as it swerves around abandoned vehicles and the occasional nomad journeying on foot. Louisa sits in the back, wringing her hands and praying something will cause them to crash and knock Bobby, their driver, unconscious while the rest of them escape. Cat squeezes her wrist to reassure her that all will be as it is meant to be.

David Junior is fast asleep but, despite the late hour, the girls are wide awake. Excitement makes their eyes sparkle. Cat entertains Louisa's daughters with tales of magic and heroism. A girl who saved a dragon with kindness, and a boy who travelled strange worlds in search of his lost love. The kids are enthralled by her stories of great adventure.

When they pull up outside the grand hotel, Cat gazes up at the towering red stone walls and large windows. The art deco lamps are all lit, and the doorway looks welcoming. Bobby talks animatedly on the radio before he steps out of the car and opens the doors for everyone to stretch their legs. When David emerges through the rotating door, arms and smile wide to welcome his family, his face is full of joy. The girls run to him. Bobby unhooks the baby seat and carries it, while Louisa grips Cat's hand.

'For the first time in a long time, I feel as though everything might be okay,' Louisa whispers.

Black-and-white tiles spread out before them. An enormous chandelier hangs from an ornate white ceiling, and three arches supported by Corinthian columns dominate the lobby. The girls run ahead. Amy darts up a wide curved staircase and calls to Bree to chase her. The older sister happily complies, and Ella follows in their wake.

'Be careful,' Louisa calls.

'They're safe here,' David assures his wife. 'It's only us in the building. Let me get you a drink.'

David glances at Cat, giving her a crocodile smile. She

knows his plan, and what the future holds for her. David's stiff nod assures her that he is well aware that she knows.

CHAPTER TWENTY-TWO

A SHALLOW layer of warm water has settled over Chokmah, crowned by a soft blue mist which invigorates Star's body and mind as she paddles. She reaches for a distant memory of a beach in summer but suffers no distress when the image evades her. What's happening now is far more interesting than what came before. The air above and around her is the shimmering grey of a freshwater pearl. Everywhere glows like the hint of sunrise on a foggy day, shining with energy and potential and humming a harmonious lullaby that opens her mind and stimulates her senses, awakening her rather than sending her to sleep. The colours of her magical cape dance across her shoulders and arms as her skin absorbs the energy of those glimpsed alternate lives until it becomes an inner robe of glory, not seen but felt as a pleasant tingle of potential.

Fear and anxiety are concepts so alien to this place that Star doesn't even notice their absence. She is safe in this world of gentle activity. A circle of seventy-three standing stones surrounds her, and pure blue mist ejaculates upwards from these columns before descending gracefully to billow across the water's surface. Star sits cross-legged in the shallows and allows her mind to join the mist and float without direction or purpose.

'Welcome.' The voice is male and gentle.

Star opens her eyes and summons her wandering mind before she answers. 'Is it okay for me to sit here and think?'

'Of course,' the giant says as he sits beside her. Golden curls frame his exquisite, glistening face.

'Are you an angel?' Star asks.

He shrugs, but the smile which lights his face certainly looks angelic. 'I'm Samael. You've reached Chokmah, few do. It takes many lives before souls are ready to become one with God.'

'I still have plenty to figure out before I'm ready. I'm a mass murderer,' Star says, as the slaughter and red rain flash through her mind before evaporating back into the mist. 'Can I do that here?'

He nods. 'Shall I leave you in peace?'

'Peace,' she says. 'Yes, that's it exactly. Coming here feels like peace has been restored. I'm ready to learn what I need to learn. All is one.'

'And everything is nothing,' Samael finishes. 'It could take you millennia to understand; it isn't something you can learn even here, but rather something you will one day know to be true. My home is yours for as long as it takes. I should probably tell you that your son is looking for you.'

'There's always somebody looking for me, Samael.' Star laughs. 'Satori found me in Binah and Edensun will find me here. I won't go back, not until I've learned how to control myself. Anyway, I love it here. What's this wonderful blue mist?'

'Do you remember the columns of mist in Binah?'

It takes Star a moment to tug that memory into her consciousness. 'Yes.'

'This is the mist before it begins organising itself. It's the ever-flowing force of the unmanifest.'

She doesn't understand, but instinctively feels she will in time and does not want to take any short-cuts on her journey. She brushes her hand across the surface and shivers as bubbles of energy bump against her own.

'Will I meet God?' she asks.

'There are many aspects of God — this mist, me, you, Lilith. He may speak to you when he feels you're ready, or you might not meet him until your spirit returns to Kether and you cease to exist. Does that make sense?'

Surprisingly, it does. Her brain expands to encompass the concept and examine it, sorting out what she already knows to be true and what she will need to meditate on, unpick and explore after Samael has left. Star's in no hurry for him to leave, but neither does she need him to stay. In many ways it feels as though she's talking to herself, and he's merely a mouthpiece for her own thoughts.

For the last time, Star thinks about her parents. Neither her mother and father nor their mistreatment of her will bother her while she stays in this place. She sees their cruel mouths and wishes they knew what she understands at last, that God is peaceful. When she lifts her eyes, Samael has gone.

Her body is idle, wallowing in the comfort of water and mist, while her mind searches the landscape for previously hidden truths. She finds these in the mist and sky, stones and water, the earth and her own form. As her brain works it discards all mortal clutter — the memories she has nothing left to learn from, and the pain that she's clung to for years. She forgets the drawings her father tore up; she forgets her parents and their church, and Raven, the woman Star murdered because she felt jealous and betrayed. Fellow students who ridiculed her at university, her hated tele-sales job, falling in love with Lilith and being tortured in Binah by her lover, abandoning her son, even Satori and all the expectations he forced upon her — all drift away, clearing space for new and divine revelations. When the boy with green eyes approaches Star, she does not recognise him or understand why he calls her Mum.

'I've mended your paintings and moved your clothes into your wardrobe at the villa. You have plenty of black dresses and skirts now. Come home with me, Mum.'

She stares at him, trying to understand his face in the context of God, and the unmanifest energy from which everything was created. She loves the boy, just as she loves the air, water and mist and those giant stones that hold vigil around her, protecting her while she explores.

'I am home,' she says.

He frowns. Does he not understand, or does he want a different answer? She has no other to offer.

'I'm your son. Don't you remember? You gave birth to me.

You left me twice, once as a baby and again after the rain, but I will always find you, Mum.' He grabs her arm, but his hand slides off her skin as if she's an eel, although she doesn't remember what an eel is either.

'You have to remember,' he begs. 'Donna, Freya, Satori, Lilith, Edensun! How can you forget us all?' He glares at the mist as if it is a toxin that has stolen her mind.

'It's just the ever-flowing force of the great unmanifest,' she tells him.

He growls his frustration and reaches for her arm again but cannot gain purchase.

'Come back with me,' he demands.

'Why would I want to leave? It's so tranquil and beautiful, and I'm learning everything I need to learn. Sit with me and see. I'm waiting for God. He'll come when he knows I'm ready.'

Star glances at the stones spurting chaotic energy directly from God, then at her legs and the pure water that laps against them. When she turns, the boy has gone. Within an hour she forgets his visit completely.

CHAPTER TWENTY-THREE

EDENSUN VISITS Samael in his tower before abandoning Chokmah. Lilith described the palace Samael's children built for him on Earth, and this tower contrasts greatly with the black catacombs the goddess described. The building looks phallic, rising above the water, and the wall is mostly glass and reflects the bright, shimmering light, dazzling any onlooker, even one who is, at least in part, divine.

Samael's chamber is at the top of the tower, thirty-seven storeys up. Edensun climbs the spiral stairs while he thinks about what he will say. *Can I convince Samael to give my mother to me?* The god of this land sits on a throne in the centre of a circular room and wears a midnight-blue robe with wide sleeves, the cuffs of which cascade over the armrests of his gold and violet chair.

'What's wrong with her?' Edensun asks.

Samael's beautiful face creases in confusion. 'There's nothing wrong with her.'

'She doesn't remember me!'

'That's natural. She must shed her mortal memories to reach God.'

'I don't want her to forget. Bring her back!'

Samael's laughter booms around the room.

'Stop laughing!' Edensun demands. His fists feel hot. If he doesn't contain his anger, he's likely to set something alight.

'Then grow up. How old are you?'

Edensun shrugs.

'A babe in a teen's flesh.'

Edensun pushes leathery wings from his shoulder blade and fangs through his gums. The ceiling is high enough to allow Edensun to attain his full demonic height. If he expects Samael to be impressed, and part of him does, he is disappointed. The god holds Edensun's gaze without craning his neck. Even though there are metres of difference between their heights, somehow Samael has no need to look up at Edensun. It makes the boy feel petulant, but to shrink back to his human form would mean losing even more face.

'I need her,' Edensun whispers.

'Hasn't the poor woman suffered enough?' Samael asks.

'Haven't I? I never asked to be born. She owes me!'

Samael shakes his head, but Edensun sees pity in those amber eyes.

'Please,' he begs. 'Expel her. I'll take care of her. She'll be safe with me. Just a few years, that's all I'm asking. I don't think she knows what she wants, not really. I'll be helping her. You have to see that.'

'I cannot.'

'Why? You are the lord of this land. Here your word is law. A whisper of suggestion, a swarm of mosquitoes, even a sprinkle of grit in the wind, that's all I need, then I can offer her shelter from her discomfort. Remember when Lilith left you. You must have missed her. All the demonic brood in the world couldn't replace her love and gentleness, could it? Yet you got to spend thousands of years with her before she deserted you. I haven't even spent one year with my mother.'

'I will not, whelp. You demand too much.'

'I ask so little. All I want is what is owed to me, Slant Serpent!'

'Do you think I haven't seen her memories, or yours?'

Edensun bristles.

'The reptile that scurried across the sand and tore his mother's breast. The jealous Oedipus who sent Satori to wake a sleeping woman before making a torch of his flesh. The manipulator who demonstrated the cruelty of mankind only to amplify it with water from the Lake of Sorrows. I will not expel Star from

Chokmah to cure your loneliness. She is healing, and you will only make her sicker. There is nothing you can say that will change my mind,' Samael promises.

Realising he has no hope of forcing Samael's hand, Edensun steps through the curtain to Chaos. He broods there for a while, thinking about the unfairness of his existence. It wasn't as though he asked to be born, and yet he's constantly rejected, pushed away by both mother and father, dismissed by Samael, used by Garlow and hunted by the Morrigu.

When will it be my turn to heal, to be protected and respected, to be loved?

Maybe Donna can reach her.

Edensun knows that a human entering Chokmah risks madness or death, but if it is the only way to remind Star of who she is and what she owes him, he is willing to risk Donna's sanity and much more.

When he finds Donna, wandering in a field, wallowing in her grief, he convinces himself that he is helping both women, not only himself.

'Donna, what happened?'

'Soldiers. They caught the others. I managed to hide then followed their trail, but I found them too late, being pulled through a village, tied to stakes, burned. I can still hear their screams. Why? Why did you and Sarah do this to us?'

'I found her. I can take you to her. Mum will be glad to see you,' Edensun says.

Donna's eyes brighten, before she shakes her head and focuses on the mud and blades of grass. 'Sarah created this mess, then left us to it. I never thought she would do anything so cruel. Maybe Freya was right.'

'Freya was wrong about Star, and I was wrong about Freya. You knew Freya could be a better person. Now I need you to help me save my mother.'

'Fuck off, Edensun. Leave me alone so I can grieve for my friends.'

'Not until I get my mum back.' Edensun grabs Donna's wrist,

opens a rift, and drags her through Chaos.

When they emerge in Chokmah, Donna falls to her knees.

'Come on,' he demands.

Why won't she get up? Star is only twenty metres away, but Donna sinks into the water as if she would rather drown than take a single step to help him. He raises his hand, wanting to slap some sense into her. His arm trembles as she turns her face towards him. Her eyes look glazed. Her hands press against her ears as her pupils roll upwards and disappear inside her skull.

'No,' he shouts, gripping Donna's shoulders and shaking her. 'You need to see Star. You have to help me.'

His fingers press deeper into soft flesh, then his thumbs and fingers touch each other as Donna becomes mist and disperses across the lake, joining with other consciousnesses which will eventually travel to Binah and be moulded into new flesh by Lilith.

'Fuck!' he screams.

Samael strides towards him, his face dark with fury. Unwilling to stay and face the god's wrath, Edensun creates a rift and disappears into Chaos, where he sits cross-legged and petulant, cursing the world.

Wiping hot tears from his face, he remembers the witch in the tower block and her enigmatic predictions. She had warned him that his mother would not recognise him. What else did she say? He thinks back, trying to remember. Cat told him Star's paintings were the key.

After retrieving them from the Morrigu's lair, Edensun had returned the paintings to his mother's cottage and spent days repairing them, laying the pieces out. They varied in size, those blades of torn canvas. Star's preferred palette was black, white, purple and red, and it had been difficult to discern which pieces belonged in which pile, and even harder to repair the paintings.

A psychologist might have read other things into the landscapes and portraits that Edensun rebuilt, but the loving son saw nothing to worry him. His favourite paintings were those which depicted a parkland full of fairies caught hard at work. They gave him a sense of calm, a feeling of connection with nature that he hoped his mother felt as she dipped her brushes into watercolours or carved and spread her oil paints across canvases. They were painted outside Star's cottage garden, where he met Donna after the rain, and she mistook him momentarily for Satori. But even the terrifying portrait of his father, with dagger-like forks of lightning that radiated around the man's cruel face, complete with the twisted sneer and emotionless eyes that Edensun remembered clearly from their battle, was admired for its skill rather than used to diagnose Star's mental agitation. If Star had seen this vision of her lover before she and Satori met, would Edensun have been conceived or Lilith brought to Earth by that jealously possessive magician?

He realises what he must do. In the end, it's all about sacrifice. He sacrificed Donna in vain. Now he must be willing to sacrifice himself.

Edensun finds Lilith in her sunken bath, surrounded by rainbows of bubbles.

'I've messed everything up, Lilith,' Edensun says, pacing the room. 'We never should have drenched the mortals with sorrow. People couldn't handle their pain, and Star couldn't handle her guilt. I found her, but she's lost to me.'

Lilith nods. 'Do you want me to get out of the bath?'

'No. I don't need to be held or comforted. I need to put things right.'

'How?' Lilith asks, rubbing scented oil over one arm.

'I'm going to alter the timeline,' Edensun says.

She stops what she's doing and stares at him. 'What do you mean?'

'If Star and Satori never get together then none of this happens. You don't visit Earth; Star doesn't kill her friend...'

'And you won't be conceived,' Lilith adds.

'What does it matter?' Edensun asks. 'I've never done anything good. I've never been loved. What's the point?'

'The point is you're part god and immortal. You're worth more than them,' Lilith says.

'Is that what you think?' Edensun's fists shake. He holds flames in his crescent-moon palms. *How can Lilith say that anyone is worth more than his mother?*

'Of course. Two-hundred and fifty souls are born on Malkuth every minute of every day. I mould the flesh of every single one.'

'Do you despise them that much?'

'I don't despise them. I barely think about most of them,' Lilith says.

'Well, I can't stop thinking about them.'

'You're just hurt and angry that they rejected you. Get in the water. I'll give you a shoulder rub, work all that stress and anxiety out of your muscles.'

'I'm not angry at them, Lilith. I'm angry at you. Star was your lover. How can you not care?'

'Okay, tell me, where is Star and what is she doing?'

He's fallen into Lilith's trap. Star is perfectly content in Chokmah, but that isn't where he wants her. If his mother finds God, as Samael suggested she might, she will be absorbed into Kether and never return. Edensun cannot bear the thought of never seeing her again. It would be easier to have never been born.

'I've made up my mind, Lilith. I will reset time. I just need to decide when to break the old line and what to adjust so history doesn't repeat itself.'

'I can't change your mind?' Lilith asks.

Edensun shakes his head. He is already staring through the rift into Chaos.

Chaos is where Edensun finds peace. Where his mind can stretch without limitation, and he can solve any problem. The puzzle he needs to unpick is how to prevent Star and Satori getting together. He must visualise how the pieces fit together, just like he did when mending Star's paintings. That chilling portrait of Satori, Star must have hated him when she painted it, poured all her rage and despair into the pigment. If she had seen his face depicted in that way before she met Satori, she would never have dated him, and may have avoided speaking to him. *Can it be that simple? What if I put that painting in Star's room before she meets Satori? If it doesn't work, I'll still be born, and I can try something else.* The agitated wings in his stomach suggest he's right. It could be that simple. He decides to try.

He leaves Chaos and arrives at the three-bedroom apartment his mother shared with Donna and Raven. The stench of decomposition lingers there, although the rooms have been emptied, perhaps by Freya and her friends. After Edensun spared Freya's life, she, Mike and a few others buried the city's dead and helped the living recover some sense of normality. Her atonement, a way to earn forgiveness for the pain and deaths she had caused. No trace of Star remains in the apartment.

His mother's energy grows faint, but he follows the last traces of it to a university. A meagre room. Was his mother happy in her temporary cell, free from her dominating parents and full of hope for the future? Donna met his mother while they were both at university, and he senses a faint trace of the other woman's presence. They talked here and became friends. The room contains the aura of his mother's hope, but Star isn't here now.

Edensun hosts a final party in Lilith's villa to celebrate the end of his existence. He's determined to enjoy the night, even if it means pretending his friends are having fun. His mind whirls with movement and drunkenness, and he ends the night under the grey sky, head supported on Siloth's belly, complaining that he is the unluckiest demi-god to ever exist.

Later, when the dizziness has passed, Edensun retrieves the portrait from the cottage and steps into Chaos. Staring ahead he sees the threads of time. Times that have happened, will happen, or might have happened if things had been different. He searches for Star's timeline. There. He traces the thread backwards, past the point where she glowed like the sun, then further back, beyond his birth. He keeps hold of her lifeline, feeling the moment she stabbed herself with Satori's blade, when she shivered in a freezing lake, gazed in wonder at the Aurora Borealis with Lilith by her side, fled from the bathroom of a nightclub after killing her friend, making love to Lilith and conceiving Edensun. Even further back, reaching a point where Edensun's lifeline, so often entangled with Star's, is absent. He sees the nightclub again and drinks that glow under black-light where Star first senses Lilith's presence while she's dancing with Donna. Further back, and he hears Star promise to help Satori return a demon to hell; her pain when she tells Satori that it's over between them; Star bleeding from her wrists in a bathtub before her friends rush in and save her life, and before that when Star moves with her meagre possessions into Raven's flat — full of hope and excitement; her first meeting with Satori in the street when her breath caught in her throat and her thighs grew damp; she's getting ready for a party at Raven's; she's in a studio painting fruit, four hours or so before she will encounter Satori on her way to Raven's party.

He places the painting against a wall beneath the desk in her student digs. She will glimpse the edge of it when she looks in the mirror and wonder where it came from, sense perhaps that the work is her own but be unable to remember painting it. Her mind is strong enough, he hopes, to reconcile the impossibility without cracking. He has to try. If not, she will fall for Satori again, and they will destroy each other.

If they do not fall in love, he will not be born. To turn back time so that he ceases to exist is a sacrifice he is willing to make. What has he achieved with the life he was given and what happiness has filled his reptilian soul? He condemned the world to violence and terror; his mother rejected him more times than he cares to remember. His existence is misery, and everyone he cares for is dead. If Lilith remembers him, she might try to bring him forth again. If not, he'll be a tendril of mist curling across the shallow waters of Chokmah. No guilt, no sorrow.

He returns to Chaos, still clinging to the perfect spot in the timeline. He told Star he could do this for her the first day they met, when they fled from Paul's house with the Morrigu on their heels. He offered to take her back to a time in her life when Raven and Satori were still alive, but he assured her that he and Satori could not exist for long on the same timeline. She chose him, and he hadn't needed to make good on his promise. Now that he's faced with the task, its complexity baffles him.

He severs the thread with his jaws and presses it to a new version of her room complete with the painting he placed by her desk. The old future separates and flaps loose in the shifting air. A different future will be made without Edensun, growing from the branch he has grafted. He hopes it will thrive.

Edensun shivers as he watches his olive skin disintegrate. He is transparent, a mere shade, then he is mist on the waters of Chokmah, aware of himself for a moment before he loses his name and memories.

CHAPTER TWENTY-FOUR

STAR HASN'T been given that name yet by Raven; she is still Sarah
— a young woman who summoned all her courage, ignored her
parents' demands and escaped to Spike Island in the vibrant city
of Bristol to study fine art. She recently started her third year and
spends most of her free time alone, afraid to make friends who
will invariably judge her and find her weird and otherworldly.
Miss-Le-Freak is the name the other art students have given
her, and she doesn't care enough to try to change their minds.
Instead, Sarah resigns herself to a solitary life, or she did before
she met a sweet and exciting young woman at the train station
two weeks ago.

Exhausted both by the luggage she dragged along the platform
and the parting words of her father, *You're going to Hell*, Sarah
sat quietly on a bench and cleared her cluttered mind. Donna
approached her while she was deep in meditation and offered to
buy her coffee. The rest, as people are fond of saying, is history.

A few days ago, Donna invited Sarah to a house party, one
unlikely to resemble any previous gathering she'd experienced
— no children and no bible-bashers. Instead, there will be adults,
music and copious amounts of alcohol.

The party is tonight, and Sarah's mood as she gets ready alter-
nates between excitement and nervousness, but she's determined
to enjoy herself and perhaps make new friends. She applies her
make up carefully, using a mirror bolted to the wall. Her room is
small, but she doesn't have to cower while the thunderous voice
of her father yells at her from beyond the door. She is free to get
drunk, listen to *the music of the devil* and paint black silhouettes

of bats and cobwebs around her eyes as she sees fit. She has never been happier.

The pale walls and cheap wood-effect furniture juxtaposes with band posters and a few of her paintings. It will never be homely, but she plans to find somewhere else to live after graduation. Maybe she can share somewhere with Donna, the fascinating and soft-spoken English student who will also be graduating this year. The artists she shares studio space with at Spike are too brash and loud for her, but Donna is different. Sarah can imagine living with Donna.

She notices something out of place in the reflection. Half-hidden under the ugly desk, a canvas has been propped up against a wall — an oil painting dominated by a terrifying face.

She crouches to get a closer look. The energy from the portrait pulses like a severed vein. It is strangely familiar although she's never seen it before. She fights her fear and grabs the edges. Placing it carefully on the shallow windowsill so its back rests securely against the misted glass, she puts a comfortable distance between herself and the window and studies the portrait. *It could have been painted by me!* She shakes her head and decides it would have to have been painted by a more confident and competent version of herself. Certainly, the brush strokes are similar and the limited palette, something she's frequently been criticised for by her tutor — *don't be afraid of using colour!* It's a man's face, she thinks, although the features are androgynous, with dark hair and cruel grey eyes. Darkness radiates from his stare. It makes her shiver. His expression is full of arrogance and contempt, as though everyone he encounters is somehow inferior — less clever, less important and far less powerful.

She moves closer and hunts for a signature. When she finds it, she shakes her head again. *Who would do this?* The signature is hers. She pinches herself to check it isn't another vision. They've been plaguing her recently, the forbidden glimpses her father tried to beat out of her before subjecting her to the humiliating experience of an exorcism. No, she mustn't think about that place, only madness dwells there.

She places the painting in the wardrobe, facing the back and hidden behind long skirts and dresses, before returning to the mirror, but her hand is shaking too violently to finish the intricate designs of her make up. Instead, she paces her room, gulping wine straight from the bottle, talking herself down until she hears a knock on the door. *Donna, already?*

A sense of calm washes over Sarah as she opens the door to her smiling friend. 'Come in. I'm sorry, I'm not ready yet.'

'Raven said nine, so it won't get going until eleven,' Donna assures her, chuckling.

Sarah glances at the wardrobe. 'What's Raven like?'

'Loud, Goth and one hundred percent authentic. It should be a wild night.'

The rhythm of Donna's words washes over her, but Sarah isn't really paying attention to the subject, unable to stop thinking about the face in the painting. Her chest is tight and her stomach churns. She pours wine into two mugs and passes one to Donna.

'Classy,' Donna says.

'Only the best at Chez Sarah.'

After a few sips, she's calm enough to continue painting her face.

'I know we've only just started the year, but what are your plans after you graduate? Will you head back home?' Donna asks.

'God no! It's painful enough spending summers there. I'll find a job and a place in Bristol.'

'We should rent somewhere together.'

'I was thinking that myself. It would be great.'

'Awesome.' Donna sounds as though she means it, although Sarah's self-doubt tries to convince her otherwise.

'Okay, make up done. Do you mind turning round while I get dressed?'

'No problem.'

Sarah chooses a knee-length tulle skirt, a bustier, and big boots, and pulls them on. 'What do you think?'

'Stunning. Want to head out?'

'After we finish the wine.'

'We're late,' Sarah says as they stride along a residential street. 'Is it much further?'

'Don't worry, Raven's parties go on all night,' Donna says.

'Donna!' a male voice calls out from across the street.

Sarah turns and stares at the source of the greeting. Her forehead creases into a deep frown. It's him, the face in the painting. Her blood chills in her veins, and she clings to her friend. Donna quickens her own pace, and they hurry away from the long-haired man.

He jogs towards them and grabs Donna's upper arm. Sarah cannot look away from the cruel smile in his otherwise beautiful face. Perhaps the painting was a vision after all, a warning to keep her distance from this terrifying individual.

'Hi,' the young man says. 'Couldn't you hear me call you, Donna?'

Donna squeezes Sarah's hand.

The man nods, still grinning. 'And you are?' he asks Sarah.

'S-s-sarah,' she stammers.

'If you're heading towards Raven's, I'll walk with you,' he says.

The women do their best to ignore him. He leers like a wolf that has never pretended to be anything else. At the end of the street, he seems to get bored and strides ahead to reach the party before them, hoping, no doubt, for more appreciative prey.

'Who the hell is he?' Sarah asks when he's out of sight.

'That's Steve, and he's bad news.'

Donna points to a discreet door nestling between identical two-storey flats in a shabby cul-de-sac. The door hangs open, and the thud of industrial beats punctuates their last steps.

'Here we are,' Donna says.

They hurry up the steep stairs. Raven's big black boots stand firm on the living room floor. Satori's arm is draped around her shoulder, and her painted lips curl into a lascivious smile. They look well paired. Donna and Sarah approach, and Donna interrupts the flirtation. Raven scowls then her pierced lip slides across perfect teeth in a smile.

'Donna,' she says. 'Glad you could make it. Oh, and you brought a friend.'

'This is Sarah,' Donna says.

'Oh, you are far too perfect to be limited by such an ordinary name, isn't she Satori? We shall call you Star.'

Sarah grins as she follows Donna to a coffin-shaped coffee table covered in bottles of alcohol.

'Is she as scary as she seems?'

'You get used to her pretty quickly, and she has a huge heart beneath the hard shell. At least she seems to have distracted Steve.'

'I imagine that ample cleavage can be very distracting,' Sarah whispers.

She plays with the name Raven bestowed on her in her mind. *Star — like that vampire in Lost Boys, the one they all fight over.*

It is a wonderful night of drinking and dancing, and when Donna helps her unlock her door, she asks her friend to stay. Sarah manages to spill cold water from the kettle over herself, giggling like a toddler as she stretches the damp clothes from her skin. Donna takes over and makes their instant coffees.

'I love you,' Sarah slurs.

Donna smiles and brushes her fringe from her eyes.

Sarah presses her lips against Donna's a microsecond before she passes out.

The next morning, Sarah wakes in her bed alone, remembering snippets of the wonderful night and her aborted seduction. She sees a note on the pillow and opens it eagerly.

I love you too. I was too nervous to ask before, but if you would like to come out with me for dinner or a movie, we could figure out whether we work as a couple. If it was the drink talking,

I am very happy to remain good friends. Don't worry, Sarah. You didn't do anything to embarrass yourself, and I left when you fell asleep.

Sarah reads the letter three times before grabbing her mobile phone. The face of her friend glows in her mind, rich with potential. Her heart is full, and her stomach and groin tingle. Could this be the great love that will make life worth living, that will wash her pain away? It is a lot to ask from one person, and Sarah acknowledges that even the most wonderful friend and lover might not be able to cure the misery she inherited from her parents, but it might give her the strength to heal herself. She dials Donna's number.

'Dinner and a movie sound perfect, and I promise not to get so drunk I fall asleep on you.'

CHAPTER TWENTY-FIVE

CAT LIGHTS a candle to remember the green-eyed boy who sacrificed his existence so that his mother and her friends might live full and happy lives.

'If we remember him, then he hasn't ceased to exist,' Helen says.

'Could he return somehow?' Catherine asks.

'Energy cannot die,' Hecate says.

'Should we hope for or fear his return?' Catherine asks.

All three distinct personalities stare at the flickering flame. Hecate finds hints of green on the outer edges, but none of her three aspects sees the answer to Catherine's question in the light.

Cat remembers everything, from being brought to this dismal flat in a tower block, and six years forward into an alternate future when skinheads drag her from a hotel prison and burn her borrowed flesh beside Morrigan and her followers on pyres in London because David Garlow wishes to rid England of magic.

What Garlow failed to recognise was the importance of magic and spirituality to the human condition. Had that future played out, it would have led only to further suffering and despair. Nihilism can break even the strongest mind.

The buzzer sounds, and Cat sweeps down the shared staircase to greet her sister at the door. Louisa looks well. The medication she swallows is a carefully balanced magic trick, an established alchemy that alters the chemicals in her brain, allowing her to offer Cat a natural smile, while never sinking into psychosis. Poor Louisa. Hecate is determined to make things better for the long-suffering woman.

'Come in, Louisa,' Catherine says, hugging her sister tightly.

She takes the stairs slowly, so that Louisa does not strain herself trying to keep up. Helen has cleaned the sofa for her mother's visit, so Louisa need not disguise her repulsion when she is asked to sit down.

'Tea?' Cat asks, already heading to the kitchenette to make it. 'How are you?'

'Glowing, thank you, although my ankles are already swollen. They tell me it's twins.'

'Do you want biscuits?'

'Yes please.' Louisa sits on the sofa and leans back.

Cat smiles sympathetically as she hands over the mug.

'Thank you, Catherine.'

'I've had a vision, sister. It won't be easy, but I need you to hear me out.'

'Is it about Helen? Is it Bree or the babies?'

'No. They are all fine. I need your help to prevent a dystopian fascist future.'

'What do you mean?' Louisa asks.

'In my vision, you and your husband have a son,' Hecate explains.

'A boy!' Louisa smiles and taps her belly.

'You're carrying girls. You will conceive this son after you celebrate the twins' fourth birthday, but the thing is, my love — having a boy changes David, and he attempts to build an empire. He murders us in this future — burns us to death — me, Catherine, and Helen. I can prevent it, but I need your consent, dear sister.'

'Of course. How can I help?' Louisa leans forwards and puts the mug on the cluttered coffee table to avoid spilling any then massages her shaking hands.

Hecate reaches across and holds Louisa's hands, calming the woman.

'It's having a son that changes David. It makes him a monster — a megalomaniac. He already has the potential, we both know that, but a son brings his lust for power to the fore. You've already given birth to two daughters, and will have two more healthy, beautiful girls seven months from now. I know you don't have Helen, not really. Perhaps one day I can return her to you. I have been thinking about it, and I believe there's a way of separating the three of us. What I am trying to say is this, please let me prevent you from conceiving any more children, Louisa.'

Louisa frees her hands and leans back. Her blue eyes darken. Hecate is silent, giving Louisa time to process the words. It will be years before Louisa conceives David Junior without Hecate's intervention. There is no rush.

Louisa licks her lips then picks up the mug and moistens her mouth with tea. Hecate tries not to listen to the woman's thoughts, but some storm out of her skull to stamp about the room like a toddler's tantrum. She wants more children. Her life is darkness, destroyed by her father and controlled by her husband, and her only joy is the happiness reflected in her daughter's smiles. Yet she is an unstable mother, drugged to keep calm. Even pregnancy hormones have made her scream at Bree and hold the two-year-old a little too roughly. Is she selfish to want more? More psyches to damage.

Louisa squeezes tears from her eyes. Crying takes effort while on this cocktail of medication, but it helps relieve excess pressure when thoughts begin to overwhelm her. Still Hecate stays silent, refilling Louisa's mug when it is empty, and waiting for the ill-used woman to organise her chaotic thoughts.

'What do you want to do?' Louisa asks.

'After the twins are born, I would like to remove every egg from your ovaries.'

'What will happen to me?'

'Nothing, your life will continue in the same pattern as before, unless you ask me to help you leave him. You simply won't get pregnant again.'

'Can I think about it?' Louisa asks.

'Of course. If you forget, I'll remind you after the girls are born.'

'Do you think I could forget something like this?'

'I do. Human minds frequently purge what they don't want to remember or cannot make sense of. Discarded memories, that would otherwise cause pain and suffering, create a great crimson lake between Geburah and Binah. It's beautiful as long as you don't touch the water.'

'Could you send my memories there, Catherine, so I can stop taking the pills?' Louisa asks.

'Would you want to believe your father and husband are good men who have never caused you pain, never taken anything from you?'

Louisa bites her lip, thinks for a moment then shakes her head. 'I suppose not. If I don't remember, I might forget to protect my daughters.'

'I wish you'd leave David,' Catherine says.

'Who else would have me?' Louisa asks.

'You! You would have you. Your children too. Don't think for a moment that your worth is tied to marriage. You're stronger than you realise.'

'He'd find me. He'd fetch me back.'

Cat shakes her head. It is not the first time they have had this conversation, but maybe one day Hecate will get through to Louisa, although she cannot glimpse it in their future.

'I should go,' Louisa says. 'Bree will want her lunch.'

Cat stands and holds her sister/mother until Louisa twitches uncomfortably, needing distance. She hands Louisa an envelope. 'Would you give this to David?'

'What does it say?' Louisa asks.

'I had a vision, not the one I discussed with you, don't worry. There's a man — the same man David used to combine the three of us. He has a young boy in his house. I know how David and his, what do you call them, lackeys choose to deal with paedophiles. I am confident they will reach the house before the boy dies.'

'How old is this boy?' Louisa asks.

'Seven. His parents are frantic.'

Louisa looks disgusted and grips the envelope. 'Thank you,

Catherine.'

Hecate smiles, able to see a little less darkness in the future.

Hecate welcomes Lilith into her sultry chamber within the black mountain of Yesod. The goddess' red hair is not covered, and her mouth is twisted in a snarl. Instead of the humility and respect she brought on her last visit, Lilith appears ready for war. She is not here for guidance, but for vengeance. Lava drips from the walls, and Lilith fails to hide her discomfort; sweat glistens on her skin.

'Good day, sister,' Hecate says. 'Would you care for some tea?'

Lilith strides toward Hecate, long legs consuming the distance between them. An arm is drawn back, then arcs forward, slapping Hecate's cheek. 'You knew! I came to you for guidance, and you knew what he would do, but did not tell me. I warned you not to make me your enemy, witch!'

Hecate lifts a cup to her lips, studying Lilith over the rim. Lilith tears the cup from her hand and smashes it against a wall. Hecate takes a deep breath, leans back against her chair, and watches Lilith smash every piece of furniture in the room, bar the one occupied seat.

Lilith screeches with rage, then falls to her knees, exhausted by her own fury. 'Why?' she asks, green eyes staring into Hecate's soul.

'Sister, I had to clean up your mess.' Hecate's voice is soft, but the heavy air carries it to Lilith's ears. 'The Lake of Sorrows was never supposed to return to Malkuth, but you let it rain just so Edensun could show off to his mother.'

With a twist of her fingers, Hecate replaces the broken table, chair and tea set. 'Sit with me, Lilith.'

'He was a child. My child.' Lilith gets to her bird-like feet and lurches towards the table, half-blind with grief.

'And you loved him?'

Lilith scoffs.

'Just as you loved Star,' Hecate adds, knowing it rubs salt in the wound.

Lilith will never admit she can love. She is the dark goddess, the terrible mother. She sees love as a weakness, a human affectation.

The ancient, wizened crone pours two cups of tea. 'Sit down, sister.'

Lilith shakes her head but lowers herself onto a seat. 'What happens now?'

'Energy never dies, and Edensun has much to learn before he can join the source. He will return to you.'

Lilith nods. 'What of the girl?'

'Her future is uncertain. Edensun changed her path, but she and the magician will not break their bond to each other in this lifetime.'

'Then, I will watch and wait for an opportunity to reunite mother and son. Pray I do not have cause to visit you again, Hecate.' Lilith's eyes narrow.

Hecate does not pray. She knows her prayers are powerless in the face of fate.

THE END

ABOUT THE AUTHOR

Carmilla Voiez is a British horror and fantasy writer living in Scotland. Her influences include Graham Masterton, Thomas Ligotti, and Clive Barker. She is pansexual and passionate about intersectional feminism and human rights.

Carmilla has a First-Class Bachelor's degree in Creative Writing and Linguistics.

Her work includes stories in horror anthologies published by Crystal Lake Publishing, Clash Books and Mocha Memoirs. She co-authored a Southern Gothic Horror novel with Faith Marlow and has self-published two graphic novels with art by Anna Prashkovich.

Graham Masterton described the second book in her Starblood Trilogy as a "compelling story in a hypnotic, distinctive voice that brings her eerie world vividly to life".

Her books are both extraordinarily personal and universally challenging. In the words of Jef Rouner (Houston Press): "You do not read her books, you survive them."

Carmilla is also a freelance editor and mentor who enjoys making language sing.

www.carmillavoiez.com